To Georgia;
Hope you enjoy the book!

The Lamb White Days

Kenneth D. Reimer

iUniverse, Inc.
New York Bloomington

The Lamb White Days

Copyright © 2009 by Kenneth D. Reimer

All rights reserved. No part of this book may be used or reproduced by any means, graphic, electronic, or mechanical, including photocopying, recording, taping or by any information storage retrieval system without the written permission of the publisher except in the case of brief quotations embodied in critical articles and reviews.

This is a work of fiction. All of the characters, names, incidents, organizations, and dialogue in this novel are either the products of the author's imagination or are used fictitiously.

iUniverse books may be ordered through booksellers or by contacting:

iUniverse
1663 Liberty Drive
Bloomington, IN 47403
www.iuniverse.com
1-800-Authors (1-800-288-4677)

Because of the dynamic nature of the Internet, any Web addresses or links contained in this book may have changed since publication and may no longer be valid. The views expressed in this work are solely those of the author and do not necessarily reflect the views of the publisher, and the publisher hereby disclaims any responsibility for them.

ISBN: 978-1-4401-5661-8 (sc)
ISBN: 978-1-4401-5660-1 (dj)
ISBN: 978-1-4401-5662-5 (ebk)

Printed in the United States of America

iUniverse rev. date: 9/17/2009

For Patricia

"What can I offer you now
except these tears?"

Acknowledgements

First and foremost, I must thank Lisa Powell, who has so directly touched this story. She is my first, and best, editor, and I have valued all of her advice—even when I was tired and frustrated with the endless revisions. It is a long, painful process bringing a novel to completion; Lisa made it feel a lot less lonely. Thank you, Isla.

I also owe gratitude to a number of others who slogged through this manuscript and offered suggestions for its improvement. *The Lamb White Days* was ten years in the making; however, and I wrote two other novels during that time, so it is almost a certainty that I won't remember everyone who had an influence on this story. With this disclaimer behind me, I would like to thank Rob Notenboom, Grant Powell, Toby-Anne Reimer, Douglas Reimer, Doug Morris, Sandi Reimer, Katie Harbron, and Peter May, who had more to say than, "It was good." Tracy Youck, you scared the hell out of me, but I made sure I answered the one question that caused you so much concern.

Lastly, I need to thank my mother, Patricia Reimer. You never read it, but you're the reason for it, and that midnight passage was taken in your honour.

THE LAMB WHITE DAYS

Prologue:

One cannot play Russian Roulette with a clip-loaded handgun. The decision is either I will do this thing, or I will not. In the final outcome, Fate will not have taken a hand. What is left then for those of us who lack the strength of will for such a decision—this nothing, or nothing at all?

Samuel J. Harris wrote that perfect wisdom is silence.

First let me tell you what happened to us that summer in Regina, the summer I met Simon. Afterwards…well, afterwards, perhaps I shall make my own silence.

BOOK ONE:
THE CEREMONY OF INNOCENCE

"When words become more important than ideas, it is time to
begin burning the books."
- *Slouching Toward Bethlehem*

I

Summer mornings in Regina were beautiful. As had become a custom of mine in the years before the war, I once again sat at a small street-side café, longing for the pre-day tranquility to permeate my senses. There was a fresh scent to the air, and the sun, which had only crested the horizon a short time before, still lay hidden behind the downtown office buildings. There was an ethereal hue to the early morning light, something altogether too delicate to last. The day was certain to be hot, but the air was yet cool.

    I had one hand wrapped about my coffee while the other absentmindedly traced the design of a hooked crucifix into the dew moistening the tabletop. Hunched forward, I studied people winding their somnambulant passages to work. In some ways, Regina was a paradox. The revolution had irrevocably changed life within the city, but the pulse of daily activity continued to beat. Like flowers revealing themselves to the light, shop doors were unlocked and propped wide, while disembodied hands flashed in windows, flipping closed signs to open. However sluggish in the early morning hours, unlike the other cities I'd seen in those last few months, Regina still exuded an air of freedom. Although it threatened, Tyranny had yet to choke the life from the city. A peacefulness presided over my musings that totally belied the underlying chaos of my thoughts and the storm that threatened Regina.

It was understandable that I'd grown accustomed to a certain level of tension, but that morning seemed imbued with a particular aura of apprehension. Most likely, I was only projecting my own fear and unease onto the people I watched. I doubt that many of them really understood what was going to come upon them. I only knew because of where I'd been before returning to Regina. At that moment, most of those people had only been touched indirectly by the revolution. The horrors of the coast were no more than a rumour to them.

Still, there were people I saw who knew something of what I'd experienced. Littering the damp grass of Victoria Park across from the café where I sat, I could discern an occasional sleeping figure, curled in against the chill. As I'd come to breakfast, I'd seen more of them scattered on the concrete sidewalk, pressed here and there into the little nooks of shop entranceways like plaster relics scattered throughout the ruins of Pompeii. They were refugees from the war, just as I was, but they lacked my good fortune in having a place to stay or enough money to buy a cup of coffee and for a moment pretend that the world had not gone to ruin. I wondered how long it would be before those streets were crowded with the displaced, driven from their homes by the implacable advance of the Coalition. They would come to Regina, the last free city, with the vain hope that life for them could continue. They'd discover instead that existence here was at a standstill, that Regina held its collective breath frozen mid-gasp, and in the silence one could hear the echoes of a futile dialectic: the rhetoric of the New Christians versus the hollow proclamations of the writers, artists and philosophers who had nowhere to be and nothing to do.

Like the other refugees, I too had been led by a false sense of hope, but hope had quickly fled. I came to understand that Regina was nothing more than a place to wait out my last days in relative peace until the Coalition arrived and brought the devastation with them. Rumour was that several kilometres from the city the remnants of the national army had entrenched itself for a final attempt to keep the Coalition at bay. It was futile, of course. The New Christian Army—the N.C.A.—could not be stopped. The revolution had become a force of nature and nothing could alter its path of destruction.

Having returned from the ruin of the coast, I knew how futile it was. Yet, I didn't blame the national army for trying, as I had tried. We must all answer to that inner drive which compels us. Maybe it didn't matter that they would be defeated. Perhaps an end was all they sought. In the coffee shops and bars, those of us gathered in Regina spoke of the fools who would fight to protect us, and we awaited news regarding their inevitable fate. Although the outcome of the battle was predetermined, the army's defiance offered us a small pretense of hope, and it provided us with a diversion from the daily nothingness of waiting.

I had particular need of diversion. I'd been in Regina for almost two weeks and was getting restless, increasingly desperate for something to keep my melancholic broodings from having their way. I had gone that route before, and it was a dangerous one; I doubted that I would escape a second descent into that depression. Absentmindedly, I rubbed my wrists, uncomfortable with the memory. The day before, I'd noticed a poster stapled to the side of the public message board in the park. It was an appeal for volunteers to work at one of the temporary hospitals that had been established within the city. It was certainly not my area of expertise, but after the things I'd seen and done, altruism smacked of redemption. As well, it would give me something to occupy my thoughts. I had decided to visit the hospital and see what I might find.

I finished my coffee, waved down the waiter and paid for my scant breakfast. I was still hungry, but whether I had the cash for it or not, rationing had been imposed. I'd been in Regina long enough to grow wise to the so-called rationing, and the idea frustrated me. One day earlier, I'd eaten my fill, but that morning there appeared to be a shortage. From my limited experience, I knew that come the next day, things could once again be back to normal. Obviously, someone was manipulating the flow of supplies—attempting to turn a profit, and the people in the city were suffering for it.

Outside the café, I passed a refugee curled into the entrance of a building, the bed of concrete softened by newspapers. He or she, I couldn't tell which, lay wrapped in a dark cloth with only a mat of tangled hair exposed to the cool morning. I thought I heard a voice and paused. Some aspect of the figure was intangibly evocative and roused within me a latent memory; something I had tried to forget that now skulked at the fringe of my consciousness. Goose bumps pricked the hair on my forearms. Set near the refugee's feet was a battered cup with a few coins lying at its bottom. I still held the change I'd gotten after paying for breakfast and bent to drop it into the cup. It clunked loudly, causing the figure to stir. "I know thy works," it muttered. I almost responded, but stopped myself; certainly, what I heard was nothing more than my imagination. With the movement, a repugnant odour of sweat and vomit rose suddenly to assail my nostrils. I lurched back, nauseated, my hunger forgotten.

I stood for a moment, confused, then looked about to see if my actions had been observed; for some reason I felt guilty. No one was watching. I shook the shiver from my shoulders then searched in my pocket for the map I'd torn off the poster the day before. I found two pieces of paper and drew them both out. One was the map to the hospital, the other, folded and worn, was the message of hope that had brought me to Regina—a thread strung out from Ariadne. Already familiar with its contents, I unfolded it carefully and ran my fingertip along the faded writing it contained. I imagined the hand that had penned those characters, then, somewhat reluctantly, replaced it in my pocket. Since I had found that note weeks before, I'd never let it out of my reach. Without it, I would wander the labyrinth with no chance of salvation.

Cutting through the park, I set off toward the hospital. As I strode beneath the trees, a leaf from an overhanging maple broke loose and spiraled earthward. I never noticed it fluttering behind me.

Not long after, I strode through a slightly unfamiliar part of town, using the map to guide my way. It named only the major streets, and I held it before me trying to fill in the gaps with my fragmented memory of Regina. I finally sought directions from a cashier in a shop and soon found myself striding down the street upon which the hospital was located.

The effects of the war had altered the city in such a way that I found myself often forgetting the circumstances of my being there. I'd quietly slip into remembrances of other times, summers before when I would have spent my days with family and friends. The reverie would be shattered, however, as I noticed another homeless figure or momentarily became cognizant of the lack of traffic. The present would then come crashing back to me—it was no longer the city I once knew. I thought again of the sleeping refugee I'd encountered outside the café. Something about the figure had triggered a suppressed memory that only that moment worked its way to the surface. I remembered that I had seen a body like that before….

I stopped walking and stood on unsteady legs. My chest felt constricted, and the shakes had returned. Knowing that I needed to bring it out, I struggled to take hold of the memory.

On my journey from the coast to Edmonton and, subsequently, to Regina, I'd passed through the Rockies, avoiding as much as possible any sign of the New Christian Army. Whenever I came upon a town, a possible checkpoint or a long stretch of road where I could be seen from a distance, I took my motorcycle off-road or used whatever viable paths I could find. It was an unsettling experience travelling through the mountains alone. Because I avoided human contact, a vast silence found its way to my side and became my only companion. The sound of the motorcycle drove it off, but the instant I shut down the engine, it rushed back to envelop me with its smothering embrace. The nights were the loneliest, and it became a measure of my intense solitude when the sound of a wolf howling brought me comfort. Travelling was difficult, and my progress was slow. Worse, I carried with me the fresh memory of the horrors I'd encountered in Vancouver.

There were times, however, when the necessity of securing provisions and fuel forced me to risk human contact. For the most part, the presence of the N.C.A. was light. At that point, they were engaged in open combat at several locations, so their forces were stretched thin; they were only just beginning to swell their ranks with conscriptions. Occasionally though, I encountered evidence of their passing.

One such place was a town called Field, where I'd stayed during vacations when I hiked in Yoho valley, and I knew it reasonably well. It was small and could be scrutinized from a distance. Located in a wide valley, it was spread out with only a few buildings over two stories high. When I studied it from a vantage point overlooking the valley, I saw nothing that suggested the presence of the N.C.A. I saw no movement at all, but that wasn't unusual with a sleepy place like Field. Seeing nothing to cause concern, I climbed on my motorcycle and kicked it into gear. The road down the valley was totally exposed—the kind of passage I'd avoided all the way from the coast, but I could see that it was clear. I knew it would have been better if I had sought an alternate route, but my dwindling supplies compelled me.

The closer I got, the further I travelled down that road, the more the hackles rose on the back of my neck. By the time I pulled into town, my heart was hammering, and my hands were slippery with sweat. There's a gas station not far from the main access to the highway, and since gas was my priority, I planned to go there first. I never reached my destination.

At first, I thought it was road-kill, odd within the town limits but the only logical interpretation my brain could arrive at, given what it saw. Gathered in a heap at the centre of a street, there was what I interpreted to be the carcass of a deer, dead for long enough that parasites had discoloured its shiny coat and torn into its flesh. I wondered why no one had cleaned it up. As I got closer, I understood.

I'd intended to swerve around it; instead, I brought the bike to a complete halt. Of age, I had no idea, but I was fairly certain that *it* was a *she*. Lying face down, the figure was grossly rounded, bloated with internal gasses. What I had mistaken for blood was the material of a summer dress, stretched taut, torn and tattered in places. Like her red hair, it was matted with dirt. One arm was hidden beneath her body; the other stretched above her head, as though she were reaching for something. In drifts of dirt obscuring the road, I could see the paw prints of dogs that had come to feed. My approach had interrupted a banquet of flies that suddenly clouded the area. In the unmoving air, my nostrils were assaulted by a stench that made my stomach lurch. How long ago she'd died, I also had no idea, but the sight of the ravaged corpse alarmed me as no number of N.C.A. tanks could have done.

I spun the bike around, almost dumping it, and escaped Field as quickly as I could. The truth was that I'd already seen worse sights, but I'd not grown accustomed to horror; hopefully, I never will. The wind whipped tears from my eyes.

I understood why there was no N.C.A. outpost watching over Field. None was needed. The town was already dead.

A horse drawn carriage clomped by breaking the dark spell of my reverie. I took a deep breath, forced the tension from my body, and tried to forget. The driver of the carriage yelled something at his horse, and I almost grinned, bemused by the irrepressible ingenuity of mankind. With a shortage of gasoline, private and public transportation had ground to a standstill. As a consequence, traffic in Regina became characterized by the rattle of bicycles. As time went on, more and more carriages and wagons appeared in order to move people throughout the city. Most were makeshift, ugly adaptations of motor vehicles, but some were the genuine article, or at least looked that way—something out of the nineteenth century. A queer step back through time. It was romantic enough, if one didn't examine the reason behind it.

As I approached my destination, I realized that the hospital I sought was an emergency facility set up in response to the war; it had once been something else. The sign out front read Luther College; it was, or had been, a high school. I don't know what I was expecting, but I was taken aback. It was a logical enough location: a school would have lots of space and decent facilities. What bothered me was the fact that it was available for use. I wondered whether the youth of Regina had forsaken the future or if they had all been sent to fight. I was so out of touch with reality that I never realized classes were over for the summer. Would the schools have been open anyway? What does a teacher dare say to a class of potential informants? A quietly uttered truth becomes a death sentence when filtered through the perspective of a fundamentalist revolutionary. When faith becomes a governing ideology, freedom of speech is the first right to disappear.

The building looked unkempt. The lawn was brown in spots, overgrown in others. I noticed broken glass in a classroom window that had been patched with cardboard. Had some kid thrown a rock through the glass, or had the school been broken into one night? I wondered what was left to steal when nothing more than the side of a box had been erected to hold back the chaos.

Approaching the entrance, I walked past several men sitting wordlessly upon the front steps. I assumed that they were patients, although they wore nothing to identify themselves as such, except for the bandages visible in spots beneath their clothing. Their garments were worn and ill fitting, obviously secondhand. One of them regarded me as I passed. His blond hair was cropped close to his scalp where an angry, red scar proclaimed a path curving back a full five inches from his forehead. He dangled a cigarette from his mouth, and the smoke shrouded his features. The others simply stared ahead, seemingly oblivious to the world around them. It wasn't what I'd expected to encounter at a hospital. I'm not sure of what image had been in my mind, but that vision of quiet despair wasn't it.

Inside, the ubiquitous, familiar scent of sterility stung my nostrils, stirring a sharp and unpleasant recollection of my last visit to an emergency ward—sometime in another life. The hallways were crowded, yet there was little noise. Men and women stood about speaking in whispers. Some sat in small groups on benches or the floor. The majority of them were alone. I hadn't entered a hospital or a high school; it was a sepulcher. Somewhere along the way, those people had already turned toward to the grave. In their eyes, I could see the same malaise that had taken hold of me since my coming to Regina; I was simply not as far gone as they were. *What am I supposed to do here?* I wondered, questioning my decision to respond to the poster.

Some of them wore uniforms, and that gave me pause. I hadn't realized it was a military hospital. I should have guessed that. It made sense: there weren't yet enough civilian refugees to necessitate emergency facilities. The fact that most of the patients were without uniforms meant that they were most likely from the Emac—the emergency army corps. This troubled me deeply, and I was seized by a sudden impulse to leave, terrified that I might be recognized by one of them. I turned about, making my way through the crowd to the open door. Before I'd strode a dozen paces, however, my way was blocked by the slim figure of a woman in a white smock. Shoulder length brunette hair contrasted with her uniform. Her eyes were hazel.

"May I help you?" she asked. I noticed dark stains upon the fabric of her clothing—blood.

"No, I...." What could I say? *No, thank you, I'm on the run, and I'm afraid I may be recognized here.*

There was such an expression of compassion on her face, however, that I stopped walking. She was young, younger than I, but whatever the war had put her through, the experience left scars. Once she would have been called pretty, but the lines upon her face spoke of too much pain for that description to apply anymore. "You must be looking for someone," she said. "Lots of people come here hoping to find someone they've lost."

She paused, waiting for me to reply, but my mind had gone elsewhere—I was thinking of my fiancée, Katherine. The doctor was right in a way; I was looking for someone. It was for Katherine that I'd come to Regina; although, it would have been a lie to say that I still believed I would find her; I entertained no delusion that Katherine was still alive. Since I'd left Edmonton and come to Regina, I had convinced myself not to hope. Six months before, I couldn't have drawn a breath without the love I felt for her swirling within my chest, but at that moment I felt only a dull emptiness. When had the passion died? When the hope had died, that was when—at the same time that the Coalition had set fire to the coast.

"I'm just making my rounds," the woman continued. "Why don't you follow me, and I'll show you around the place."

The doctor, or nurse, I wasn't sure which, stepped closer to me and took my arm in her hand. It was a gentle touch.

"Come along," she said. "We'll look together."

Even today so many years later, I can't explain to you why I stayed there, why I let her take me through that silent testimony to tragedy. War with the Coalition had decimated that tiny cluster of humanity. The broken bodies only hinted at the wounds beneath. Their past had been destroyed, and what was there for any of them, any of us, to do except await the inevitable coming of the end?

Amidst it all, however, there was that woman who had taken me in hand. I marvelled at her strength. Seeing my pain, for the thought of Katherine had assuredly marked my features, she moved closer and touched me, silently asking me to suspend my hopelessness and for a moment simply look with her. I couldn't deny that, and I let her take me along. The deep-set lines of suffering on the faces of those we approached softened as she passed. It was curious that she evoked such a response, for she seemed as damaged as the rest of us. I sensed a void within her. What had she been through? Maybe by helping others, she could forget her own emptiness.

"Who is it you're looking for?" she asked as we entered a stairwell heading to the second floor of the school. It was a natural enough question, and perhaps something she would have normally asked a little sooner. Under the circumstances, however, I could understand her reluctance to inquire as to anyone's past.

"I'm not…." But how could I speak to her of a nihilism I'd not yet fully admitted to myself? "It's my fiancée, Katherine," I said. "We were…separated when the fighting began, and I was never able to get back to her. I hoped I'd find her in Regina, but…."

I recalled the days I'd spent searching when I'd first come to the city. I'd sought her in those places that we'd once frequented together, in those summers now past and trivialized by the malevolence of the Coalition. The ghost of her laughter rattled with every woman's voice that passed me by. I had turned a dozen corners to find her standing there, then I'd blink, and she'd be gone. When I walked those streets, thinking of her, seeing her but not seeing her, my heart broke. It was more sadness than I could bear, but I never stopped watching the crowds for her face. I never stopped looking. It was simply that hope had given way to an aching melancholy, and my actions in Regina became little more than a parody of my initial purpose for going there.

"This war has touched all of us in some way," the doctor whispered to me. "It tears my heart to come here everyday. There's nothing that we can really do for these people. I've patched up their bodies, but that's all. Most of them shouldn't even be in the hospital anymore, but if we turn them out, they'll have to sleep on the streets.

"What worries me most is the possibility of disease. The more refugees who come into the city, the less sanitary things become and the greater the chance of an epidemic. If that happens, anything the Coalition could do to us would seem insignificant."

Not true, I thought. *You haven't seen what they did to the coast.* At least in every epidemic, there were always some survivors. While the image of Vancouver played for the thousandth time in my head, she left me for a moment to speak with another doctor whom we'd approached in the hallway.

I watched the two of them talking. Seeing her discuss matters with a colleague, her smile replaced by the grim face of reality, I could see how truly haggard she was. My heart went out to her. She had taken the time to help me, futile as it was, and I decided then to return the favour.

She came back to me, smiling once more. "Shall we continue?"

"No, there's no reason to. What I'd like, though, is to help out in some way." She looked confused. "I saw a poster," I explained.

The sudden light in her face was beautiful to see. "Oh, right, I'd forgotten. That would be wonderful. Do you have any training?"

I braved my first smile in months. "I have a doctorate in philosophy."

She frowned, shaking her head, "Sorry, we can't have any philosophy here, it's much too morose. Besides, that's what got us all into this mess in the first place." I flinched involuntarily. It's odd how such comments, even in jest, can accidentally strike so close to the truth. I stepped back. "Oh, I'm so sorry," she said. "That was just a little joke. I didn't mean to offend you. Listen; if you're serious, there is a way that you can lend us a hand. It's what I was thinking of when I put up those posters."

I nodded, "Sure, what can I do?"

"We have a patient who…well really, he just needs someone to talk to. He's blind and can't get around on his own."

"I can handle that. Where's he from?"

"We're not really sure. My guess is he's Emac. He came in with a head wound—unconscious. He's recovering now, and physically he's fine, but he has amnesia and hasn't regained his sight. I'll admit that we don't have access to the best equipment, but as far as I can tell he should be able to see. Frankly, I don't know what to do. He needs a psychologist, not a doctor."

"Can't you bring someone in?"

"Tried, everyone's too busy, and no place in the city has an open bed. We're stuck with him."

"So what can I do?"

She shrugged, "Talk to him. I think he's lonely. If anything, you can just help him move around. Sitting in the library must be driving him crazy."

"Sure, what else have I got to do?"

"Okay, well, I should talk to him first. Can you come back tomorrow?"

"Tomorrow would be fine."

We discussed the time when I should arrive, then she escorted me downstairs and out of the front doors. The steps were empty. Quietly, I made my way down to the street.

"Excuse me," I heard her say.

I turned and looked back.

"You must have a name."

"It's Harrison," I lied, "Jacob Harrison."

"Good," she said, "then I'll see you tomorrow, Jacob."

Hours later, when the sun was close to setting, I made my way down to Victoria Park to have something to eat and hopefully meet with some people I knew. I don't usually enjoy small talk, but during those times the diversion of conversation acted as a necessary respite from the torment of my internal machinations. In short, I needed the distraction of others to keep me from going insane.

Victoria Park was located at the city centre, just south of the downtown core. It was fairly small, just a city block of grass and trees with a cenotaph in the middle. On the northeastern corner there was a glockenspiel that rang periodically throughout the day. Beside it was the public message board where I'd seen the doctor's poster. Surrounding the park were several places that I'd grown used to frequenting during the years before the war. Facing the park on the south road was the old and regal Hotel Saskatchewan. On the west side, beneath a public library, was a small theatre with second-run movies or artistic films that never made it to the big studio outlets. Across the park from that was a coffee house with tables set on a small terrace along the side of the street. After movies, people would either gather there or stroll a block north along the paving stones of a pedestrian mall called Scarth Street and convene at Dante's wine bar. There was an amateur alternative art gallery close by, where impromptu performances were held and people often spilled into the street drinking and talking into the night.

It was an oddity of Regina that the approach of the Coalition did nothing to keep its citizens from frequenting the city's bars and cafés. The effect was antithetical to what I'd expected upon arriving there. Instead of deserted shops, places were often crowded, as if everyone needed the company of others to dispel their apprehensions.

When I arrived that evening, Victoria Park was full of people. There must have been news and the city had gathered to hear or gossip about it. I recalled the doctor's concern of an epidemic, thinking it curious that people didn't leave Regina and escape up north or go to the mountains. It would certainly be cleaner and safer than taking chances with the Coalition. So why didn't I go myself? I had as much and more reason to leave than anyone in the city. When it came down to it though, really came down to it, where was there to go? If you fled, they would find you. Sooner or later there would be a reckoning. At least if you stayed in Regina there was a chance that the Coalition would let the citizens convert to the New Christianity. They had done it in most of the places I'd seen. It was only the West Coast that got annihilated.

Still, there was that risk. The jihad that swept over Vancouver could as easily be repeated in Regina. It was the last free city, and perhaps they had saved it to serve as a final example to discourage any future uprisings. A bloody finish here would go a long way to cementing public subservience in the future.

There was considerable speculation as to why Regina had been left for the end. To me the question was moot; the killing spree of the Coalition had to end somewhere. The final stage of the revolution was simply a matter of coincidence and geography. It did, however, seem appropriate to me that I was there at that time. I had been born in Regina; I'd left it when I was young, but more often than not returned for periods of time during the summer months. Teaching university had allowed me that freedom. The city held a kind of a fascination for me. My brother used to live there, which is why I started my return visits; after he moved, however, I never stopped coming back. There was a Fringe festival every July that always gave me an excuse to return. Truth was, though, I attended fewer and fewer plays with each passing year.

So, at the end of things, I was back again. There was no festival planned for that year, and it was hardly the Regina that I once knew. The quaint charm of Victoria Park had been obliterated by the homeless, the hungry, and the threat of invasion. Worse, the crowds that gathered at the city centre always evoked within me a sensation of unease. Like a slumbering beast, violence was only a push or a shout away.

I maneuvered my way through the crowd, headed up the street and slipped through the doors of Dante's. There was one thing to be said for the Coalition, it had forced together a fascinating collection of refugees: artists, philosophers, teachers and poets. Anyone who could not see their way through to swearing an alliance to the New Christianity was there, and they outnumbered the less fortunate wanderers who I'd seen sleeping on the street earlier that same morning. Many of these free thinkers frequented Dante's. The future was bleak, but the conversations were good.

That night was no exception. Sitting at the bar, locked in conversation with a man I didn't know, was William Thomas, a local writer—it was always easy to spot his unruly blond hair from within a crowd. Writing was something that we had in common; although, he was more into avant-garde fiction than I. I'd met him through my brother years before when he had lived in Regina. A fair bit of William's work had been published, and I supposed that he made money at it. Other than that, he didn't work much, more of a professional student. I made a habit of getting in touch with him whenever I came into town. We'd seen quite a lot of plays together and spent long hours discussing literature. He had a cynical edge that I liked. When I returned to Regina that summer, it was Will who had found me a place to stay in the downtown. It helped that I had a lot of money, but if not for him, I could have been one of those poor souls sleeping under the stars.

Will knew things about me.

He had a pint in one hand; the other was wrapped about his square chin. From that bit of body language, I knew whatever the two discussed was disturbing to him. I called his name, and then made my way toward him. I wasn't sure if he'd actually heard me, but by chance he looked up and saw me approaching. There was nowhere to sit, so I simply stood beside his stool and waved above his shoulder to catch the attention of the bartender. Will glanced up and leaned toward me, raising his voice over the din of the bar.

"They're rationing."

As I stated before, rationing in Regina was an on-again, off-again phenomenon. Except for gasoline, it was pretty obvious that supplies were reaching the city. Quite often, however, prices were jacked-up, and we were told that stocks were low. Will suspected it was all a scam, but with a lack of alternatives, we just lived with it and paid what we had to pay.

"It's time to start brewing our own," I said.

He grinned then turned back to his companion. I arranged for a drink, a meal, then was lucky enough to notice a table emptying before anyone else beat me to it. In a moment, the three of us were sitting and moving the dirty glasses out of our way. Their conversation interrupted, Will made introductions.

The man's name was James Braxton. His eyes were too close together, reminding me somewhat of a hyena. I took in his black hair, squat, thickly muscled frame and felt an immediate sense of unease. Beside Will's lanky height, he looked short, but he didn't seem small. He said that he was from the Emac, but I was certain I hadn't known him. Shortly after the beginning of the revolution, and the split of the military, the Prime Minister realized the seriousness of the threat posed by the Coalition. She decided that what was left of the military, already stretched thin by Canada's obligations overseas, would not be sufficient to deal with the New Christian Army. In desperation, she passed martial law and began conscription. The influx of fresh bodies overwhelmed the infrastructure of the army and, of necessity, a new branch of the military was formed: the emergency army corps, which quickly became known as the Emac. There wasn't time to properly train the new recruits, nor was there money to outfit them in regular army apparel. What the government ended up with was a rag tag collection of armed civilians, most of who went to battle in jeans and Nikes. They were given rifles, pointed in the right direction, then set loose on the N.C.A. I had fought as an Emac, but my career hadn't lasted for too long a time.

Apparently Braxton's career was also at an end. He explained that his company had been devastated by the Coalition, and that was why he was now a civilian. Of course, that was everyone's story. It spoke of the desperate times, but in the field, desertion, regular army or not, was punishable by a summary execution. I'd seen it on the Island, and it was a prospect that left me cold. It was a modern Catch 22. Once you were in the military, you either died fighting, or you were shot for not dying while fighting. I guess if we were winning the war, things would have been different. But we weren't and things were the way that they were.

"Braxton here," Will was saying, "just got back from the coast."

The coast wasn't a favourite topic of mine, but I thoughtlessly replied, "What company were you in?" Stupid question.

"The 23rd." He grunted. "We were stationed out on the Island."

I sat back nodding, terrified that he might recognize me. The 23rd had been my company. I exchanged a brief glance with Will; a flicker of anxiousness twisted his features. His carelessness had put me in sudden jeopardy, and he realized it. Still, I hadn't recognized Braxton. There was a slim chance that we hadn't been fighting at the same time. Careers in the Emac were notoriously short.

His feral eyes narrowed. "Why weren't you fighting?" Braxton asked me.

It was an indelicate question, but such conventions didn't seem that important in those days. "I'm a prof," I replied. "Or at least I was. There doesn't seem to be much of a need anymore."

"You should have been fighting. Maybe we'd have had a chance if people like you hadn't taken an easy out."

I bit down hard on the "Fuck you" that rose as an instant reply. There were a lot of other things I could have said as well, but I made the wise decision not to respond. I decided that I didn't much like Braxton. It was odd that he didn't go after William, but perhaps they'd covered that ground already. I was considering making an exit when my meal arrived. I paid and then immediately began to eat, hoping that a full mouth would excuse me from further conversation.

The food was good, but I ate it so quickly that I hardly noticed. I paused momentarily, looking up and away from our table, avoiding eye contact with Braxton. I caught the flash of a familiar profile and quickly turned away, worried that it was someone whom I knew from before the war. Up until that point,

I had been lucky, but I knew such luck couldn't hold out forever. I stole another look and realized that the face belonged to the doctor I'd met that afternoon. Welcoming an excuse to leave Will's guest, I excused myself and made my way toward her.

She was speaking with another woman when I interrupted. "Hello, doctor, I didn't expect to see you again until tomorrow."

She stopped in mid-sentence and turned to me with a puzzled expression. For a moment I was afraid that she wouldn't recognize me, then she smiled and extended her hand, looking quite formal. I shook it, relieved. "Of course, Mr. Harrison, isn't it?"

"Jacob is fine."

She gestured to her companion, "This is Samantha. We work together." I recognized the other doctor from the hospital.

"Jacob?" Samantha asked. "That's an unusual name. Biblical, right? Jacob and the whale?"

The doctor grinned, "I think that was Jonah, Sam."

"My friends just call me Jake."

Samantha frowned. "Oh, that's not unusual at all."

This wasn't proceeding much better than my encounter with Braxton, and I was beginning to wonder what I'd gotten myself into when the doctor took my arm for the second time that day, and the inanity of the conversation didn't seem to matter so much. She had a beautiful, if somewhat sad, smile, and the illumination in the bar was more kind to her than the fluorescent lights of the school had been. When she smiled, the tired wrinkles about her eyes disappeared, and her entire face was transformed. I guessed her age to be in the early thirties, but I was certain they had been difficult years.

"I'd rather not continue thinking of you as 'the doctor'," I said.

"But I am a doctor," she replied. I must have looked frustrated for she smiled again and added, "My name is Christina." That was it, no last name. "It was very nice of you to volunteer today. I think you'll find Simon an interesting case."

"Simon?" I asked. "Isn't that biblical?" As with half my jokes, it died an awkward death. Both women regarded me with slightly confused expressions. I could feel my cheeks redden and was thankful for the dim light.

Christina mercifully terminated the uncomfortable silence, "We don't actually know his name. Like I told you, he came to us with amnesia, but we had to call him something, and he reminded me of character from a Golding novel, so I started calling him that. He overheard me one day, liked it, and the name stuck."

I hadn't read *Lord of the Flies* for a long time, but I was pretty sure Simon hadn't come to a good end.

The other doctor stared at Christina, "You read a book?"

Christina wrinkled her nose, "It was for a class."

Samantha regarded me. "So you're matching Jonah here up with Simon?" she asked.

Christina nodded, "We spoke today, and he said he'd be glad to have someone take him sightseeing." She frowned, "That wasn't quite the way that he put it, of course. You don't think that's a bad idea, do you?"

Samantha shook her head, answering slowly, "No, it's a good idea." She studied me carefully for a moment, and I realized she was not as vapid as she first appeared. "Has Christina told you what to expect?"

I shrugged. "He's lost his memory and vision. He needs a guide and someone to talk to. That's about it."

She chuckled, "Oh, I think you'll find a bit more to it than that. When do you meet him?"

"Tomorrow."

"Well," she smiled slyly, "good luck with that."

I excused myself a short time later and rejoined Will at our table. To my relief, Braxton had left. The expression on Will's face was truly pathetic. "Christ, I'm sorry about that."

"Forget it. Nothing will come of it. Where'd you meet that guy?"

"Years ago in university. He used to be an idealist, now he's all whacked up with bitterness."

"No kidding."

"He got after you a bit, didn't he? Sorry; he's not the same guy I used to know."

"Who is? Listen, if they're rationing here, can we go somewhere else and try to get a few more pints?"

He nodded, "Sure, I'm in." Standing up, he glanced at Christina. "Who's your friend over there?"

"Nobody really. Just someone I met at the hospital this morning."

"So you're going to do that?" he asked. Will had been with me when I'd seen the poster.

"Got to do something to pass the time."

"You're a writer, get back to it."

"Not likely, Will."

"Sometime, you know. It's in your blood."

"Then I'll get a transfusion."

When we walked out of the bar, Christina glanced over and caught my eye. I smiled, but she seemed lost in thought.

Out on Scarth Street, I paused to appreciate the evening. The night was lovely. The air was still warm, and it hung about us without a stir. That's an unusual occurrence—a windless day on the prairies. If I was to identify one thing that I hate about Regina, that would be it; I can't stand the wind, so to walk out to a calm night was like a blessing. I looked skyward at the fragmented constellations. Orion was up there; some limbs had been washed away by the dim city lights, but he still held his station. I wondered what the constellations would be if the ancient Greeks had possessed electricity. The night would have lost its fear, but it also would have lost its fascination. Sometimes less really is more. I could see the hazy glow of the moon sitting like a halo over the buildings.

Will spotted a carriage and made the executive decision that we would take a ride to our next watering hole. He whistled, waved when the driver looked, then we trotted over and climbed on board. The term carriage was a bit of an exaggeration. True enough, there were two horses tied to the front of the thing we sat on, but I was certain that the makers of the Volkswagen Beetle had never intended for their vehicle to serve such a function. It was a convertible and had probably been considered trendy in its day, but it hardly created that impression any longer. Battered shocks groaned under our weight, and one side of the carriage rested appreciatively lower than the other. I clutched at the door handle, fearful that a bump in the road would send me sprawling onto the street. In case the downtown bars were in collusion regarding the rationing, we decided that we should head to another part of the city. Will gave directions to the driver and the horses set off into the night. Their hoofs clomped on the asphalt in a muffled tattoo.

The downtown fell away behind us as we rode into Wascana Park. The moon came out from the shelter of the tall buildings and watched us furtively from behind the trees. Its pale light washed the world of colour and turned the branches and leaves above us into silhouettes. Will's angular features, half obscured beneath three days of stubble, appeared ghostly, as though I was riding with one of the undead. We had made our way southwest through the park then turned onto the Albert Street Bridge.

It wasn't that late in the evening, but the bridge was almost deserted. Perhaps it was the lack of other people, but my attention was immediately drawn to a small knot of men clustered by the side of the road, halfway across the bridge. The poor light made it difficult to be sure, but I counted six of them skulking in and out of the shadows. Although I couldn't identify anything specific that would substantiate the assumption, my immediate impression was that they were military. Their intentions may have been innocuous enough—there was little else for people to do during the evenings, but the sight of them prompted me to glance around the floor of the carriage, searching for a weapon.

I nudged Will and nodded in their direction. "What do you think?"

When he saw the group, his face registered surprise, and I noted the fleeting passage of something else—recognition, maybe? He turned quickly away, as if afraid that our curiosity would somehow draw their attention.

"Not good," he muttered. "We probably shouldn't come back this way."

Returning via a different route would mean crossing Wascana Creek by another bridge, and that would extend our ride by at least half an hour. I was about to suggest we turn back downtown when Will drew a sharp breath and grabbed my arm. "Look at this!"

I followed the direction of his gaze and spotted two people on bicycles approaching from the South. I shrugged, and looked back at Will, saying, "What's the big…?" But the sentence died half-formed on my lips. We had drawn close to the men, and I could see them when I looked over in Will's direction. The group had also noticed the approaching cyclists, and their collective reaction set off warning bells in my mind. There was nothing overtly aggressive in their reactions, but whereas before they had been slouching with hands in pockets, they suddenly assumed an air of alertness. The difference was so subtle, that I wasn't sure I hadn't imagined it, but the simple act of pulling their hands from their pockets spoke volumes concerning their intentions. They seemed to draw in on themselves, like lions crouching to spring.

Alarmed, I considered shouting to the cyclists, but Will knew me too well. He turned and growled, "Keep your fucking mouth shut."

I'd like to say that I was surprised at Will's reaction. I'd like to say that I ignored him and did the right thing. The truth of it, however, is that I was afraid. If I had intended to shout, I would have done it before he spoke. I hadn't, for I knew full well the consequences of my intervention. If I'd cried out, whatever demon of violence had those men in its thrall would have simply turned its attention toward us. The carriage driver must also have noticed what was happening, for he gave his team a quick lash of the whip. We jerked forward, and I stared in horror as the cyclists rode on to the bridge. The gang of men seemed to disperse, but I could see that they were simply spreading out to cover the width of the road.

We pulled away from the gang and drew closer to the cyclists. Time slowed to a crawl, but I was unable to react. I forgot Will and the driver, focused only on the two that approached. They were teenagers, a boy and a girl—the girl was laughing. They both had long hair; the girl's hung down, framing her face, but the boy had his tied back into a ponytail. That's how I saw it. As they pulled abreast us, just yards away, I caught a clear glimpse of his profile, and I gasped at what I saw. Tattooed onto his temple, clear even in the moonlight, there was a small cross. I quickly glanced back at the waiting men and understood. This was not to be an opportunistic attack, not arbitrary; this was an ambush. The tattoo on the boy's temple proclaimed him to be a New Christian. Most likely, the girl was too. I had no idea what had transpired before, but obviously those men knew that at this time those two would be coming this way. If my earlier assumption was correct—that the men were military, then the boy's desire to flaunt his brand could turn out to be a final, fatal act of hubris.

Ultimately, however, this was all on my shoulders.

I realized with a start that I was standing in the carriage, twisting backward as the teenagers passed by. I was yelling, but I couldn't tell you what words I used. Will clutched at one arm and tried to pull me back onto my seat, but I struggled against him, suddenly determined to intervene. The carriage driver must have realized what I intended. No doubt concerned for his own welfare, he snapped his whip and shouted at the horses. When they jumped forward, I lost my balance, and Will gained the upper hand. He dragged me down beside him then threw his weight on top of me.

Twisting back, I saw the gang surge toward the teenagers. We sped away, and I could do nothing more than watch.

II

I slept restlessly, so I didn't leave for the hospital the next day until a little after noon. The streets were clean and fresh. Overnight, thunderclouds had piled skyward over the prairies then rumbled down and vented their fury on the city. My apartment windows had rattled with the rain. Hangover non-withstanding, I arrived at the hospital feeling refreshed and eager to see Christina once again. Simon hardly entered my mind. Had I known what he would come to mean to me, and the fate that awaited him, I wonder if I'd have ever returned to that building.

The entrance to the erstwhile high school had no sentinels as it did the day before. I noticed that no flag had been raised over its front lawn. There was an overall air of neglect about the place, and I had an unsettling intimation that it had been evacuated sometime during the night. Once inside, however, the impression was dispelled, although it took some time before I'd shaken the residual emotions.

I couldn't find Christina immediately, but after wandering about the hallways, I ran into her near the entrance to the school library. She stopped dead in her tracks and regarded me with a surprised expression. "Well, if it isn't Jacob and the whale."

"Very funny."

"Someone gave you directions?"

"No, I've been looking for you."

"Coincidence. This is the place. Simon's in here."

"I thought we could talk a bit before you introduced me to him."

"Oh, you must be nervous," she concluded mistakenly, "but I don't have any time right now. This day has been frantic." She pulled open the door to the library and escorted me in.

The room was tight with beds. The counter behind where a librarian should have stood was cluttered with boxes and piled clothing. Books still lined the walls, but the shelves that once would have filled the room had been removed and replaced with cots. At the moment we entered, most of them were empty. At the far side of the room, however, a small group of young men were gathered around a figure lying face up upon one of the cots. Three of the youths stood; a fourth, with his back to us, sat upon the makeshift bed, holding the hand of the boy who was lying down.

"There's Simon," Christina said, "but…."

We walked closer and what had appeared a scene of little consequence suddenly assumed great import. Almost certainly, the boy upon the cot was dying.

If that's Simon, I thought, *he won't be needing me after all.*

None of the youths looked up when we approached. The one sitting, slight of build and with blond hair, was speaking so quietly I couldn't make out his words. The boy lying on his cot gazed up at the speaker. He was smiling, seemingly enraptured.

When I had first thought to come to a hospital, at some level I was aware that people died there. On that day, however, after what I had experienced the evening before, my soul was too raw to face such a reality again. Yet there it was before me—oblivious to my needs or desires—that boy was dying. I wanted to turn away, to leave, and yet there was something about the tableau that transfixed me.

This was no morbid fascination like gawkers driving past a car accident. Something of a spiritual wonder had taken hold of me, and it found its cause in the particular aspect of that boy upon the cot. I sensed a luminescence; it was as though he had been washed clean, and whatever it was inside of him that would carry on after he left us was being allowed to shine through. I don't know if Christina experienced anything of what I saw; somehow I thought that she didn't.

We came close enough to hear snatches of what the blond boy sitting on the cot was saying. His words came to us as from a distance, a voice more like music than words. I couldn't have repeated what he said, but I could sense its meaning, the soft strains of a farewell. Quiet and serene, the phrases brushed against us and then receded, whispering like waves. Christina stopped, and as if expecting me to interrupt, lifted her hands for silence. The blond boy swayed ever so slightly side to side, leaned forward, kissed the boy upon the cot and whispered too quietly for us to overhear. The boy stopped breathing.

Christina gasped and moved swiftly to kneel beside the bed. She pressed fingertips against his throat. The one who had been speaking reached down and took her shoulder in his hand. I saw his face, and, like the voice I'd just heard, it too had an ethereal quality. His were the eyes of seraphim. It was, of course, an absurd impression, no doubt a product of the gentle surrender I'd just witnessed.

Christina looked up, the lines of pain so clear. She began to speak, but the youth shook his head. "It's out of your hands, doctor," he said. "Just let him go." Tears welled in her eyes.

Feeling like an intruder on something intimate, I backed away, then turned and left without saying a word.

I stepped out onto the street with the full intention of getting drunk. There was little reason not to. There I was in that strange city awaiting the coming of the Apocalypse, suffering the loss of a woman I'd loved my entire life, and trying to drive the image of the doctor from my mind. I didn't know why the death of that young man had upset me so. Maybe it just reminded me too much of what I'd seen on the Island. I hadn't known the boy. I really didn't know anything about him, but I'd watched his beautiful face grow dim and understood…understood something. I wasn't sure what.

In any case, I left the hospital determined to obliterate the memory of the past few days.

And I was close to obtaining that goal hours later when Will found me at the Free House, a café on Albert Street, a little distance from the downtown core. Unfortunately, Braxton was with him. After what Will had said the night before, I was surprised to see the two of them together. Perhaps they had some connection I wasn't aware of. The rationing from the previous night was no longer being enforced, lending credence to Will's suspicions. With a glass of chilled whisky swishing sweetly, I'd forgotten the death in the afternoon and was sliding smoothly into the evening.

"Heya Jake, where've you been hiding out?"

Where haven't I been hiding out? I thought, bitterness welling. "Hiding out?"

"Yeah, I've been looking for you since before dinner."

I shrugged, slurring, "I've been here all afternoon. There was nothing I had to do, nowhere I had to be."

Braxton nodded at me. *Fuck you*, I thought, returning a curt nod. *Why weren't you fighting?* I wanted to spit into his face. I had been on the Island. I'd stood in the night. I had blood on my hands too.

"What happened at the hospital?" Will asked.

"It didn't work out. I left."

"Ah." He sat and Braxton followed suit. They signaled the waitress and ordered drinks. "There's news."

That cut through my drunken haze a little. News in Regina was a precious commodity. The Coalition controlled communications, so there was no contact with the outside world. We were in the dark, but every once in awhile, fragmented bits of information reached the city. All of it was suspect, but we hungered for it nonetheless.

"What is it?" I asked.

Braxton took his whiskey from the waitress and began talking. "Word is that the army has been routed. You know that the military set up their defense south of Regina?" I nodded. "Well, the N.C.A. arrived last night." I grunted—the N.C.A. As far as I knew, only the Emac called them that. It was short for the New Christian Army, but most people just referred to them as the Coalition. Technically, that was a misnomer. The Coalition was the political party; the N.C.A. was its muscle. When it really came down to it, however, they were pretty much the same thing. "The military was obliterated in a couple of hours."

It was much as I had expected—everyone recognized that it was a fait accompli, but I had difficulty accepting Braxton's word. The telling of it seemed to satisfy him too much. At the time, I thought it made him feel self-important. In retrospect I came to understand that the triumph of the Coalition excused him in some way for having failed as a soldier and not returning to the war after the 23rd fell. Apparently, there is no shame in losing to an invincible enemy.

I glanced at Will for confirmation. He nodded. "It's what everyone says. Hell, you could hear the artillery all afternoon." Locked inside my own musings, I hadn't noticed a thing. "The wounded have been streaming into the city for hours. They didn't even see it coming, just got the shit blown out of them. They were so under supplied that they could hardly return fire."

"Poor bastards."

Will said, "Curtain call for madmen."

I saw Braxton frown, then he snapped, "What the hell is that supposed to mean?"

"It was a suicidal gesture," I said. "They must have known they didn't have a chance."

"At least they had the guts to fight." His hostility, which had flashed at William, was just as suddenly directed toward me.

"I guess that's one way to look at it." I was about to ask Braxton why he hadn't been out there too, but Will interrupted.

"The Coalition could be here by nightfall."

"There's talk of setting up a resistance," Braxton added.

After what he'd just told me, the suggestion was ludicrous. I laughed bitterly. "Remember Tiananmen Square?"

Somehow he missed the allusion and continued, "There's also a rumour that Joseph Adams is coming. That means he'll most likely lead the troops into Regina." The idea shocked me, but it was certainly possible: Adams was the founder of the Coalition, and I supposed that also made him the commander of the New Christian Army. I knew he had been in Vancouver, but I doubted that he followed the army everywhere it went. Still, Regina would mark the end of the revolution. It stood to reason that he would want to be present.

I wasn't sure why Braxton found this piece of information significant. As I regarded him, he leaned forward and said, "Somebody needs to put a bullet into his skull." The expression on his face made me feel somehow dirty.

My God, I thought. *This guy is dangerous. If someone kills Adams, they'll raze this city to the ground.*

Fortunately Will was there to speak before I framed an appropriate comment. "It's not likely that he'll ride in at the head of the troops."

"I wouldn't doubt it. The guy's got a Christ complex. By this time, he probably considers himself the Second Coming." That sounded too intelligent for Braxton; he'd no doubt heard it somewhere else.

"Are they going to allow people to swear over, or are they going go burn us down like Vancouver?" I finally asked.

Braxton was silent. Will took a long draught of his beer then answered me, "I guess that's the question, isn't it?"

An hour later, we walked from the Free House and William suggested we head to Wascana Park. A few blocks south from the café, the street intersected a pathway that followed the serpentine windings of Wascana Creek as it made its way through the city. The banks of the creek had been set aside for parkland. We set off in this direction. At some point, Braxton left us, but I wasn't clear headed enough to take note of it. It was a beautiful night, incongruous with our circumstance. Will and I walked for about an hour before turning back. Neither of us spoke much. We could see the light of the city as a pale glow on the underbelly of low hanging clouds.

That night, I slept a fitful sleep, undisturbed by dreams, but restless nonetheless.

As they often did, my thoughts the next day drifted toward memories of Katherine. I had been a fool to leave her before the revolution and a fool to stay away after the fighting began. Of all people, I should have been able to predict the desperate actions of the Coalition.

After breakfast and coffee in a corner shop, I set off walking and soon found myself wandering near the hospital. The sun slanted eastward. I stopped at the edge of the school grounds. The grass was moist. I lay upon it, letting the dew seep through my clothing and shivering with the chill. The sky swept above in an incredible arch those not from the prairies could never comprehend. At the edge of my sight, treetops rested quietly in the still air. And, once again, I thought of Katherine.

"Let me go with you," she had argued for a final time.
"And put you in danger too?"
"We'd be together."
"But we *will* be together. This will pass. They'll forget about me in no time."
"Not soon enough."
"You can't just give up your job."
"What about you?"
"Are you kidding? I'm as good as fired. Besides, I can never go back into the classroom. I need you to be my anchor, Kate. Together we have a life here, and I want to come back to it."

She kissed me and nestled her face against my neck. Her thick, red hair smelled like honey. "I don't have a life here without you."

"Don't be so melodramatic," I said, unintentionally callous. She grew silent, angry. "Anyway, there might be another book in this."

"Oh Christ, that's all we need."

"They've made the last boarding call," I said. She didn't let go. "Come on, Katie. We'll be back together in no time."

"Let me have just another moment," she said, and then held me a heartbeat longer.

Moments pass. You rarely recognize the importance of a moment until long after it's gone. I had touched her back, kissed her neck, all the time looking over her shoulder and worrying that I'd miss my flight.

If only I had stayed, but leaving seemed the safest thing to do. A week earlier, we had been eating a late dinner when the sound of the doorbell interrupted our conversation. I'd been startled to find two detectives standing at my door. Drawn by our terse exchange, Katherine came after. When she saw my expression, she hesitated and her hand drifted up to cover her mouth. "What's happened?" she asked.

I moved closer so that I could touch my hand to her waist. One of the detectives began to speak, but I silenced him with a gesture. I looked Katherine in the eye and spoke slowly, "These gentlemen believe that there's a plot to take my life."

I watched the deluge of emotions flow across her face: surprise, worry, anger and resignation. I knew she didn't blame me for all that occurred, but she wasn't happy about it either. "We're not leaving," she said. "I'm not letting some neo-fascist moron drive me from my home."

I nodded in agreement. "You're right. We shouldn't leave...."

One detective interrupted, "These are not empty threats; we know...."

I ignored him and completed my thought, "but maybe I should." Katherine's green eyes flashed, and I ignored her too. "Listen, if I stay, they'll know where to find me, and sooner or later they will. You know as well as I do what kind of people we're dealing with." As I said the words, the thought occurred to me that there was nothing to guarantee the two detectives were who they said they were. The New Christians had infiltrated all aspects of society. More accurately, they came from all aspects of society. The two men I'd let into our home could have been assassins themselves. I looked at Katherine, and fear tightened my chest.

She glanced at the intruders, "How do you know this isn't a hoax?"

The older of the two sighed and shook his head. "Believe me, this is for real." He nodded his head toward me, "We've been watching your husband for months, and the Coalition has been following him for over a week. They know everything you do."

I looked at him in surprise. "Why haven't you picked them up?"

He hesitated, evidently uncomfortable with his response. "We thought it more prudent to let them think they were undetected. This allowed us to keep track of their movements, and it's how we uncovered the intended assassination."

Katherine tried to mask her anxiety with anger. "So why are you here now? They'll know you've contacted us."

"Because the situation has become unmanageable." He looked me directly in the eye. "It's time to take you into protective custody."

"The witness protection program?" I quipped sardonically.

"You're no witness."

"No," Katherine hissed. "He's a prophet."

I turned my back to the detectives and pulled her further into the house. "We knew this was coming, Katie,"—she took a deep breath—"and we can't just ignore it."

"Then I'm coming with you."

"I don't think you should." I glanced over my shoulder. "They're certain that the N.C.s have no interest in you. If you come with me, you'll be putting yourself in unnecessary danger. Both of us, actually; two can't hide as well as one."

"If we're being watched, they'll know where you go."

"No, they'll know when I go, which is good because they'll have no reason to come after you. But they won't know where; I'm pretty sure I can shake them. They're not that bright."

Katherine regarded me quietly for a moment, then she shifted her gaze to the detectives. "Don't trust them."

I shook my head. "No, when I go, I'll go on my own." I could see her shoulders drop ever so slightly; her eyes misted.

"I don't want you to go," she said, and I knew then that she was decided. Like a fool, I was relieved that I'd changed her mind. I should have paid heed to the sick feeling in my stomach.

As I lay on the grass trying to bring Katherine's image to mind, I couldn't remember whether or not she'd been crying that day in the airport. There beneath the magnificence of that eternity of sky, made all the more sweet by the approaching fire of occupation, all that mattered was the sad sound of her voice, the image of her face. And all that I could not bring to mind were those things. I had left her once. I discovered then that my memory had forced me to leave her a second time.

Who was to blame for that?

"Jacob?"

I looked up to see Christina.

"That *is* you. What are you doing out here?"

"Waiting."

"Waiting for what?"

"Godot."

"What?" Confusion clouded her features.

I sat up, smoothed the grass out of my hair. "Why aren't you inside?"

"I might ask you the same question. I thought we had an agreement." She sat beside me.

"After what happened yesterday, I didn't think...." My voice trailed off and faltered.

She nodded, laying a hand on my arm. Not understanding why, I resented her touch. "Don't worry; I understand," she said. "It's not easy to watch someone die."

You need to tell me that? I moved my arm away. "How are you doing?"

She frowned. "It's part of the job. We knew it was going to happen soon, and I didn't know that boy very well. Maybe that shouldn't make a difference, but it does."

It was my turn to be confused, "Oh, I got the impression he was something special to you."

Christina looked at me strangely, then ventured, "Simon asked me about you."

I returned the look then abruptly realized my error. "That wasn't Simon."

"No, Simon was sitting on the cot." Sudden realization lifted her features. "Oh, you thought he was the one who...? No wonder you left like that." She paused, considering. "Are you still interested in helping out?"

I nodded, intrigued by the thought of meeting the youth who had spoken so earnestly at the death of his companion.

It was later than I realized. Christina had come out to the grass to eat her lunch saying that she needed to escape from the madness of the hospital. Since the collapse of the army, they'd been inundated with casualties; the building was terribly overcrowded and noisy. Unexpectedly, I had an appetite, and she shared with me what little she had with her.

The realization that Simon was alive unsettled me. I was still committed to helping but felt too unprepared to see him that afternoon. I told her that I would stop by the next day and spend some time there. A little after that, she left, and I was alone again.

I spent the rest of the afternoon in the park, thinking.

Hours later, as I returned home, I came upon William sitting outside my apartment building. He was perched on the front steps, his knees pulled up to his chest, and his blond hair tousled by the wind.

He grinned as I approached. "Busy day?"

"Where's your buddy?" I returned.

"Uh? Oh, Braxton. I think he's still scouting out the encampment."

I felt sick. "What encampment?"

He started to laugh, albeit bitterly, then saw my expression and stopped. "You don't know? Where have you been all day?"

"Hung over and in the park. What's going on?"

"They're here."

You've heard the old cliché about how a person's blood runs cold. When he said those words, I realized that it isn't not true just because it's a cliché. The N.C.A. had arrived. "In Regina?"

"No, outside it. There's an encampment about a kilometre outside the city limits."

"How do you know it's the Coalition?" He just looked at me. "All right, well, what have they done?"

"Nothing, just set up camp. Someone said, and this is coming from someone who heard it from someone else, so take it for what it's worth, but apparently this is how they operate."

"Why? What's the purpose of waiting?"

William shrugged. "To freak us out, I guess. How should I know? Maybe to give the people a chance to swear over."

"We'll never get that chance if Braxton has his way."

"How's that?"

"Taking pot shots at the new Messiah."

"Ah, Braxton's full of hot air. It'll never happen."

"Sure, you say, but how many madmen with guns have shaped the course of history?"

He shrugged again. "Wait and see what happens tomorrow."

I sat beside him on the steps. His leg touched mine, and I moved away. With all that was happening, it was still a beautiful day. I closed my eyes and let the sun bake my skin.

A little later I asked, "So why are you here? You didn't come to tell me about the Coalition."

He was quiet for a moment. "No, I didn't. I have a proposition for you." I'd heard one or two of his propositions before and didn't feel in the mood to reject another. I said nothing, but he continued anyway. "Do you remember my friend Roland?" I didn't. "He owns a riding school near Maclean. He's a young guy, married with one kid. His parents live on a ranch near Kananaskis. It's a beautiful place, I've been told, hidden in the mountains. Pretty self-sufficient."

He had my interest. "And?"

"They lost most of their hands to the Emac and have asked Roland to come and help them out. He's going to do it, join his stock with theirs and live on the ranch."

"How will he transport them?"

"By trailer."

"They'll be spotted by the Coalition."

"Not if they use grid roads and travel at night." He paused, "And why would the Coalition care once they've taken Regina? No one would be suicidal enough to try to get across the border, and where else is there for people to go?"

"Okay," I nodded, "so what?"

"It would be a safe place, Jake." It sounded funny when he called me that, but I understood why he did it. "As likely a place as any to hide from the Coalition."

So he was leaving Regina and wanted me to go with him. I felt strangely unmoved by the proposal. "When?"

"Roland's not ready yet, but soon, before the occupation."

I felt empty inside. "Let me think about it?"

"Sure," he stood up, "but you need to decide soon; we've got to get supplies together, and we don't know how long they'll wait out there."

I nodded, said goodbye and watched him go. The whole discussion had a surreal quality to it, as if it would never happen, even having seen what I had seen. After all that I had been through, and after finally arriving in Regina, it didn't seem right that I would have to move on. I was so tired of running.

Westward, I could see the rough edge of the horizon. I studied the clouds for a long time, deciding nothing.

I arrived at the hospital the next day shortly after lunch. Christina couldn't be found, but her friend, Samantha, escorted me through the converted high school. It was a lot more crowded than it had been when I'd come the other day. Refugees from the army's ill-fated last defense against the Coalition filled its hallways and beds. The place was dark with uniforms—most of them tattered and stained. There were other wounded, not in uniform, whom I took to be deserters from the Emac—people like myself.

We arrived at the entrance to the library where I'd first met Simon. "He's expecting you," Samantha said. We entered the room and searched through the forlorn faces for his quietly closed eyes. Patients lay moaning; some sat slumped on the edges of their cots, their eyes dim and without hope. Simon was nowhere to be seen.

I looked around. "Should I wait?" I asked, hoping she would say no and not leave me in that place.

"I don't know. I suppose you should, and I'll go find Christina. She'll know where he's at." She smiled and left me alone. I stayed for less than a minute, then decided to go search for myself. It was better to be with the walking wounded then with that battered parody of humanity in the library.

The high school was a poorly lit place, but outside it was another beautiful summer day, and light made its way in through windows at the end of each hallway. The effect was an eerie one, for as I made my way through each dim corridor, those before me, silhouetted as they were by the illumination of the windows behind them, took on the aspect of phantoms. I walked through a hallway of ghosts. And it was in such a hallway of ghosts that, appropriately, I saw Simon for the second time. Recognizing him, I was at first nervous. We hadn't spoken before and hadn't been introduced. What was I to say? How do you approach a blind man? As I came nearer, however, my hesitation faded.

Simon sat upon a low bench set before the window and nearly stretching the width of the hallway. The window faced south and warm sunlight flooded through it. The floor was tiled and reflected almost as much light as there was above. The effect was that Simon appeared bathed in luminescence. When he moved an arm, the light shifted with him as if he were clothed in it. When I came close enough to actually discern the features of his face, I realized with a start that I couldn't have known it was Simon before that. For a short span, I had been blind as he was, yet I had recognized him. Stranger and stranger still....

He had his head tilted back and eyes closed. There was a serenity about his face that was not lessened by the stark brilliance of the sun. I sat beside him. From the slight movement of his head, I could tell that he had heard something, but he didn't say what it was. I used the moment to study him.

He was young, certainly not more than eighteen; his jaw looked like it had never been scraped by a razor. It was a thin, clean face, the face of an aesthetic, yet it wasn't hard at all. Almost delicate, I thought. Long, sandy hair framed it. I found myself wishing that I could see his eyes.

"Are you through?"

Although I'd heard it before, his voice startled me. No doubt I moved away. "Pardon?"

"Are you finished?" He lifted his hands toward me. "Here, it's my turn." I was only momentarily confused, then I sat and took his fingers in mine, guiding them to my face. Gently, he touched my features, like a butterfly brushing my skin. Delicate touch on cheek, bones, nose—smooth over my blinking eyes. Here he hesitated, then followed the lines of my face to touch my lips. "So you're Jacob," he grinned, and I assumed that Christina had told him I'd be there. "The name doesn't suit you."

My skin crawled, fearful of discovery. "It's the name my mother gave me," I quipped. I hated lying; but now, in retrospect, I know that even then he suspected the truth. Everything else that followed just confirmed it. He simply waited for the right time to let me know.

"Well, I've looked forward to meeting you," he said, smiling. "I appreciate you coming here."

"I don't...."

A voice interrupted me. "Hello, boys." I looked up to see Christina. I hadn't noticed her approach.

"Hello, doctor. How are you today?"

"Same as I was an hour ago, Simon." She sent me her smile. "I'm sorry I wasn't around to meet you, Jacob, but you two seem to have found each other all right."

She stayed then for a time, and the three of us exchanged useless bits of information. Don't infer that it was unpleasant for me. Simon struck me as intriguing, and I had already decided that I enjoyed Christina's company. It's just that I've always hated small talk, and there was little more that we could hope for during that first meeting. I sensed that Simon felt the same way. We ended the discussion with my commitment to return and help him extend the limits of his life beyond the hospital.

III

For some reason, the encounter with Simon left me altered, yet I could not exactly identify what had changed. We'd only spoken briefly, but as I walked home through the city, so much of everything seemed new and different—a resurrection of sorts. We'd voiced pleasantries and then quit each other's company. So what had he done to me? What was it about that exchange, prosaic as it was, that had affected me?

Uncomfortable with the incomprehensible, I struggled to push the feeling aside.

People passed me on the street, and I found myself giving them a wide berth. The action brought back an unpleasant recollection of my time on the Island. Did I recognize a more desperate look in their eyes than what I'd seen earlier that week? The arrival of the Coalition would explain such panicked glances. Perhaps I was seeing some of the new flood of refugees. Certainly they would understand the tentative nature of our respite in Regina.

I decided I needed some familiarity to help centre myself, something of comfort. I remembered that not too far from the downtown there was a small coffee shop where I had often gone in the not so distant past. All things considered, I supposed that some of my worst writing came out of that place, but it was also true that some of the best things I had written had come to me as I'd sat on its outside terrace sipping coffee and scratching notes in my journal. I decided to go there, fairly certain that I would not have my deliberations disturbed by anyone I knew.

As I walked, and the more I saw, bits and pieces of memory began to fall into place. Had it only been the summer before when I'd been there last? It seemed like so much more time had passed. I remembered that across from the café there was a cathedral, and I began to look for its spires as I drew nearer my destination. It hardly justified being called such, by European standards anyway, but in Regina it stood out as a fairly significant landmark. I wondered how the parishioners of that church would react when its walls were torn down. They didn't know it, but the destruction had already been decided upon. The N.C.s would not leave it standing. There was a chance that I was mistaken, but after seeing the burnt out husks of churches stretching westward, I doubted that such a monument to the old religion would be allowed to survive.

I spotted the spires of the cathedral from several blocks away. They emerged between buildings and trees, like some distant beacon guiding me back from a far-off destination, but the mood I felt was not at all like a coming home. Certain aspects of Regina had changed too much in too short a time. Perhaps the coffee shop would no longer even be there: before I left, the owner, Peter, had been trying to sell it. The closer I came, the more nervous I grew.

I finally turned onto Thirteenth Avenue, the street where the cathedral stood. It was as it had always been. The road lead straight west, and as the sun sank lower and lower toward the horizon, it became increasingly more difficult to see. I'd lost my sunglasses, so was forced to walk with one hand sheltering my vision. When that arm grew weary, I simply switched to the other or squinted my eyes and carried on half blind. I hadn't realized just how tired I was. Walking thus, and with the sunlight warm on my face, I found myself slipping into a somnambulant state.

For some reason, returning to the cathedral stimulated a memory, and I recollected, dreamed of a time a decade before when in Regina I had decided to visit the home in which I'd spent the better part of my youth. My parents had moved to the interior of the mountains six years before that. I had my own house, and until that day it never occurred to me to go see what had happened to the place where I'd spent so much time with my family.

It was a Sunday afternoon. Some errand brought me to the neighbourhood and, out of curiosity, I'd gone in search of my past—or at least the memory of it. I drove slowly down the street where we'd lived, not wanting to hurry the experience. My strongest impression was of how quiet everything seemed. It was summer. The air was still and heavy—thick with humidity. I drove with my window open, hearing the grinding of the car tires upon the pavement. Children played along the side of the way, but their voices were curiously muffled, as if I heard them from a great distance. Time slowed.

Each house I passed added to the collective memory of my youth. That house was where the Brocks lived. I had known their son. In this other house, a friend I'd gone to school with would stop and call out to me whenever we happened to arrive home at the same time. It didn't matter how late it was or that we lived a half block away from each other. We'd shout to make up the distance. I frowned to think of the neighbours who had woken to our voices. In each patio and doorway I passed there lay shadowed rich histories and half forgotten faces.

As I drew close to my home, as though in precognition of what I would eventually discover, my mood turned dark, a touch melodramatic. I found myself taken with the sensation that that street was a river, and it drew me with a sluggish but irresistible current down to an inescapable destination.

Finally I arrived at the yard and the house where I'd spent my childhood. As I feared, it had been changed. The new owners had painted over its blue with a dark brown. The tree, which I had seen placed into the earth as a seedling and then grow to stretch a yard above me, was gone with only a depression in the newly planted grass to indicate where it once had stood. I envisioned that such a spot in the earth would, some day, also mark my passage. Other aspects of the place had also been changed, but they swirled together in my mind producing the aching acceptance that my memory had been gutted.

I sped away, suddenly sickened with the realization that my youth was forever gone, and try as I might, I could never return to that innocence which I had once taken so much for granted. Years later, the death of my parents would evoke in me the same sensation. While they were alive, I had always, albeit at an unconscious level, been able to fall into the role of a son—to play the child. With them gone, I stood next in line for death and nothing could protect me.

In my youth, I was prone to such melancholic broodings, but the truth is that we are young once only, and those days, the lamb white days, fall from us like autumn leaves.

I wondered how I'd react if the coffee shop were gone as well. *Is this the last thing I have to hold on to, a coffee shop?* It was almost too sad. Unlike in my memory, however, Peter's was still there, and the neon sign out front continued to cast its eerie glow. It was an old, wartime house that had been renovated into a café. The door to the kitchen had been replaced by a countertop, but on cool evenings, the fireplace still burned, as it must have done when the first family occupied its rooms. Across the street stretched the spires of the cathedral. In front of the café, a new sign had been erected that read: The Thirteenth Avenue Coffee Shop.

I mounted the steps and entered. Just to the right inside the door, there stood a five-foot high statue of a man, holding his hand out as if begging for money. I'd forgotten he was there and almost slammed my elbow through the opposite wall when I jumped away in surprise. Hand clutching my chest, I laughed and cursed at the same time. Plastered on the wall beside the craven figure, there were a multitude of posters announcing upcoming events within the city. On the surface, they were a cheerful display of colour and artistry—fabrics of a cultural mosaic, but a closer examination belied that superficial impression. Every event advertised on that wall had already come to pass. There was nothing new. I was looking at the artifacts of a world that had slipped into oblivion. What was once a celebration had become a memorial. I turned away.

Inside the coffee shop nothing had changed, a little more worn perhaps, but otherwise the same. How much could change in a single year anyway? At one of the two small tables near the bay window at the front, a man sat alone writing in his journal, as I had been wont to do. He looked up at me, smiled, and I turned away. Further in, sitting beneath a side window, two girls sat chatting with their heads close together. Telling secrets, no doubt. *That'll have to stop when the Coalition arrives.*

Standing before the counter, I became apprehensive that Peter would be there to serve me. It was certain he would ask questions, and what could I tell him? I decided to leave, cursing the sentimentality that had led me into danger of discovery, when a dark, shaggy-haired young man strolled out from the kitchen and asked for my order. Relieved, I told him, then walked out to the patio.

There was no one out there. I sat near the entrance, removed my sandals and propped my feet up on the heavy, cement tables. After a moment, the waiter brought out my drink.

Few people passed by; fewer still stopped and entered the shop. I sat alone. With no one to watch, I found myself studying the street.

The day had passed into late afternoon. Though the air itself was beginning to grow cool, the light of the sun had a reddish hue to it that made the day seem warmer. Light at that time of day always fascinates me. It creates shadows like modern art—contorts and stretches, makes what is common, strange, what is beautiful, grotesque. It throws a floodlight on the west face of things, leaving the opposite side to the night, an interesting study in contrasts, and yet not a contrast at all, for appearance is not reality. Westward to the setting sun, the richly coloured light was sprinkled with clouds of insects floating on the air. Where I sat, I could see none of them, but I knew that they were there, hidden by the shadow. It was only the unusual cast of the light that allowed me to see what was otherwise hidden. I wondered what else of that mystic world was there which I knew nothing about.

Something large appeared to cross the street; I saw its shadow move in the corner of my eye. I glanced up to see nothing, then looked further down the road to spot a cat jumping up the sidewalk some fifty feet away—its doppelganger stretched by the long light. A few minutes later I heard its meow and saw it leap on the table next to mine, searching for food. I had none to give it.

I turned my attention to the cathedral, taking a moment to study its architecture and the sharp lines of light and darkness. I supposed that that was appropriate, though not in such a literal sense. There were two spires, each reaching over a hundred feet and ending with an ornate cross. The western height was alight with the golden sun; the other, shaded by the first, was in shadow. As a backdrop, the deepening blue sky framed them both. Between the towers was the main part of the church. The flight of stairs at the front led up to a large arched doorway with darkly stained mahogany. Above this, there was a window with stained glass set within a red, wrought iron frame. It was illuminated from within. The roof came to a triangular peak, at the top of which was a statue of Christ. He looked down upon me, his hands spread in supplication. He was wasting his time.

When the coffee shop first opened, Peter had commissioned an artist to paint a watercolour of the cathedral. As the story went, the man had procrastinated, then finally started working too close to the date of the café's opening. In his anxiousness to get done, he'd painted the blue of the sky over his penciled detail of Christ. The finished work was fairly large, and Peter placed it so that it was the first thing everyone would see as they entered the building. No one noticed that part of the image had been omitted. It was the painter himself who first drew attention to his mistake, but by then Peter hadn't the will to change it. The painting stayed as it was. I thought of it as the Church Without Christ—appropriately enough.

When the Coalition arrives, it will be Christ without the church. In the future, all that will be left of this cathedral will be an inaccurate painting and a few frightened memories. Perhaps I was being too pessimistic, but I'd seen enough of their handiwork to justify such a bleak point of view.

I heard a noise and glanced up to see the man I'd noticed writing in his journal opening the door of the café. He caught my eye, smiled again, then a look of surprise lit up his face. My heart sank when he approached. "'Ello, 'ow are you?" he said. It was what I had feared since coming to Regina. So far I'd been lucky, so many people had gone and so many refugees had flooded into the city that I had been afforded some degree of anonymity. But I was discovered. I wondered how long it would be until I was called to account for my role in the whole tragedy. I frowned and looked away. Funny thing was, he did look familiar, but I didn't think I knew him from Edmonton or Regina.

In response to my reaction, I heard him say, "Sorry, man," and the French Canadian accent made my memory click.

I blurted out, "Adam," before thinking to bite my tongue.

He turned back, grinning. "Yes, I know I recognize you. From Tofino?"

Flood of relief. He didn't really know me at all. When I'd left Katherine in Edmonton and went into hiding on the Island, Tofino seemed as far away from civilization as I could get and not entirely die from boredom. I met Adam working at a place called the Whale Station. It was a small company that arranged charters for sightseeing and whale watching. Adam was an expatriate Quebecois. He summered in Tofino and returned home during the winter. I had found him rather fascinating. He was well read, though not particularly educated, one of the throngs of neo-hippies who peopled the coast. We had struck up an immediate friendship that ended just as abruptly when I joined the Emac and set out to make war against the Coalition.

I had my foot on a chair and pushed it out from the table so that he could sit down.

"Jake, it 'as been a long time."

It hadn't actually been that long, but so much had occurred. We shook hands.

"Jesus, Adam, what are you doing in Regina?"

"What else?" It was a stupid question. What else indeed? He'd come to Regina for the same reasons as everyone who hadn't lived here: there was nowhere else to go.

"When did you leave Tofino?"

"Just before de occupation. Remember Frenchy?" He was a friend of Adam's who ran a one-boat charter company. We'd spent the better part of a day together unsuccessfully fishing for salmon. When we'd met I was surprised to see that he was a West Coast Indian, not French at all, so he stuck in my mind because of his inappropriate nickname. "Well, before de tanks come into Tofino, we ship out. We only travel by night, so it take us two day to reach de mainland. Frenchy keep going sout', but I get off and 'itch my way east."

I laughed, "You hitched here, all the way from the Coast? You've got horseshoes up your ass." I had gotten through the mountains too but had stolen a motorcycle to do it. I could hardly believe he had thumbed for rides, but that was Adam. "How did you know about Regina?"

"At first, I know not'ing, but I did not want to stay on de Island. I was on de prairie when I 'eard de Coalition left one free city, so I come 'ere."

"It appears you were misled."

"Yes, but what else can I do?"

We talked for awhile after that, sharing stories of our different experiences since leaving the coast. He told me that he hadn't passed through Vancouver, a blessing for him. Good for me as well, since he didn't know enough to press me for detail of my experience there. It was a relief to talk about my past without having to watch every word I said. I found out that he was living near the cathedral, being one of the lucky ones, like myself, who had found a place to stay. He rarely went downtown, which was why I hadn't run into him. I wondered who else was there that I'd missed, and, in retrospect, I wish I'd dwelt upon that thought a little longer; it could have saved me a lot of heartbreak.

It was getting late by the time I decided to leave. I finished my coffee and got up. "Good seeing you, man. I hope everything works out."

He looked at me oddly, saying, "Yes, for you too. See you around."

We shook hands again and promised to look for each other around town. I left. The sun had set and the city before me was clothed in darkness. Thick clouds had formed overhead, but in patches where the sky was clear, stars had begun to salt the heavens.

Adam. I hadn't really wanted to leave; I wasn't sure why I did. It was good to see someone that I knew without worrying about revealing my past, and we'd had a lot of fun together. I wondered what that expression on his face meant. Was he just lonely, like I was, or something more? If the former, I empathized, and I guess I should have committed to a definite meeting sometime, but I couldn't get a handle on that part of me which wanted to keep people distant. I'd developed a justified case of paranoia over the previous few months, and it had served me well. Still, I knew it was something I would have to work on.

Part of me felt it had been a mistake to come to Regina, that I should have stayed on the coast and accepted my fate. All I had done would only serve to prolong the inevitable. I had gone to Peter's to find an element of familiarity that would lend me some comfort for the evening, yet I left as tense and confused as ever.

I had only walked a few blocks from the coffee shop when I heard the sound of shouting echo down one of the southbound side streets off Thirteenth Avenue. After what I had just experienced on the bridge, I was at once curious and full of dread, but I turned from my path and set off to find the source of the disturbance. When I got closer, I was able to discern a number of voices and realized that some manner of crowd had formed. I saw a group of perhaps twenty people gathered before a man standing on the front steps of an antique furniture shop. I increased my pace, now anxious to discover what was going on.

As I drew close, it became evident that the man was arguing with the others, and the mood of the crowd was antagonistic. He appeared to have been chased and was now cornered on the steps. A few feet closer and I could see that he wore the black and white colour of a priest. That in itself was a dangerous thing. Since the first outbreak of violence by the New Christians, religious tolerance had disappeared, replaced by a deep and vicious resentment of anything non-secular. The priest was a fool, perhaps a courageous and idealistic fool, but a fool none-the-less.

One step closer and I could guess his age at the mid-forties.

A few more steps and I stopped walking. From a distance I hadn't seen the body slumped at his feet. Slight of build, it was bent forward, unmoving, with long hair obscuring its features. I got the impression the person was young. The hair was matted with blood. Dead, unconscious? I couldn't tell, and no force in Heaven could motivate me to go closer in order to find out.

What had happened there? Possibilities raced through my mind. Had the priest attacked the youth and the crowd intervened? Was the opposite true? Had the priest and youth been set upon? It was impossible to tell. Trying to piece together the sequence of events, I backed away a few feet and looked around. That's when I noticed the smear of blood on the sidewalk. Whatever had transpired, it appeared that the youth had been dragged to his or her position upon the step.

And what had happened then? I felt a strong compulsion to act, for really, wasn't I the underlying cause of all the violence? I was, but knowing that intellectually had little influence on my actions. Much stronger then my rationalization was my fear. Not just that I might become a victim of the violence, but that I may also have to witness what was almost certainly to occur. The fear was a near palpable force that pressed against my chest, driving me in halting steps back onto the street.

What was said or done to break the tableau, I didn't see, but before I'd gone far enough away to turn my back and leave, as though I wasn't a part of what was happening, the mob let loose the gathering violence. They surged forward and dragged the priest from the step. There was almost no sound, and the priest gave only a grunt before they were on him. Then there was nothing but a cluster of struggling bodies. Sickened and trembling, I staggered away only to collapse and vomit on the street. Once my head was down, I didn't have the courage to look up again.

A long time passed as I hunched in my own filth. The sky dropped a light rain that in no way made me feel clean. At some reptilian level, I knew that the crowd had disappeared, and when I felt nearly well enough to do so, I dragged myself to my feet and walked blindly home.

I never looked toward the antique shop to see what remained there, and I never walked that southbound street again. It became a path that was closed to me.

IV

Over a week had passed since I'd first been introduced to the enigmatic Simon. During that time, no word had come to us from the Coalition encampment that hunkered like some beast outside the city. Speculation was that they were waiting for something or someone—Joseph Adams most probably. I suspected that it was psychological warfare, and if that were the case, it was certainly working. The atmosphere in Regina grew increasingly tense. The influx of refugees had created a pressure cooker of disparate and desperate people. The downtown was overcrowded, and its facilities were beginning to falter. The streets were thick with the homeless; garbage had begun to clutter the roadways. An undercurrent of nihilism and violence heaved the stagnant waters of my birthplace.

Bored and uneasy, sleepless, overwhelmed by ideas yet unable to write, I sought distraction at Luther College. The makeshift hospital had grown to become a refuge for me. I realized that my main reason for going there was to see Christina, and, although I had rationalized the death of my Katherine, the growing attraction I experienced to the doctor caused me no small amount of guilt. I was close to stopping my visits when Simon himself gave me the incentive to return.

To say he was an enigma would not be accurate: that would make him appear too intellectual of a mystery. The more I saw him, the more Simon engaged me at all levels of my awareness. Samantha had been right when she cautioned me in the bar that evening before I first saw him. He was as open and unreserved as I was guarded; yet after a week together, he had come to know me perfectly, more than my deception should have allowed. Of him I understood nothing. He sought to discover his past; I sought to elude mine. Sometimes we would walk out in the neglected football field across from the school. Often, although it was crowded now, we'd just sit in the hallways and talk. Simon was a good listener. I guess he had to be, since he had little of his own experiences to add to a conversation.

When I was in his company, the other patients never came near us, and I wondered at their behaviour. From a distance, they'd watch us talking but would never approach. I knew they were simply awaiting my departure. I could understand a certain degree of fascination with Simon, but they appeared to idolize him in some way, something almost akin to worship. I wondered if they saw something in him that I did not. Now, of course, I know that they did. At the time, I was just too blind to recognize the obvious.

The past interested Simon. He was desperate for something to stimulate his memory. I had no desire to speak of the war, and he accepted that, but anything else was fair game. He had a voracious appetite for details. At times, I fancied that he actually didn't have a past—that he'd just been reborn somehow, so eager he was to live out my memories. Certainly more eager than I was. Life in Regina also occupied us for many hours.

He was most intrigued, however, by philosophy, and this subject matter figured predominantly in our discourse. The two of us were a dichotomy. There I was with a philosophy cultivated through years of study, thought and experience, face to face with a youth whom had none of those things. He was a total innocent. Well, not so innocent, in that hospital, he'd already seen more of death than anyone should. Still, his ideas were absolutely his own, free from outside influence—until he began speaking with me. Ironically, although I knew so much, I believed in very little. Everything I had ever thought, read or experienced had led me to the ultimate realization that philosophical and theological speculation was all a colossal waste of time. I worshipped the void, and, once or twice, had attempted to join it. At those times, even the void had failed me.

When I was a child, my parents had given me, absolute in its perfection, a beautiful image of the world cupped in the tender and protecting hands of God. Years later, my mother was diagnosed with cancer and after suffering terribly, lingering horribly, finally succumbed to the inevitable. The subsequent death of my father, also from cancer, and at a time when he had seemed to rediscover the wonder of life, destroyed that image as surely as a stone thrown through the stained glass window of a church. Years later when I tried to reconstruct the ideology, the pieces of that window no longer fit together. Subsequent events had ground the shards until I was left with nothing but mounds of dust and utterly without faith.

But Simon, Simon fairly shone with faith. His was an almost overpowering belief in…something; he just had no idea what it was. Still, he was determined to find out, and without my realizing it, I had been conscripted to serve as his guide. It was the blind leading the blind. If I could have been honest with myself, I would have realized that I was envious—Simon had something that I never did: he'd been touched by an illumination, but, due to his amnesia, he lacked the theological context necessary to apprehend what he was experiencing.

On a personal level, Simon's singularly particular circumstance evoked within me a sense of pathos, and I wished that he would recover his memory; intellectually, however, I was fascinated by his difficulties and wanted them to continue. His was the quintessential epistemological question: how do we know what we know? Everything he experienced came with some meaning attached, but how he interpreted that meaning, with no conceptual framework, was difficult for me to imagine. He did not approach any of the philosophical or theological texts he read from the bias of a preconception—there were no established ideas to be reinforced or contradicted. Everything might be true; everything might be false. I couldn't wrap my head around it, but I could appreciate that Simon offered us a unique opportunity to view the religions of the world. At times I felt like a Judas by helping him to make sense of things. I thought, hoped, that if he was left to his own interpretations, he might merge those disparate teachings into one pure belief that would unite the world instead of divide it.

At my prompting, he found a copy of the Bible then coerced nurses and fellow patients to read it to him. He devoured it in just a few days. I brought him *Zarathustra* and Lao Tzu, reading him lengthy passages myself, and then leaving, wearied by his insatiable curiosity. Each morning after, he asked for something new. One day, I was startled when he showed me a copy of *Slouching Toward Bethlehem* that one of the nurses had found for him. Since it was the catalyst that had started the revolution, it surprised me that some fanatic hadn't burnt it. When he brought it out, I experienced a moment of trepidation, then realized once again, as I often forgot when we were together, that he was blind. He hadn't found someone to read it to him yet, but I quoted him bits and pieces. When I left, I took it with me and threw it in a trash bin outside the college. I should have burned it myself.

Over the span of days, his strength increased to the point where Christina thought that it would be good to take him beyond the hospital grounds. I was at a loss as to where we should go. Busy streets, uneven walkways in the park, crowded cafés; these things seemed too inaccessible or inhospitable for a blind man. Still, it became increasingly obvious that the confines of the hospital were becoming tiresome for him; his insatiable curiosity demanded more stimulation. We set a date for his first outing and waited for inspiration to strike.

On the designated morning, I arrived at the hospital to find a carriage, a real carriage, parked outside the front hedge. The sight of horses on the streets still gave me pause. Though it was common enough, for some reason I had trouble growing accustomed to the image. As I drew close, I realized that Christina and Simon already sat within the carriage. They'd been waiting for me.

"What's this?" I asked.

"A buggy," the doctor answered me.

"So I gathered. You don't work today?"

"There are times when I don't."

There was an edge to her voice; something had upset her. "What's the plan?" I asked.

"Simon wishes to visit an old friend."

Odd, I mused, *for someone without a memory,* but I let it ride. "I'd thought we'd go to the Free House. It's not too busy early in the day."

"There's no reason we can't do both," Simon said.

"I'm easy." I climbed in, sitting opposite them, with my back to the driver. Christina asked him to get started, and the buggy set off, almost pitching me into her lap. "Where are we going?"

"You remember the boy who died that first day you came to the hospital?" Simon asked. It wasn't necessary to answer. "I'd like to pay him a visit."

It wasn't the type of outing I had anticipated, but it was Simon's call. I wondered if that was what was disturbing Christina. "All right," I said. "Which cemetery?"

"It's just north of downtown. Do you know it?"

I nodded. "I know it. Do you mind if we go to the cathedral afterward? I'd like to stop at the church, and the Free House is just down the street from there."

Simon's face brightened. "Good, I'd like to go there too."

The carriage rattled along, jostling us from side to side. I noticed that the driver was taking us on a circuitous route to the graveyard, but I didn't mind the extra time with Simon and Catherine. I'd travelled by foot so often that Regina appeared different from that height. I felt somehow removed from the problems of those poor pilgrims on the streets. Facing to the rear of the carriage, I wasn't able to see what lay ahead; I could only watch the world that slipped away from us.

The scenery was lost to Simon, but I could tell he was receiving pleasure from other things: the sun on his face, the wind and the sounds of the city. He wearied of this soon enough, however, and his thoughts turned to other matters. "Jacob?" he said.

"Yes?"

"I have a question for you."

I sighed; at times with Simon, I felt like I was teaching again. I made a meaningless gesture toward Catherine. "Why don't you ask the doctor?" It was an ineffectual half-formed joke.

Christine must have known what he was thinking and quipped, "This isn't my area of expertise."

"I take it this isn't a medical question," I said.

"Do you think he actually meant that there was no God, or that he just didn't know for sure?" Simon had an odd habit of picking up conversations hours after they had lapsed, in this case, a day later. Still, I knew who he was talking about. When this topic had first come up, I thought it troubled him. Evidently he had spent some time mulling over it.

Ah, it was a sunny day. The last thing I needed was to debate Existentialism. I closed my eyes for a moment, appreciating the warmth upon my skin. Surely summer wouldn't last too much longer. *Zarathustra* seemed so out of place in such a setting. I rarely taught it, and it had been so long since I'd read it, I couldn't remember exactly what Nietzsche had said. Did God even come up in that piece, or had Simon read something else? I finally responded, "I think the former, but the question's moot."

"How's that?"

Christina flashed me an accusing look. "Since you started visiting, he never lets up."

I grimaced. There was obviously something on her mind, but I chose not to respond. She seemed to have forgotten who'd originally brought us together. I said to Simon, "He's not really talking about God, just our faith in God. There's a big difference. One can be observed; the other cannot." I added, "I suppose he's figured it out by now anyway."

"Who has?"

"Nietzsche."

"Why's that?"

"He's dead. One way or the other, all of his questions have been answered."

"According to rumour, Harris' have too."

"What the hell are you talking about?" I snapped.

The question startled me; Simon had taken a completely unexpected turn. It occurred to me that the connection to *Slouching Toward Bethlehem* was not totally illogical, but comparing Samuel J. Harris to Friedrich Nietzsche was a considerable stretch. Regardless, it was not a conversation I intended to pursue.

"Couldn't you two save this for later?"

I thanked Christina silently.

"You don't find it interesting?" Simon asked her.

"No, it's useless conjecture. All those books you read, your so-called experts on the subject have never experienced what they're talking about. Where is their empirical evidence? Without that, this discussion is meaningless."

It was an old argument, valid for all that, but the lack of an answer does not belittle the question asked, perhaps the opposite. In any case, I didn't feel at all like playing the game. "She's got a point there, Simon."

"You don't really believe that."

"No, I...." I hesitated. Years before, I wouldn't have, but at that moment, looking within, I was surprised at what I found. "I guess maybe I do. It's all just rhetoric, Simon. It pays the bills, or at least it used to." He didn't respond, and I couldn't read his expression.

The horse and buggy clomped along the outskirts of downtown. The driver had taken a wide loop south of the graveyard and was now heading back north. We were not too far from Wascana Park and passed through an area, little more than a dozen city blocks, that I'd always thought was an embarrassment for the city. The people who hung around that area always looked so wretched that, at night, I would never walk alone through that part of town. As we rode through on that particular day, I saw a row of pathetic souls stretched in a ragged line that ended at the entrance to a small building that had the sign: Souls' Harbour Mission. I directed Christina's attention to it.

"It's like a line of refugees. What's going on there?"

She smiled a wry smile. "The same thing that always goes on there."

"What is it?" Simon asked.

"It's the Salvation Army. They give out food to the poor. It's been there for years."

"Huh, I never noticed it."

"You never lived here."

"I did, once. I was born here. I just never come by this part of town." For some reason, I couldn't tear my eyes away from the entrance of that building. I half rose from my seat.

"What's wrong with you?"

"I don't know. I wonder how they get food with all the rationing."

"People still give. I'm sure they always will. Anyway, the rationing's a farce."

The carriage swayed around a corner and the scene was lost to my sight. I looked back to Christina. "How do you run the hospital?"

"Same way. It's city funded, but we get donations from other sources too."

I felt immediately guilty that I'd never given them money. "Are you ever short of supplies?"

She shrugged. "Day to day. I'm sure one morning I'll show up for work and find the doors locked."

I nodded. *Day to day sums it up for all of us.* Simon was silent, either listening or lost in his own world. "Penny for your thoughts, Simon of the Flies."

"Oh, God, Jake, don't say that," Christina snapped at me. Simon just smiled.

"You gave him the name."

She just called me Jake, I realized. It was bad enough to lie about my name; the added familiarity made things worse.

"You know, it's not really fair that I'm named after a character from a book I've never read."

"He gets beaten to death by a mob of savages."

Christina ignored me. "He was a noble character, kind of a prophet."

"That's me," Simon said, "a blind prophet." The term struck a raw nerve in my memory. He laughed, "Isn't that what the Coalition called Samuel J. Harris, the Blind Prophet? Maybe they got it wrong: maybe it's been me all along."

I felt sick. I looked away from Christina who was shooting ineffectual daggers at Simon. We were silent for a time, a tense silence for all of us. I looked back when Simon called my name.

"What is it?"

"I had Samantha re-read part of the Revelations to me last night." He leaned forward in his seat, wrapping one hand about the other fist. "When Christ returns, do you think it will be as the lion or as the lamb?"

"It's the lion, Simon, and his name is Joseph Adams."

Christina cut off Simon's response, "We're nearing the cemetery."

I turned and looked ahead to our destination. *Here's one place that hasn't changed since the revolution*, I thought. *No, I guess that's not true. It has a lot more graves in it.*

The carriage came to a halt at the wrought iron gates of the cemetery. A short hedge served as a fence. Years before, it had stood ten feet high, but there came a rash of vandalism; gravestones were overturned; others had swastikas and pentagrams spray painted on them. The city was forced to cut the hedge down to its roots. The vandalism had stopped, but a terrible knowledge remained in the minds of the families affected by the vandals' actions.

The height of the carriage allowed me a fairly good perspective over the grounds, and I paused to study our destination. Freshly placed flowers splashed colour across the greens, making the place appear almost cheerful. I wondered where Simon would find his friend. Had he been buried, cremated? The sardonic thought struck me that with the high mortality rate plaguing the city even the dead would have difficulty procuring accommodations.

Christina climbed down to the street, extending a hand to grasp Simon's arm. "Let me help you down." Somewhat clumsily, he descended and stood at the curb, his head drifting from side to side. I could sense him soaking in the sensations of that world outside the hospital. What else did he know? "Don't let go of me, Christina."

"Don't worry, Simon. Here's my arm."

"Where do we go?" I asked.

"I'm not sure, but there must be a groundskeeper around here somewhere."

As we stood there looking over the rows of gravestones, it occurred to me that my presence might be an intrusion. I decided to leave them to their mourning. "Do you two mind if I don't tag along?" I asked. "I have some business at the cathedral, and I can just meet you there when you're done."

"I don't mind," Simon said. "We'll see you later."

I walked away, leaving them to search out their friend's grave.

Walking, it took me a half hour to reach the entrance to the cathedral. I'd lost track of the days, but I guessed it was Sunday, for the doors were open. I walked within.

The interior was dark. It took a moment for my eyes to adjust, then I made out the shadow of a couple praying midway up the rows of pews. Otherwise, the church appeared deserted. On the right hand side of the hall, close up to the altar, I saw a rack with candles illuminating the gloom. I walked to these and set down a dollar as a donation. A thought had formed during the ride from the hospital. Taking up a taper that was unlit, I palmed it and contemplated the significance of what I was about to do.

For me, symbolism has always had particular impact. Gestures often carry more meaning than words. Since arriving in Regina and after a month of searching its streets, countless hours of waiting in places that we'd once frequented, I'd finally grown close to admitting that Katherine was gone. En route from the hospital I decided to make a gesture, to light a candle in her memory, yet, standing there, I found that it was too terrible a statement to make. I trembled. By lighting that small flame, I knew I'd be extinguishing something else. In my heart, beyond rhetoric and lies, I would know that her death was true, and I just could not bring myself to surrender her to the darkness.

I gulped for a breath; my knees felt weak. I knelt on the carpet, bowing my head and struggling to bring her image to my mind. The candle trembled in my grasp. I brought both hands together before me, stood one up against the other that their strength could be united. My eyes clenched shut. It must have appeared that I was praying.

I can never remember a person's face. No matter how long I've known them or how much I cared for them, my memory always draws a blank. What I can remember are photographs. Kneeling in that church, I could not envision Katherine, but I could see a picture I'd taken summers before—one static image—and focusing upon that alone, the brightness of the day the photograph was taken flooded my senses.

"Water break," she had declared.

"Already?" It was three years before, midway up the ridge hike in the Yoho Valley. Katherine had suddenly stopped on the trail and dropped her daypack to the lichen covered rocks.

"I thirst; therefore, I drink." She plopped herself down on a nearby boulder and began rummaging through her pack. I walked back. "Cookie? They're wafer thin." We'd picked some up that morning at the Field bakery shop near the hotel where we'd spent the night.

"Sure." I slipped the weight from off my shoulders and sat beside her, facing out toward the valley below. The trail we were on ran along the edge of a rock cliff that dropped straight for two hundred feet. There was a fair bit of exposure, but the trail at that level was flat and dry. If vertigo set in, one could move away from the edge and scramble along the chaos of boulders that lifted up and away to a less accessible height on the mountain. The void bothered Katherine not at all. I was sure she'd be caught daydreaming some day and just step out to her death. I was affected to a much greater degree. I didn't find it so bad when we walked below the tree line, where I had something to hang on to if need be, but up there, the sheer volume of air sometimes made me dizzy. We'd gone rock climbing once. A good friend of mine had taken us up some easy routes in a valley not too distant from the place where we were that day. When I had finished my first climb and come back to earth all pallid and wan, Katherine said that I should consider myself lucky. The way that she saw it, I got twice the thrill for half the energy.

Regardless of my unease, the view was worth it. From our vantage point, we could see the white mass of a distant glacier that toed down into a perfectly flat alpine lake. The run-off from the lake fed the spectacular Takakaw waterfall that dropped several hundred feet to the valley bottom. I had read that it was one of the highest on the continent. I took out my binoculars. Near the top of the falls, there was a part where the water struck a lower ledge and shot straight out from the rock face. The water covered such a distance that, when I studied it through the glasses, it appeared to move in slow motion.

A sharp cry came from the valley. I stood and moved cautiously to the edge. There, sweeping in great, wonderful spirals, I spotted an eagle gliding below me. "Look." Katherine joined me, staring silently into the abyss. She sat, and when I turned to join her, I noticed a curious expression on her face. "What is it?"

She shook her head. "Never mind, you'll laugh at me."

I sat on the trail before her. "There are a lot of things I'd like to do to you right now. Laughing is not one of them."

She smiled that funny smile where the edges of her mouth turned down when they should have been curling up. "I know what you think, but when I look around at all this, I just feel like this should be our church, you know. Never mind building cathedrals and synagogues, just have everyone hike up these mountains and find the truth."

She was a smart girl, my Katherine. I pretty much decided on that trip that I would marry her. Of course, it took me another year before I built up the courage to actually ask the question.

"Maybe they'd let me bring my classes up here."

"Life on the prairies is a long ways away."

"Golden wheat fields and blue sky."

"Heavy oil up-grader and landfills."

"Yeah, but 'God is in the details.' Who's to say you won't find a flower in the garbage? Wouldn't that argue for the existence of a supreme being?"

She hooked a foot under my knee and lifted. I tipped, lying flat and looking at the endless azure above. The sun was brilliant. I whispered, "Crushed by my superior logic."

"Shall we go, Copernicus?"

I took hold of her ankle, reached up to squeeze her lithe calf muscles. "Wait a bit, Kate. I want to soak this in."

"Okay."

After a moment, I heard her searching through the pack a second time, then there came the click of her Yashica. I sat up. "Here." She passed it to me, and I snapped the picture of her. It was that picture that had stimulated my memory. Lowering the camera, I studied her face—her hair, auburn and cut short about her head. It glistened with the light, the strangest thing. Her lips made me shiver. Thick and rouge, the thought of kissing them sent me on a more precipitous spin of vertigo than the mountain ever did. Her skin was flawless, except for the small scar beneath her lower lip. When she was a child, a toboggan had lost its rider and struck her on the chin, splitting the flesh to the bone. I sometimes studied her, finding it difficult to believe that she had made the decision to be with me. With me. The scar helped. It was the one imperfection that let me accept that she was mortal.

"I love you, you know?"

"I know," I said.

She gave that grin again, "That old woman down at the hotel said we'd come across a small lake up here somewhere. I'd like to go for a dip."

I climbed to my feet and grabbed my pack. "Sounds good to me." She too stood, and I kissed her. "But I didn't bring my trunks."

She kissed me back. "Well, damn," she said.

I stood and placed the candle, unlit, back on the shelf where I had found it. "For you, Katie," my voice rasped, and I left the building. My vision, confused by the ambiguous illumination of the church, needed to adjust to the honest sunlight, and for a moment I was as blind as Simon. I blinked and shielded my eyes. Simon and Christina hadn't arrived yet, so I sat upon the top of the stairs that led down to the street. The city was quiet; the streets were almost empty. I thought of our times in the Rockies. *Up there*, I thought, *one can see more clearly, but here....* I thought of going back to the Rockies. A cooling wind stirred. Eyes closed, I let its gentle touch dry my cheeks.

It was some time later that I looked up to see Christina and Simon opposite me on the street standing beside the carriage. I hadn't seen them come. Had she called? Had I heard her voice? Christina checked for traffic, then led the blind prophet across the road. It struck me as odd, not so much that she stopped to look when there was no longer any traffic in this city, but that I had noticed it. Had the common place become so unusual?

They climbed the steps, Simon holding her elbow and walking slightly behind her. I could hear her whispered directions. It was good to watch them together. She couldn't have been more attentive; he couldn't have been more faithful. In the midst of all the insanity, I found comfort in their mutual trust. Although I was a lie, they trusted me too, and I believed it was too late to tell them the truth. My refuge had become a trap. There's a special place in Dante's pit for people who lie to friends.

"Sorry we kept you waiting."

"You didn't. Did you find what you were looking for?"

"Yes," Christina said, but Simon was silent, his face drawn. I motioned with my head, brow furrowing. Her weary eyes looked up at me.

"Simon?" I asked.

He shook his head, quiet, as if gathering thoughts—finally, "It was a mistake to go there, Jacob. I thought it would be…something…better, you know? But it wasn't like that at all."

"What did you expect?"

"I had no idea, but not what was there."

I looked to Christina, seeking her help, but she gave nothing in return. I didn't know if he wanted to talk about it, and he offered us nothing more. After an empty moment, I asked him if he wanted to go home.

"No," he replied. "I'd like to go inside first. Will you take me, Chris?"

"Of course."

"Jacob, you come too."

I didn't want to go back inside. "I've already been."

"You can describe it for me." Christina could have done that, but I capitulated and rose from the steps, then held the heavy door wide so they could enter together.

We stepped into the cool twilight of the cathedral.

The same couple knelt in prayer. At the front, by the cloth-covered altar, a priest stood talking to a young woman. I wondered where they had been. What work they had been doing? My face flushed. Had they seen me kneeling? We'd only walked a short distance down the aisle when the girl spied our approach and excused herself from the priest. She came toward us.

"Maybe we're not supposed to be in here," Christina said.

"No, I think we're about to get a sales pitch."

"You've got to be kidding."

"What's going on?" Simon asked.

"Someone's coming to speak with us."

"Who is it?"

"I don't know. A girl," I said quietly, watching the predator close in. "She's going to give us a spiel about joining the church. I don't want to listen to this." I stepped away, frustrated. The memory of Katherine was still fresh in my mind; I didn't want to lose it to this little churchgoer.

She came upon us. "Hi, is this your first time here?" Her voice was deeper than I'd expected. Up close, she didn't look so young as I'd thought at first.

Christina remained silent, watching her charge. On an angry impulse, I moved toward the girl, held out my hand, and she took it. I didn't let go. For a moment she seemed confused, then frightened. I asked her name.

"It's Diana."

"Is this your church, Diana?"

"My church?" She frowned, momentarily confused, then smiled. "Oh, yes, of course." She tried to pull her hand away.

"I mean, do you own this church?"

"Own it? No, no. No one owns the church. I'm just one of the congregation."

"People come here to see you?"

"Please let go of my hand."

"Jacob, what are you doing?" Christina asked.

I insisted, "Do they come here to see you?"

"They come here to be with God."

"Then what are you doing?"

"*Let go of my hand!*"

Christina's voice was angry now, "Cut it out, Jake."

The priest was looking our way.

"We don't need an intermediary."

The woman finally managed to jerk her hand away. Her expression, which had been confused and frightened, now seemed hurt. "I was only trying to be nice."

At that point, Christina stepped forward and took my arm. "I've heard enough," she said and yanked me toward the door. Pulled off balance, I almost stumbled, stretched a hand forward to catch my weight. As Christina moved us out, she glanced back at the girl and apologized.

Once outside, she squared up to me, inches from my face. "That was inexcusable."

I'd never seen her like that, and it startled me. Anger was not an emotion that I'd ever associated with the doctor. Caught off guard, I resorted to professor mode. "It certainly was," I said. "She had no right to do that." Christina said nothing, but I swear her eyes smoldered at my sarcasm. "I wanted her to understand what she was doing. Her actions are indicative of the Church throughout history. It's never helped people to understand anything, only interfered with the process." I hated sounding so pedantic, but her reaction had surprised me.

"It was none of your business."

"She made it my business."

"You didn't have to scare her."

"Sometimes you have to shock people to get them to listen."

"There's never any reason to hurt someone."

Somewhat clumsily, Simon had followed us outside. "Jake has nothing to apologize for," he interjected. "I would have rather just walked away, but she had no right to confront us like that."

"All she did was say hello."

"No, it's not as simple as her just coming to say hello. Spiritualism isn't a community event."

"It *is* that simple. Life is simple; it's made up of simple things. What's the point of all your philosophy if it doesn't teach you to be civil to each other?"

"Christina, you're taking way too narrow a viewpoint. Who…?" She left before I could finish. I watched her cross the street, this time not checking for traffic, and climb into the carriage that awaited our return. She sat with arms folded, her head turned from away from us.

"She's wrong," I said.

"Everyone was wrong," Simon mumbled.

"Perhaps."

He took hold of my arm, and I escorted him down the cathedral steps.

V

The carriage set off with the driver following our initial instructions to take us to the Free House. I didn't know if Christina would still want to go, but I was hungry and didn't intend to say anything if she didn't. She sat looking away from me, staring but not seeing the buildings clomp by. The muscles of her jaw worked stoically. I wanted to explain myself to her, justify my actions, but for all my rhetoric, I knew that the strength of my reaction to that mislead girl had indeed crossed the line. Simon saw the truth—everyone was wrong.

It took only five minutes to get to the café. I told Simon that we had arrived, and he lifted his arm for me to assist him. When we were both standing on the sidewalk, I reached back and offered the doctor my hand.

"Mademoiselle?"

She made eye contact with me for the first time since we'd left the cathedral. "You're a rogue," she said.

"You've got a temper."

"And you're a troublemaker."

"You don't know the half of it."

"Oh, yes I do."

"Regardless, are you going to join us?"

Without comment, she took my hand and descended.

The bar was almost full, but the atmosphere was subdued. Out of habit, or perhaps intending a statement, Christina guided Simon's hand to the crook of her arm. I held the door, letting the two of them pass before me. We stopped inside the entrance and looked over the crowd, hoping for a place to sit. I hadn't expected to run into him anywhere except the Thirteenth Avenue Coffee Shop, but I noticed Adam at a table against the far wall. A young woman sat beside him. He saw me as well and waved to get my attention. As we approached, I realized with a shock that I knew his companion. I smiled, calling out "Moe!" and she smiled too, standing to give me a hug.

"Jacob," she said with her light French accent and almost perfect English. "Adam said that he'd seen you. I'm glad to see you too." She looked no different since first we met several months ago in Tofino—tie dyed tank top and wrap around print dress. Half her left forearm was covered with hemp bracelets, and between her breasts she wore a pewter moon design hanging on a leather thong. I'd been with her when she'd purchased that. Her hair was sandy and constrained in dreadlocks that didn't quite hold together. She was as eccentric and as beautiful as ever.

Moe had been with friends in Tofino, two other girls like herself who had dropped out of university and headed west to see the rest of the country. That was before any news of the Coalition had begun to shake the peace. The three of them had left the Island before I'd joined the Emac. I was curious why she was alone but afraid to ask what had happened to her companions.

Adam invited us to take a seat. Christina assisted Simon while I went in search of a fifth chair for the table. When I returned, Christina was explaining how she and Simon had come to be there with me. As she spoke, I caught the attention of a waitress and took the liberty of ordering us drinks. Adam had made sure that everyone knew each other. He'd introduced Moe as Moe. It wasn't her real name. When we'd first been introduced on the Island, I'd found it impossible to pronounce her French name. She shortened it for me. After awhile, everyone started calling her the same thing. Despite our difference in ages, we had become immediate friends.

"It is good you join us, Jake," Adam said, and I chuckled to hear him speak. He and Moe both spoke so well, but Adam, aside from his thick accent and difficulty with verb tenses, always sounded like he was reading from a textbook. Moe, on the other hand, sounded entirely natural.

"Why is that?"

"We are finishing a conversation dat begin months ago."

"Okay, that narrows it down some."

"Do you remember Moe de Samuelite?"

I groaned. Conversations always seemed to come around to my least favourite subject. Moe and her friends, Adam excluded, had formed their own New Christian sect that they called the Samuelites. They had discussed it tongue-in-cheek, but at the heart of things, I believed they were sincere. It was a dangerous thing for them to be saying. Sentiments against the New Christianity were strong enough that any type of affiliation to the movement could get someone killed. Moe was very courageous, very foolish or just suicidal. Adam was wrong; it wasn't good that I was there. It had made me more than uneasy to discuss it on Vancouver Island, and Regina was a much more dangerous venue. I didn't feel like resurrecting the topic.

"You'll have to fill the rest of us in," Christina said.

Adam explained, "Moe is a defender of Samuel J. 'Arris."

Christina rolled her eyes and tilted her head back to stare at the ceiling.

"Why is that so unusual?" Simon asked.

I spoke thoughtlessly, "Christ, Simon, take a look around you." His sightless eyes stared through me.

Simon smiled, angling his head forward. Moe had been studying him; abruptly she understood and blurted out, "Oh, tu es aveugle," then put her hand to her mouth, embarrassed at the outburst.

The smile remained on Simon's face. He extended his hand, palm up, and with sudden trust, Moe reached forward and took it. "It's okay. I'll bet I'm the only one here who can appreciate that wonderful perfume you're wearing." She looked confused, then grinned.

Adam leaned closer to her. "I smell not'ing."

She lifted her bare shoulder to him. "Elegant, don't you think?"

"What is it?"

"Baby powder."

Simon said something in French, and she laughed. I was startled; in all the time we'd been together, I'd never heard him speak another language. I wondered at the function of memory that would allow him to retain a second language but forget his own name.

Moe reached her other hand to clasp Simon's. She squeezed his and held on. "You lose one thing," he said, "and another steps up to take its place."

I'd grown so familiar with Simon that I had forgotten how young he was. Seeing them holding hands like that, I was reminded that he was really little more than a teenager. He should have been attending classes instead of waiting for Armageddon. Our drinks arrived. I sat back uneasily, looking down. Thinking of the two of them together, I experienced a flash of unreasonable jealously.

"So what's a Samuelite?" Simon asked.

Shut up, Simon!

Moe looked at Adam, "I'll explain." She took a deep breath, actually looking nervous; evidently the experiences of the summer had left their mark of caution on her. "There's really no such thing as a Samuelite; it's just me, but my point is that people don't understand what Harris was trying to say. For certain, the New Christians have gotten it all wrong. Even between the five of us, I doubt that we can agree on what he means." She looked around the table. "Who's actually read *Slouching Toward Bethlehem*?"

I nodded. Adam said that he had too.

Simon cocked his head. "I had a copy, but someone stole it." *Was that for my benefit? Does he realize I stole his?* "Am I the only one?" he asked.

"I haven't either, Simon," Christina said; she glanced from face to face until her gaze rested on me. "Care to summarize?"

I squirmed, "Why me?"

"You're the expert."

I regarded her sharply, "How's that?"

She afforded me an unusual expression. "You're the philosophy prof."

"Oh, yeah, well…."

Simon said, "What does it say? Nobody seems to want to talk about it."

That was also for my benefit.

"You must 'ear somet'ing," Adam said.

He and Moe appeared a little confused, so I offered an explanation, "Simon had a head injury; he's lost his memory."

"I think I just got hit on the head—the same way I lost my vision, but everyone considers it psychological—post-traumatic stress syndrome. No one's explained anything about the N.C.s to me; Jacob always avoids the topic, and Christina has trouble being objective."

Adam let out a long breath. He leaned forward with elbows on the table. "I am not sure where to begin; it is complicated."

Simon was alert, listening intently. "Keep it simple," he said.

"Well, all right. Two year ago, a company in Vancouver publish *Slouching Toward Bet'le'em*, by Samuel J. 'Arris. It is just a small book, a hundred page, but everyone start talking about it. 'Arris become famous overnight—everyone know 'is name."

I cut in, "Infamous is a better word for it."

"Most of de reaction is negative," Adam continued. "'E say in dis book dat dere is no God, and in Western Civilization we 'ave not'ing left to give us meaning." I brought my fingertips to my temples. Was that really how people interpreted *Bethlehem*?

It had all seemed so clear to me. "'Arris write also dat dere will be a Second Coming, but it will be de Devil and not Christ."

It pained me to hear it. Adam was an intelligent person; how could he have read it all so literally, even in a second language?

"That wasn't what he said at all." Moe appeared to read my thoughts. "First of all, he never said that God was dead. He wasn't really talking about religion at all; that's just how the media interpreted it. His whole argument, his whole point was," she struggled over the words, "sociological not theological. People misread the book."

Adam insisted, "'E did say God is dead. I remember dat."

Moe leaned forward, speaking very deliberately, "Harris said that Christ hadn't died for our sins, he died because of them." I was surprised at how well she knew the text. Perhaps the Samuelites had a point.

"'Ow is dat different?"

"Because he wasn't talking literally, he meant the..." she paused, searching for the word, ". . . ethics of Christianity. His point was that our society is the product of moral decay. The reference to Christ was just a metaphor." Regardless of her youth, I had always found her quite clever. Aside from Katherine, she was the only person I'd ever spoken to who had really understood *Bethlehem*. In addition to her grasp of the concepts, her command of the language had increased since the summer. Obviously, this conversation had been repeated in various places since the last time we had met. She had spent years travelling in western Canada, but I was still impressed.

"What about de Second Coming?" Adam asked.

I was curious as to how deep her understanding went, but she said she didn't know. That would have been too much to expect. I felt obligated to clarify things. I hated to join in, but Moe deserved that much.

"That was a metaphor too," I said. Adam looked at me, one eyebrow lifting. Moe smiled, surprised at the support. I'd never before shown interest in these discussions. "'The Second Coming' is a poem by W.B. Yeats. Yeats had this idea that the Second Coming wouldn't be Christ; instead, it would be the Antichrist. The title of the book is actually one of the lines in the poem; Harris took this idea and played with it, but he still wasn't talking about religion. He was making a comment on society; he said that Yeats' Second Coming was here, except that the devil was us, the society that we had created. He was just trying to bring about change in society, to make things better."

"'E brought about change," Adam said. "Dere is no question of dat."

Simon was shaking his head. "I still don't understand how this led to the revolution."

Moe continued, "He wrote some other things too."

"Like what?"

"He said they should burn the books and the churches."

I was already in it and couldn't let that go. "He said no such thing."

"Tell me how that could be misinterpreted," Moe demanded.

"I remember the actual line. What he said was: 'When words become more important than ideas, it is time to begin burning the books.'"

Simon was listening; he smiled and asked, "How do you remember that?"

I shrugged, "I was a teacher."

Simon repeated the line quietly then said, "So he was talking about adherence to dogma rather than...what? Faith? The ideal?"

"Yeah, something like that."

"How could that start a revolution?"

I sighed. "Because people are fucking stupid, that's why. Because the quotations were taken out of context, and his work was misinterpreted. Because the moral majority was looking for any justification that they could use to impose their beliefs on the rest of humanity. A group formed, a cult really, that called itself the New Christianity. They touted *Bethlehem* as the next testament, as a kind of modern day Bible and claimed that Harris was a prophet who foretold the coming of the Apocalypse. They understood his social commentary, but made the mistake of interpreting the theological allusions literally. They believed that Satan was actually coming, or that he was already here. That became their justification for a holy war. They fixated on a single line from the text that said Jesus was going to be reborn. Harris meant that there was hope in society for moral and ethical rebirth, but the New Christians claimed he was foretelling the actual Second Coming. They decided it was their duty to prepare the way for Christ."

"And to do that, they had to kill the unbelievers," Simon said.

"Not originally. When they first formed, they were like the Jehovah Witnesses and just stood on street corners trying to get converts. As *Bethlehem* became more popular, the group got larger. Six months after publication, they had chapters all across North America."

"Where was Harris during all this?"

"Originally, he didn't want anything to do with it, but the N.C.s claimed him as their figurehead. He began to feel responsible and tried to stop it."

"But he just wrote what he believed. He's not responsible for how people react to his ideas."

"Maybe, Simon, but it's a moot point now. Even if he didn't feel responsible, he felt it was necessary to disassociate himself from the movement. He had his publishers arrange a press conference, which they didn't want to do by the way, because the book was making so much money, and he made a public statement denouncing the New Christian movement. It almost worked: there was serious in-fighting over what the response should be to what he said. One faction claimed that the government had forced him to make the statement, and they used that idea to fuel their antiestablishment movement. Probably the largest number of members claimed that Harris was their "blind prophet" blessed by God to foretell the Second Coming, but unable to see the truth of it himself." Simon smiled at this, no doubt recalling his earlier comment. I continued, "It was a classic display of doublethink. The final group felt that he had betrayed their cause and should be killed." Simon's smile disappeared. "That was the first time violence was ever mentioned. If people had been paying attention, they would have seen the genesis of the jihad. In the midst of it all, Harris disappeared. Apparently, the police caught wind of an assassination plot and helped him to go into hiding."

"Dat is just one t'eory," Adam said. "Most people t'ink 'e is really Adams."

This brought an outburst from Moe. "Good God, Adam. Nobody actually believes that. Did he get plastic surgery? Why would he go to all the trouble? Instead of denouncing the movement, he could have just taken control. I think he was murdered. Otherwise people would have heard from him by now."

"Not necessarily," I said. "Right after the fighting started, the Coalition took control of communications and shut everything down: Cells, blackberries, Internet, television, everything. I don't know what kind of juice you need to pull that off, but they had it. So, even if Harris had wanted to, there was nothing he could have done. Besides, he already said what he had to say. Who would have believed that it was really him anyway?"

"Yes, I guess, but it is funny how 'e just disappeared."

"How did Adams get in control?" Simon asked.

"No credit to him; he was just there at the right time. After Harris disappeared, the New Christians needed a leader. Adams lucked out. He had the right look, and he said the right things. He does get credit for the Coalition though. The New Christian movement was splitting apart when Adams formed what he called The Coalition for Ethical Purity. Some saw shades of the Klan and called it ethnic purity. This pulled the N.C.s back together. The

Coalition was a strong vocal group responsible for bringing to the attention of the government anything that the New Christians felt 'endangered the ethical development of the nation.' Their mandate, as they put it, was to return us to the lamb white days of Christ, before the advent of our depraved Western Civilization. Basically, they sought to abolish free thought. At first they did this through censorship, eventually they resorted to violence.

"When the revolution finally came, it was highly coordinated and brought the government to its knees in just a couple of days. The military was split and Ottawa declared martial law. The N.C.s had their fingers in every aspect of society; all they had to do was make a fist, squeeze, and the country was crippled."

Simon let out a breath; his blind eyes were closed. "All this because of a book."

"That's depends on your interpretation of history," I said to him. "Great man or great event? Maybe the time was right and Harris was just the tool of change."

"What about Adams?" Simon said. "He fits the role better than Harris does. Harris just wrote the book; Adams is the one that made everything happen. He's the 'great man.'"

Adam grunted. "I am sure 'e would like to t'ink so."

I nodded, "No doubt he would, he probably thinks of himself as the new Messiah, but he didn't come along until after the whole movement had already formed. He kept it from falling apart, but he can't take credit for creating it. Really, he's little more than an opportunist and a common butcher."

"A butcher," Christina said, "who's close to ruling the country."

There was a moment of silence.

"It all come back to *Slouching Toward Bet'le'em*," Adam finally said, "but de bottom line is dat no one know what Samuel J. 'Arris mean in dat book except 'Arris 'imself, and 'e is nowhere to be found."

We didn't stay too much longer after that. I had another drink and tried to bring the conversation around to a different topic, but nothing seemed worthy of discussion. I'd lost my appetite. Finally, Simon said that he needed some rest, so the three of us excused ourselves and left the Free House.

It had cooled a little, and the carriage ride was less enjoyable than it had been leaving the hospital. Simon said little. Christina appeared uncomfortable. We rode home in silence.

As the carriage neared the dark husk of the hospital, Simon finally spoke. "I have one more question," he said, quietly enough that the driver would not hear him.

"What's that, Simon?"

"What did you really mean?"

"I don't get you," only I feared that I did.

"When you wrote that book, Samuel, what did you really mean?"

Book Two:
The Blood Dimmed Tide

"The most convincing testimony to the elusive nature of
Christianity is the overwhelming number of hypocrites who
claim to live according to its precepts."
- *Slouching Toward Bethlehem*

I

With Simon's hand clutching my arm, we walked for a distance down the bank of Wascana Creek. The current was sluggish, as it always was that time of year. The spring melt was long over, and the dry summer had reduced the flow of the creek down to a meander. Along the walkway, between clumps of trees and the water, there was a nice view of the city skyline. Dusk was still a ways off, but the sun had dipped low enough that its glow had a rich hue, and it cast an amber haze on the downtown. Fireflies, an unusual sight in Regina, had begun to flash along the shoreline. I drank the beauty like a heady wine and spared a thought for Simon who could see none of it.

As we walked, silently, I enjoyed the subtle play of light that hazed the horizon and dusted the western, low-lying clouds. Simon scented at the air, turning his head with the caress of passing winds. I noticed what he was doing, and it occurred to me how we came at the world from such different perspectives. We approached a lone figure sitting on the grass by the creek, gazing into the distance. When we came near enough, I recognized William. He'd told me earlier that day to look for him near the park, but I hadn't expected to actually find him. I really shouldn't have been surprised. Without dependable transportation, most people limited themselves to a small area of the city. My area was the downtown core, and it wasn't uncommon to run into the same people several times in a week.

I called out, and he looked up to us. We came closer. Even from a distance I could tell that he'd been lost in his imagination. His body had a kind of slackness to it, as if it had been forgotten, and his expression was void of emotion. Finally, he shook his head, as if fighting his way out of a trance. He smiled. "Hey, I'd given up on you." I helped Simon to a seat upon the grass, and William studied him. "This is Simon, I presume."

Simon nodded, extending his hand in the direction of William's voice. "You have me at a disadvantage."

They clasped hands. "Not really. I'm Will, an old friend of Jake's."

"You're the writer. I've been looking forward to meeting you."

"Me too. Jake's told me a lot about you."

I interjected, "You can drop the alias."

Will looked up, studied me a moment before talking. I couldn't read the expression on his face. "Don't get lax, Sammy. I know people in this town who wouldn't hesitate to put a bullet into you."

My knees felt suddenly weak; I sat down beside Simon who said, "He didn't tell me. I figured it out."

"You must have said something." Will shook his head, still staring at me.

"I said a lot of things."

He glanced at Simon, "How did you know?"

Simon shrugged, which struck me as ironic. "When we first met, I got the impression that he was lying to me. Maybe because I could only hear his voice; I don't know." His sightless gaze moved in my direction. "The more we talked, the more suspicious I got. Then you stole my copy of *Bethlehem*."

I grunted, "So you did know that was me?"

"Who else? You were evasive enough to make me curious, so I had someone dig up another copy. When they read it to me, I could almost hear your voice. Then, after our discussion that night in the Free House, I was pretty sure. Couldn't you tell I was baiting you?" I remembered wondering at his behaviour, but I never imagined what he was really thinking. "When I asked you on the ride home, it was still just a hunch. Your reaction confirmed it."

I blew out a quick breath.

"Does anyone else know?" Will asked.

"Christina."

Will nodded, apparently remembering her and satisfied that she was safe. I wondered at his reaction, even while I agreed with it. I had talked about Christina often enough, but Will had never actually met her. Or so I thought. I occurred to me then that they might have gotten acquainted on their own. Will had seemed interested in her that night in the café, maybe they'd run into each other sometime after that, and he'd introduced himself. Inexplicably, the thought made me angry, then just as quickly I recognized that what I felt was actually jealousy.

"What are you doing out here?" I asked, in a vain attempt to change the subject. He ignored the question at first, apparently still trying to decide just how dangerous my situation had become. I could feel myself beginning to sweat before he answered, "I'd been struggling with a new idea and needed to get away from distractions. I thought I might have something for you to look over."

"Any luck?"

"No, but it's all in my head. I was just about to head home and sketch it out." He stood and stretched. I noticed that he carried a little notebook with him. Funny how similar we were. He was flipping it shut when a note must have caught his eye, "Oh, hey, have you heard about the poetry reading at the Thirteen Ave. Coffee House?"

"You're joking."

He gestured, lifting his hands and spreading his palms. "What else is there to do?"

"I guess. When is it?"

"Tomorrow night. I've got a few pieces. Just show up. Anyone reads."

I shrugged, "Sure, it might be a diversion. Simon?"

He nodded, "Okay. We should bring Christina along; she needs the distraction."

"Good, bring her." Will folded his journal under his arm and started off. He looked back, "Nice meeting you, Simon."

Simon waved. "You too."

William began to walk away, then paused and glanced back. "Don't forget how dangerous a place this is for you, Sam. And Simon, unless you're willing to take a bullet for him, keep your secret to yourself." Without waiting for assurances, he turned and left.

We were silent for a moment, watching his retreating figure.

"You don't have to worry about me, you know," Simon said.

"Just forget about it. So, you want to keep walking?" I asked.

"No," Simon said. "Let's stay here for a bit. How long have you known him?"

"William? Long time. Years."

"That's why he knows who you really are?"

"Yeah, we were friends before the war."

"Does he know Christina?"

I frowned, still troubled by my reaction five minutes before. "I don't know, Simon. Up until ten minutes ago, I'd have said no. Now I'm not so sure."

"Is she attractive?"

"What?"

"Christina, do you think she's attractive?"

"She's beautiful—in a melancholic kind of way."

"She has a thing for you, you know?"

"Yeah. I know."

He was quiet for a moment, and then asked me, "What was her name?"

"What's gotten into you?" At first, I didn't know who he was talking about. Sometimes speaking with Simon drove me crazy. Not only did he pick up conversations hours after they had been dropped, he also skipped sequential steps of logic. If I understood him, he was asking who it was that kept me from reciprocating Christina's affections. *Has the doctor put him up to this?* I wondered. It was funny, if true, with everything she knew I had done, everything I was responsible for, Christina's only question was about Katherine. "Who wants to know?" I parried.

"Both of us."

"It's not 'was,' it's 'is.' Her name is Katherine."

"We've all lost something, or someone. It's not a betrayal to move on."

I felt a flash of anger. "Let it go, Simon."

He did.

The dusk lengthened, and after a time, he asked me to describe in detail all that I could see. I did my best. He listened with eyes closed, making soft noises of recognition, as if remembering the beauty of it. When I was done, he was silent, his head tilted, still listening. After a time, I grew impatient.

"Let's move."

He put his hand up, "No, wait," then he drew a deep breath and let it out slowly. "Listen, Samuel." After so much time it felt odd to hear him use my actual name. "You've missed so much."

"What do you mean?"

"You depend too much on your sight. Can't you feel that soft breeze coming from the west?" he asked. "It's running along the creek and spilling over the banks. It's just a little bit cooler, and I can feel a touch of moisture on the left side of my face." He was right. When I paid attention to it, I could feel what he was describing. The wind stirred my hair. "Now smell. What are those? Flowers from the park? I can even smell the grass. Feel it, it's damp like it was watered today, or maybe there's dew already." He was quiet for a moment, and the silence settled on us. I could feel my impatience easing from me like a long sigh. It was a relief, after so many months, to lie back beneath the summer sky and be free of deception. Until Simon had torn down my façade and called me by my true name, I hadn't realized the crippling weight that that lie had been.

That afternoon in the carriage, when he'd called me Samuel, I'd glanced quickly to Christina, frightened at her reaction. She'd only smiled, albeit wryly, and nodded. Obviously, they'd discussed it before I met them that day. I had thought back over the course of the day's discussions, and their behaviour, which had seemed odd to me, then made sense.

I'd sworn the two of them to secrecy. There were so many people who would want to see Samuel J. Harris dead. I thought of Will's friend, Braxton. What would he give to exact retribution on the author of *Slouching Toward Bethlehem*? I couldn't blame him for thinking me responsible. Would the Coalition want me dead as well, or could I serve them better as a figurehead to be erected aside Joseph Adams? The Blind Prophet and the New Messiah. The thought made me choke on bile.

"Tell me about the Island," Simon said, breaking my reverie.

"It's a large land mass off the western coast."

He laughed quietly. "If you don't want to, don't, but I'd like to know what happened out there."

"Christ, how much time do you think we've got?"

He didn't respond.

Do I want to tell him this? I wondered, but immediately I realized that I did. Like the lies, that story, everything that had occurred after I had fled from Edmonton, had been bottled up inside of me for too long. It took several moments for me to collect my thoughts, then I began talking. As the words came forth, they began to resonate like a chant and swiftly I was drawn into the past relieving those terrible moments.

* * *

The Lamb White Days

After I denounced the New Christian movement, I explained to Simon, and the death threats started, I caught a plane from Edmonton, where Katherine and I lived, to Victoria, which is located at the southern tip of Vancouver Island. It was a difficult decision to leave Katherine. I obviously grew to regret it, but at the time it seemed safest for her not to be with me. The police took the threats very seriously. The Island has always been a place apart from the rest of the country. The pace of life is different, or was anyway; I think that being ocean bound tends to slow the people down somewhat. You know the feeling when there's nowhere you need to go, nothing that you have to be. You're already there, at the end of the country. The next stop westward is Russia, and that's a few thousand kilometres away.

From Victoria, I rented a car and drove to Tofino. It's a small fishing village, halfway up the western side of the Island. The Trans-Canada Highway ends there. From that point on, you need to either rent a plane, a boat or just swim if you want to go any further north. It seemed a good choice for seclusion. Plus, I'd visited there several times before, so I felt comfortable with the location. For awhile, I enjoyed my stay there—lonely, but otherwise fine. Most of my time was spent writing. Often, I'd just hang out at the pier and sketch portraits of people who I saw. I'd take notes, I mean—try to capture them with words so that I could use them later in something I might write. That's where I met Adam. We'd go fishing or hike in the Pacific rain forest.

Nobody in Tofino seemed too concerned about what was going on nationally. Hardly anyone I met had read *Bethlehem*, or if they did, they didn't consider it worth conversation. Naturally, I kept an eye on the news, but ultimately it didn't matter how informed anyone was, the revolution came so suddenly there was little that could be done anyway.

The fighting on the Island started in Victoria, but I didn't hear about it until a half-day had gone by. Believe it or not, I was hiking by the coast. Even on the drive from the trailhead to my hotel, I listened to a C.D. rather than the radio. I got my first inkling that something was wrong when I noticed that the streets of Tofino were almost deserted. I didn't think much about it, just sort of thought "huh" and gave it no more mind.

Twenty minutes later, the phone brought me out of the shower. The only person in town who had my number was Adam, so when it first started ringing I ignored it, thinking I'd call him back. But when it kept ringing, I wrapped a towel around myself and went to answer it. It went silent just before I picked up. Again, nothing unusual registered on my consciousness.

When I think about it now, I'm certain that it was Katherine trying to get hold of me, and that number was our only line of communication. I had left my cell behind, worried that somehow I'd be tracked to the Island, and we were afraid to use e-mail or web-cams for the same reason. The agreement we had was that we would never use my number in Tofino unless there was an emergency. Katherine only had it because I had written it on a postcard and sent it to a friend of ours, and then they had given her the number. It was all pretty cloak and dagger, but the cops had convinced me that the danger of assassination was real.

Now I have to ask myself the "what ifs?" What if I had stayed in town that day? Would I have known right away what was going on? Maybe, but from all accounts, the networks down played the events of the revolution, either not piecing together the big picture or not grasping the enormity of what was occurring. If I had known, I would have acted before it was too late. I would have phoned Katherine; we would have made a plan, and we would be together right now. But I didn't figure it out right away. I didn't answer the phone when she called; I went back to rinse the shampoo from my hair, got dressed, cooked a meal in the small kitchen of my room and then flopped down in front of the television hoping for something mindless to numb my senses.

The screen flickered to life, and images of violence splashed light on the hotel walls, people fighting in the streets. I thought I was on a news network, so I flicked to another station—same scenes. Obviously, I reasoned, fighting had broken out somewhere in Eastern Europe. It took a few minutes for the truth to sink in—that I was looking at images from North America.

My first thoughts then were of Katherine. I tried phoning, realizing as I did, the significance of the call I had just missed. The lines were dead. I guessed rightly that communications had been cut across the country. I tried the operator, anything I could think of, but nothing worked. I ran to the nearest cyber café, and my heart sank to see it closed. It had seemed to me that that place *never* closed. I was looking for something to smash the window with when the owner appeared from the shadows to unlock the door. It was only because I insisted that he let me try the computers, but as he told me, the system server was down.

By the time I returned home, there was no longer any signal on the television. They'd gotten to that too. I must have sat in stunned defeat for a good ten minutes before the resolve formed to get back to the mainland. Hoping he would know more than I did about how things really were, I sought out Adam.

He'd spent the day watching events unfolding on the small screen, but instead of planning to leave Tofino, he'd come to the conclusion that it was the safest place to be. He said that the airport and the Island ferries were reported to be under Coalition control, as was most of the country. There was no way back to the mainland unless I had my own boat. I pursued this option too, but no one I approached cared anything about how much money I had, and the armed guard posted at the marina precluded my more desperate plans. I was trapped on the Island. My refuge had become a prison.

Time passed, and I went crazy in Tofino, feeling desperate and guilty and needing to fight in some way against the Coalition. The guilt. You can't imagine how I felt. I paced the streets like a jaguar in a cage. I debated for a long time what I should do; eventually I decided to join the Emac—the emergency army corps. As it turned out, it was a futile gesture, and, in retrospect, I realize now it was also a terrible decision. My motivation was right: I thought I could do something of value to try and stop the

Coalition, but I found, when it came right down to it, I couldn't deal with the…realities of war. I joined to alleviate my feelings of guilt. As it turned out, a much more powerful emotion drove me to my desertion, and they shoot deserters.

The Emac was a travesty—people signing up for slaughter. I had all these Hollywood images in my mind detailing every stage of the process from enlisting to actual combat. None of them were accurate. The day I signed up was the same day they slapped a weapon in my hands. We were given less than a week of training—more propaganda than anything else, which struck me as odd since everyone there had volunteered. I guessed that they were trying to root out New Christian sympathizers. I suppose it was a real concern, but if there were any in our troop, they didn't show themselves. The bottom line was that when I finished my so-called military training I was no better equipped to deal with the realities of war than I was when I signed up.

The major fighting on the Island was going on in Victoria, the capital, and that's where they sent the company I was assigned to. Looking back now, I see clearly how badly organized the whole endeavour was. It would have made more sense to travel by boat, but instead we were loaded into a ten-vehicle convoy and sent across the Island to go fight for freedom.

None of us doubted that that was what it was all about—freedom. Even though this is a civil war, it seems so clear-cut in other ways. It's a classic Good versus Evil thing, although I guess if you try to argue whose side God is on, things get a little confusing. Anyway, we were all armed and inspired, ready to fight for freedom and stop the blitzkrieg of the Coalition. I had a ton of equipment strapped around me, but they hadn't been able to issue us uniforms, nothing to identify us as who we were; there just weren't the funds for that.

My company was a very diverse group, teenage girls to middle aged men, construction workers to executives. A testament, I suppose, to how desperate things had become. I befriended two men in particular: a young student named Stephan Low, an Asian kid, and a truck driver named Ben Hallings, kind of a burly guy. I think Stephan drew me because he possessed an obvious vulnerability that sparked my teacher complex and made me want to take him under my wing. Ben displayed a frank honesty that I found refreshing. He had an explosive temper, but it was never directed at me. The three of us spent a lot of time talking. I found out that Ben had a boy living in the east and that they had lost contact when the fighting broke out. I think Stephan became a kind of surrogate son for him. In any case, we looked out for one another.

The convoy left Tofino in the early morning. There was a hummer carrying the officers, a medi-truck, an armoured car at the lead, and another one bringing up the rear. The rest of the vehicles were trucks, loaded heavily with Emac personnel. We were in the second last vehicle. I remember how odd it felt to be travelling down that highway in the spring weather, constantly having to remind myself of our destination. The road follows the coast for about fifty kilometres then cuts inland and weaves through a beautiful landscape of trees, rivers and lakes. The sun soaked into my pores. No one spoke and, for a moment, I closed my eyes and tried to imagine that I was anywhere else but where I was. It was impossible: reality intruded on my thoughts.

The rumble of the trucks was loud in my ears. Every time we hit a bump, the metal seat I perched on sent a jolt up my spine. The wind was hot, and it stank of gasoline. Under the gear that was strapped to my body, sweat soaked my shirt. When I opened my eyes, the first thing I saw was the frightened face of the teenager who sat across from me. She stared straight ahead, right at me, but I could tell that her vision was turned inward. I wondered what hell she was reliving.

She wore a Mickey Mouse t-shirt.

I glanced away and caught the flash of brightly coloured billboards that swept past us on the side of the road. God, I'd gone down that route so often with nothing more on my mind than finding a beach, or a nice spot to eat lunch. The probability of killing people who had once been my countrymen was almost too difficult to comprehend. It didn't help that the sun shone over a fleckless blue sky, and the cry of birds floated on the air. My life had become an impossible jumble of paradoxes.

After the highway to the capital cuts straight east across the Island, it then follows the east coast down to the southern tip where Victoria is located. The reality of our situation became less and less difficult to apprehend the closer we got to our destination. We passed what looked like ghost towns on the sides of the road. I remembered an open market, situated just before the southern turn off, where I had often stopped and spent hours browsing through the craft shops and gift stores. It was usually so crowded that I'd have to park on the side of the highway. It was deserted when we rumbled past. The windows of some of the buildings were broken, and their shelves looked empty. I couldn't help wondering where all those people had gone. Did they make it to the mainland in hope of escape, only to find nowhere to go, or did they die fighting, waiting for people like us to come and help them? There had been rumours of work camps, but I never saw any evidence of them as I came back from the coast. I discovered later that the U.S. coastguard had been overwhelmed by refugees fleeing Victoria. What we did see was evidence of sporadic warfare—burnt out vehicles, gutted buildings—for the most part, however, the land seemed untouched. It was a though a plague, rather than a revolution, had swept the country.

We were more than an hour from Victoria and approaching one of the major docking sites for the mainland ferry when the first rocket hit the convoy. I was facing forward, staring with a cold horror at the burnt out buildings we approached when a light burst from the ruins and sped toward us. I didn't even react, too startled I suppose; I just watched it race forward and strike the vehicle two ahead of us. There was a loud, deep sound like the bark of a bear, then a searing blast of air hammered into my face. The breath was sucked from my lungs, and I lurched backward as though I had been kicked in the chest. Momentarily, my senses failed me. My eyes were struck blind, and my hearing grew muffled.

The carcass of the truck was catapulted to the ditch on the far side of the road. Where it had been, a great billowing cloud of flame erupted and filled the highway. I gasped for breath, and the superheated air scorched my throat. The transport directly before us was flung back by the force of the explosion. Its front end lifted, and the whole thing came flying backward. You know how they say that a moment freezes, or slows down and you experience things like they're happening in slow motion? It's true, and that was one of those times. I still have this vivid image of that truck, almost vertical, twisted at an odd angle, sailing down upon us. In the back of it, a young soldier looked back in stunned desperation and caught my eye. She couldn't have been older than sixteen. The Coalition had stolen her innocence; it was about to steal her life.

I said that I was too shocked to react; fortunately, our driver was more alert. When he saw the first flash from the roadside, he cranked the steering wheel in the opposite direction. By the time the explosion tore up the asphalt, we were already veering crazily away. He managed to swerve out of the flight path of the transport, but the sharp turn sent us careening into the ditch. The front tires caught in the soft shoulder; our truck spun and flipped onto its side, the bottom of the vehicle facing the direction in which we had been travelling. I suppose that saved our lives. We were tossed roughly to the ditch, but the vehicle itself protected us from the devastation of the explosion.

Ignoring bloodied skin and twisted limbs, we scrambled to our feet, ran back the way we'd come and then up the side of the ditch and into the cover of the burnt out buildings on the far side of the highway. There was gunfire, ours or theirs I wasn't sure. I thought I heard the sound of another rocket and the screeching of tires, but everyone around me was shouting and the sound of my own heart drowned out almost all other noises. It was absolute madness and cacophony. Terror clutched at my chest.

We dashed into the blackened husk of a house. I stopped and threw myself against a wall while the others ran in behind me. A soldier, older than me, started yelling, "Go through it! Go through it!" and yanked at my clothing. We scrambled out onto a suburban street with the house we'd just passed through shielding us from the highway. We ran south for sixty metres, then inched our way back through the houses to check the site of the ambush.

It was already quiet. The remainder of the convoy, which had preceded the truck hit by the rocket, was nowhere to be seen. They'd run out on us. There were a few bodies scattered on the road, unmoving. The vehicle that had been hit lay half off the highway, flames and black smoke billowing into the bright summer sky. It looked like a child's plastic model that had been stomped on, then set on fire. Debris lay scattered about it, smoking also, and from where we stood it was impossible to tell if we looked at pieces of the truck or bodies. I supposed that they must have been soldiers. The truck that had been blown backward, lay flipped, its front blackened by the explosion of the rocket. Its cargo also lay twisted and dead upon the road. Of the last armoured car, there was no sign. They too had left us. There was no sign of the enemy either; they hadn't advanced on the wreckage.

I can hardly describe the emotions I experienced as we lay there studying the devastation. We were deserted, left alone in the midst of no man's land. We had no communications or anyone among us with any real military experience. My first thought was that we had to get away from that immediate area. However large the troop was that had ambushed us, they had superior firepower and almost certainly more fighting experience than we had. We hastily discussed our options, decided to table any major decisions until we had made our way to a less hostile spot—if any existed on that part of the Island. There were twelve of us. Ben Hallings stepped forward to take command, and the rest of us were willing to let him. We formed a column and set off at a jog through the gutted suburbs.

It was a harrowing march. We were in totally unfamiliar country with no idea as to how numerous or concentrated the enemy was. The group that blew up our convoy, if a group it was, could have been the only N.C.s in the region. On the other hand, we could have been marching straight into an enemy stronghold. This did seem unlikely, however, as the area didn't appear to be of any strategic value, just a sprawl of middle to upper class houses, mostly looted and burned.

It's strange how frightening silence can become. We kept close to the houses and travelled as much as we could on the ragged lawns. Even so, I felt exposed and the sound we made seemed to echo thunderously between the houses. There should have been children playing on those streets, not terrified, half-baked soldiers running with loaded weapons. I'd seen lots of films on Vietnam, and had some impression as to how horrible it must have been for soldiers to find themselves dropped in the middle of a foreign jungle, but I think what we went through was worse. For us there would be no end to our tour of duty, no home to return to. Every moment that we spent in those suburbs made it more obvious that the life we'd all known had been irrevocably changed. Nothing could ever be the same again.

Our top priority was shelter. After what seemed like hours, Ben settled on a mid-sized two-story house located at the end of a little cul-de-sac. He argued that it was the most defensible location we had passed, and in a relative sense, that was true, but I considered it a death trap. Not one of those houses was safe. We entered cautiously and did a sweep. No one was there. We set up sentries back and front, on both levels, then searched the house for supplies. In the basement we located a freezer with meat in it, spoiled, but also a cool room with canned food. Everything in the house was electronic, so we were forced to open the tins with a knife. It was a cold, despondent meal where no one spoke.

Afterwards, those of us who had not drawn first watch separated and searched for places to sleep.

Thinking it the safest location in the house, I descended into the basement and went to a bedroom I had noted earlier. The previous owner had been a teenage girl, or a boy with a predilection for pink paint and posters of female rock stars. The decorations left something to be desired, but if the N.C.A. opened fire on the house, the concrete walls of the basement would offer some degree of protection. I dropped on the bed and ran my flashlight around the room. Bright eyed starlets smiled down on me, one after another, then I noticed a blank space upon the wall. I widened the beam of the flashlight and confirmed that there was a conspicuous absence in the bare skin and glitter—as though a poster had been removed. Despite my exhaustion, my imagination began to churn. Most likely the poster had been taken down months before when some idol had fallen from favour, but I imagined other less likely scenarios ranging from a weeping teenager hurriedly clutching at the favourite vestige of a disappearing life to a Coalition soldier stealing contraband for his daughter. Immersed in my speculations, sleep took me. Midway through the night, I was awoken to take my watch.

I used to camp fairly often up north in the prairies, or in the mountains, so I've gotten used to seeing a sky unpolluted with city lights. I've always loved it, but sitting on the second story of that house, watching over the darkened street, the empty houses, I experienced a profound sensation of abandonment and loneliness. Aside from a glowing sky low over the distant eastern horizon, I could see nothing but stars and the impossible abyss of the cosmos. What had happened to all those people? And what was it that caused this? A book. Just a book. It was incomprehensible to me. When my relief came, I crawled onto bed and, afraid of falling asleep in the dark, lay awake until sunlight.

Gathered together that morning, we attempted to reach a consensus as to what we should do. I suggested leaving the Island altogether. We were already near the coast, there was a chance that we could locate some type of ship and make it to the mainland. My one desire was to get back to Edmonton and find Katherine. Another soldier, I can't remember her name, argued that we would be leaving one bad situation for another that might be worse. There had been no communication with Vancouver for almost a week. Anything could have happened in that time. At least where we were, the fighting was mostly over, and there was a chance that we could survive if we stayed. Although we had no idea at the time, I know now that she was right. None of our alternatives were acceptable to Ben. He felt that we had committed to a cause, and we should follow it through. Obviously, the war had been lost where we were, but if the fighting continued in Victoria, that was where we had to go. It didn't seem to matter to him that the distance would easily take a week to travel on foot, or that we lacked the necessary supplies. It was a matter of responsibility and loyalty. Whatever the cost, we had to do what was right.

What was right; his use of the phrase was infuriating. I considered the idea madness and said so, but surprisingly, I was voted down. It was insanity, but when I think back on it now, I realize that the decision had implications beyond our limited circumstances. Those people weren't just making a commitment to keep on fighting; they were making a declaration that all hope was not yet lost. I guess that at that point I had already given up on society. All that seemed realistically within my reach was a few more moments of life, as many as I could collect, and that end wouldn't be served by marching on to Victoria. My meaning would be found with Katherine. Still, I had no choice in the matter. The consequences of desertion had been hammered into us during our training. We ate, collected all the food we could carry with us, then set out.

Days passed. We drew nearer to our destination, though this accomplishment only served to make us all the more despondent. The closer we got to Victoria, the worse things became. It was

Armageddon. I doubted it not. It was the Second Coming. We passed lots of bodies, some fresh, some old, some almost unidentifiable as human. Based upon the condition of a few we passed, I concluded that there were wild dogs in those haunted streets. And the flies never seemed to have enough. I worried about disease and more sudden deaths.

Then we came upon…well, we came upon something that resembled a scene from some cheesy spaghetti western, and a part of me had a difficult time accepting that it was real. At first all we saw was a cluster of blackbirds flapping around the side of a fence, but they squawked and flew away as we approached. By the time I understood what we had found, it was too late to turn away—a grisly fascination held me in thrall. There were three bodies propped side by side against the boards. Two had been shot in the chest, one in the head. All of their eyes had been torn out—birds, I assumed. Only one of them wore a uniform; the others were obviously Emac. They'd only recently been executed. We stood in a semicircle regarding their mute testimony. A piece of paper, weathered a little and ripped, fixed with a knife through the shoulder of the soldier on the left, had scrawled upon it the single word: *Deserters*.

"Poor fuckers," I said.

Ben snarled, "What are you talking about? I'd have done the same thing."

A week before, I had considered him a friend, at that moment I feared him. "How do you know what happened?" I argued. "You can't judge them without at least…."

He cut me off, his face twisted with distaste, "What do you want to do, Jake, let someone else die for you? You don't think freedom is worth dying for?"

"I'm here aren't I?" I snapped. I was going to comment on the obvious irony, but the coldness in his eyes made me understandably reticent.

"They didn't have the right to run out. They deserved what they got. What do you think Adams does to deserters?"

"I thought the point was not to be like Adams."

"They signed up. They should have stuck it out." He started walking, taking point. The others filed past, several of them staring me down. One soldier, a woman with whom I'd hardly spoken, hesitated and touched my arm. She joined the others without speaking. Stephan stopped by my side, hardly able to take his eyes off the corpses. He'd slung his rifle over his shoulder and was wringing his hands together subconsciously. After a moment, he looked up at me. "I wonder if they gave them blindfolds. When I go, I hope I don't see it coming."

"You're not going to die, Stephan." I joined the column. He stepped in behind me.

Although I couldn't understand why we'd want to hasten our arrival at Victoria, we often talked of appropriating vehicles that we found abandoned on the way. The too recent memory of our ill-fated convoy, however, kept us on foot. We felt camouflaged by the relative silence of our passing. On foot, we'd travelled over twenty kilometres that day and entered into the thick of an urban area. We passed makeshift roadblocks that had been erected then broken down. We saw more corpses on the streets, and in some places there were the charred remains of bonfires. It didn't appear that wood had been used as fuel to feed the flames. The houses bore the marks of gunfire and explosives. Obviously, some fires had been set and just as obviously kept from spreading. Occasionally, we encountered the broken down husk of a tank. I found considerable satisfaction in this, happy that at least a few of the N.C.s had gotten their own, but I was thinking like an Emac who was forced to fight with leftovers. The tanks could have easily been regular army; we had no way of knowing.

It was unsettling not being able to differentiate enemies from allies.

This consideration was on my mind, when the N.C.A. opened fire on us.

It was terribly quiet, a condition we'd come to expect that nonetheless frayed my nerves, when I heard a buzz speed past my ear and then the thump of something striking flesh. The woman who had touched me earlier, grunted, slumped forward, then collapsed to the earth. I stopped, bewildered, and Stephan came up behind me. He must have been lost in thought, such as I was, or equally traumatized by the constant stress. In any case, neither one of us understood what had just occurred.

"What are you…?" he began to say, then the report of the rifle cut him off. Someone yelled, and we both spun about, running for cover behind an abandoned vehicle in the driveway beside us.

I dropped down against the far side of the car, then slid over so that the rear tire hid me from view. Stephan crouched at the front, breathing heavily and staring at me with an expression of utter confusion. There had come a cluster of weapon fire, then more silence.

"Where are the others?" he gasped.

I shook my head. I wasn't confused; I was terrified. I pressed back into the metal of the car, trying to sink into its protective cover. Fighting total panic, I struggled to assess the situation. Everything seemed wrong; our lives should not have been in danger. Except for the untended grass, and as long as you didn't see the dead sprawled out on the street, it was as prosaic an image as you could imagine. Near the top of the driveway, the sight of a tricycle caught my eye. It sat there as though waiting for a child to come play. The echo of the gunfire had died quickly, but the silence was replaced by panicked voices from across the street.

Except perhaps to sink even lower, Stephan didn't move from his crouch. Suppressing the fear that we were being advanced upon, I spun about and rose slowly to peer above the level of the trunk. Two corpses lay upon the lawn of a bungalow, another face down on the asphalt. I thought perhaps it was Ben Hallings. Aside from those three, the street was empty. A trace of smoke or mist hung in the morning air just outside a broken second story window of a house on the same side of the street of where we hid.

I sank down and studied the street behind us—deserted. "Nobody," I said. "There's a sniper on the second floor of a house two down from us. It sounds like others made it across the street."

"What are we going to do?"

I considered running to the house nearest us and then making our way back in the direction we'd just come. At least we knew it was clear. I told Stephan and asked what he thought.

He glanced quickly above the hood and just as quickly ducked down. He was shaking, and his lower lip quivered. "If the others are across the street," he got out between deep breaths, "then whoever is up in those windows is probably focused on them. We can move up behind these houses and come up from their rear." It wasn't the suggestion I had expected. "They only got three of us," he continued. "There can't be that many of them." Before I could add anything else, he was up and running to the cover of the house. Regardless of how I felt, I couldn't let him go alone. The two of us at least had a chance of success. He slammed against the white siding with me close on his heels. As I ran, I heard the crack of a bullet hitting the car, then the sound of a second impact on the concrete sidewalk just behind my foot. Our team responded with a short burst.

We inched our way along the side of the building then rushed to the back. There was a gate that led into the yard next to the house where I thought the sniper was. Stephan placed his hand over the latch and lifted it with his whole palm. The click of the metal was muffled, and we made no sound going through—no sound except for the rasp of my breath and the drum of my heart. I could hardly hear anything else. I felt exposed and hoped that he was right about the number of N.C.s in that house. We moved low and were hidden somewhat by the fence and trees in the yard; still, an awful number of blank windows stared down on us. Any one of them could have hidden a rifle.

I was surprised at Stephan. It wasn't that he'd given any indication of cowardice in the time that I'd known him, but his young age had seemed to me to preclude such decisive action. He made me assess my own motives. Was it really that I saw no sense in what we did, or was I just afraid? How much of a coward was I? The self-analysis was brief.

He paused before reaching the corner of the house adjacent to the sniper. "How do we go in?"

"Basement?"

He nodded. We moved in long, silent strides, our rifles up; and, for a brief, naked moment, we were exposed to the upstairs windows next door. I was breathing open-mouthed with short hollow pants. My body was soaked and clammy with sweat. Then the fence afforded us a small degree of cover once again. Stephan slipped the stalk of his weapon between two boards of the fence and slowly pried one loose. It came out with a grinding sound, infinitely loud. We froze, listening for the answering echo of gunfire. Silence. I worked the next one out slowly with my hands. We squeezed through.

The basement windows had bars across them; the result of big city living I supposed. No one trusted anyone anymore. "I guess we go in through the backdoor," I said.

"That's suicide."

"The front?"

"That might work."

"I was joking."

"It might work. Obviously, they're watching, but I doubt if they can see the front of the house. The angle is too steep, and with the others across the street, no one upstairs is going to stick his head out a window and look down."

"You're assuming that they don't have someone on the ground floor. We can't make that assumption. We shouldn't; if I was in there, there's no way I'd leave it unguarded."

He began to respond, then stopped, quickly lifting his hand to silence me. "Listen."

I did and heard the faint mumble of a voice and then the even less audible click of a lock. The sounds came from the back of the house. "They're making a run for it," Stephen hissed.

Just let them go, I thought. *What does it matter?* But he rushed to the edge of the house, took a deep breath, then snapped his rifle around the corner. He fired a short, violent burst, then dashed from my sight. I heard shouts and two more explosions of gunfire.

When I spun around to the back of the house, I saw the body of a small man, maybe a boy, laying face down just outside the door. Stephan had already gone in. I bent low by the side of the house, flipped open the screen door and followed the barrel of my rifle into the interior of the house. There was no one there.

I stepped cautiously further, entering the kitchen, and I saw Stephan standing with his back to me. I came up beside him and discovered a grisly tableau: there were two other people in the room. One was dead, I assumed, sprawled halfway into a hall. Blood pooled on the tiles. A teenage girl sat on the gray kitchen tiles; she too was armed. Stephan stood with his gun aimed but silent.

I didn't comprehend what was happening, then I heard her whispering, "I'll swear over. Please don't kill me; I'll swear over." She kept repeating those words. I was stunned. She thought we were N.C.A. Was it a ruse? I turned to stare at Stephan. His face was blank, as though somewhere inside of him a switch had been flicked off. His weapon lowered a fraction of an inch.

As if in reply, hers snapped up, and she shot him.

Within the tight confines of the room, the sound was thunderous. Stephan spun away, and I dropped low, squeezing off a burst of gunfire that spattered the girl across the counter and then tore wildly up the wall into the ceiling. The roar of it died before I wrenched my finger from the trigger, then a heavy silence swallowed the room.

Stephan, crumpled up against the wall, made no sound. I searched for a pulse and could feel nothing. His chest was still, sodden with blood. He was dead. This boy who I had felt such a need to protect was dead. I had failed him like I'd failed everyone else.

The girl was dead too. It became terribly important to me to prove that she was not just another civilian but that she was N.C.A. What she'd said had to have been a trick. She had to have lied. I rose from Stephan and went to her twisted corpse. In the early months of the war, Coalition infiltrators wore no uniforms but carried black armbands that they could use to identify themselves when it became necessary to do so. She most certainly had one hidden within her clothing. Her shirt was heavy with blood. I tore it from her, tore at the pockets of her jeans but found nothing. Nothing. When I was done, she lay semi-nude, clothed in little but her own blood.

Carefully, I set my gun down beside her, then left the kitchen and sat upon the couch in the other room. The ringing in my head had stopped, and it was quiet again.

I had killed someone. Murdered someone. During training, the entire week of it, they had told us over and over that this was what we had to do. Well, I had done it.

What did it feel like? It's almost impossible to answer that. I didn't feel...anything. It was just so much that one thing was piled upon the other. At the time, I don't think I was capable of anything beyond a vague realization of the crime that I'd just committed. I guess I just gave up. Murdering that teenager was the last step I could take in the direction that I had been going, and I simply had to go a different way.

There came a shout from across the street. I recognized Ben Halling's voice, and I fled through the open back door.

After I fled the Emac, I couldn't return to Tofino, and, really, there was no reason to go back there. I came to Regina looking for Katherine, but I can't deny that I was also on the run.

* * *

I stopped speaking. An hour had passed. Clouds wheeled above, and as I drifted back from my recollections, the brilliance of the sunset drove away my nightmare. My fists were clenched. I stretched out the cramped fingers, breathing deeply to ease the tension in my chest.

"And that's how you deserted?" Simon asked.

"Yeah."

"The term hardly seems to apply."

"Argue semantics with Ben Hallings, or to those three bodies on the highway. I'm a deserter. Do you think they'll shoot me because I'm Samuel J. Harris or Jacob Harrison? Either way, it doesn't matter.

"It's getting dark, time we headed back."

"I'd like to hear the rest, that is, if you want."

It was all there, near to speaking, wanting to be told. "Well, let's start back, maybe I'll try to get through it as we walk."

We arose and set off for the hospital. I continued with my story, breathing life into those cold memories of the coast. Walking steadily, clasping my elbow, Simon followed me into the night.

II

I wandered for days, I told Simon, in shock, not really cognizant of my surroundings. I have a vague recollection of awaking in ditches, covered by shrubs, scavenging through houses and once of running from a pack of dogs. When I finally worked through the shock and became aware again, I found myself on an eerie, haunted shoreline that at moments, at certain places, seemed no different from the coast that I remembered. I would experience brief periods of delusion, forgetting all that happened, then I would see a small detail, a car abandoned at an unusual angle on the road, a broken window, and then it would all come back to me.

The cold waters of the pacific swelled and rolled between me and the mainland, keeping Katherine from my arms. Blue sky above, below, the green of the distant shore. Often in the past, I'd looked at the same image and felt that I was the only person left on the planet. The solitude used to be calming.

Originally, I had entertained the vain belief that I'd find a deserted boat and be able to make my way to the coast, but in all the distance that I travelled, I saw nothing. Whatever had happened there, the locals must have been forewarned. Enough to clear out, anyway. It was a ghost town, sans people, sans bodies, just overgrown lawns and bushes, blank windows.

I walked for several days, only occasionally hearing the sound of passing cars or trucks. Once, I swore I heard a train, though I couldn't remember crossing any tracks. When I first heard that deep shunting of the wheels on the tracks, I thought that there was some kind of monster loose on the Island. You can see what state of mind I was in. Hours passed in a surreal collage of feet scraping on concrete walkways, the tumble of waves, hiss of rain and, in the night, disembodied cries of pain. Over it all there was silence. It crept about everything, smothering each noise before it had properly ended. Everything seemed muted, cut off, like some great hand snatched its echo from the heavy air.

Eventually I reached the district nearest the dock that used to house the ferry to the mainland. It was here that I first began to run into other fugitives. They shuffled down the streets like extras from a George A. Romero movie. I was afraid of being found out and punished as a deserter, and I wasn't armed; I'd left my rifle back with…. As it turned out, there was no need to defend myself. No one ever spoke to one another, suspect, I suppose, of what we might discover. I guessed that everyone I came across was a deserter like myself—cautious rather than afraid. When meeting upon the street, people circled by each other like scorpions in a pit and then continued in their separate directions. I guess we all did carry some kind of poison within us, deadly to no one but ourselves. I was still plagued by the image of that poor girl's blank face, but the expressions I saw as I waited hopeless by the harbour were almost as disturbing.

On my first evening there, I watched a storm over the water grow immense and slowly make its way to where I waited—in the bend of a tiny bay upon the edge of the sea. It was an anomaly to see any kind of weather moving east to west. I looked out to the mainland coast and, lifting my fingertip, I traced the far curve of the bay where it sent a thin line of earth out into the void between the ocean and sky. The thunderclouds rose like the gargantuan mountains of a surreal landscape, massing one upon the other, mounting to the darkening heavens where the pale gods trembled. Beneath the malevolent shadows of the storm, the cold, flat sea heaved, and with each heavy swelling of the waves, the leviathan breathed.

I spent the second day at the dock without food, having found nothing in my half-hearted looting. Drawn by the motion of the tide and longing for release, I walked out onto the planks of a pier some short distance from the main dock for the ferry. As I strode out onto its damp surface, I heard the faint strains of a saxophone being carried to me on the breeze. It seemed so ethereal that at first I thought I was hallucinating. I searched around and spotted a man sitting in front of a shed on a lower dock, adjacent to the pier. With one foot stretched out, his back pressed against the faded planks, he sent out these heavenly, mournful, wisps of sound. They floated with the air, and, like the barely perceived aroma of a wild flower, faded, then were gone.

Oh, in that brief moment, how my heart soared. My eyes misted, and as the music undulating with the breeze, waves of sorrow flowed from within me.

That evening, I heard the startling whistle of the ferry.

I had spent the previous night in a house that rested on an outcropping of land overlooking the harbour. I'd felt secure there and returned the next evening to sleep. Midway through the night, I awoke suddenly, not immediately realizing what had shocked me from my nightmares. My first thought was that someone else had broken into my refuge, and that I was in danger. As I crawled out of bed, the whistle once again tore through the silence. I scrambled to a window. There, slowing gliding into shore, illuminated by a cold moon, was the ferry I hadn't even dared to hope for. I ran from the house, more asleep than awake, still doubting what I'd seen was real.

When I arrived panting to the large loading area, asphalt crisscrossed by traffic lines, the ferry was still there, actually there, and its loading doors were down. A thin line of rag-tag refugees was making its way to embark. Some bizarre impulse led me to get in line, rather than walk straight onto freedom. A man in a tattered steward's uniform stood at the edge of the pavement and spoke briefly to each of us before we stepped on board. The interior of the ship was in heavy shadow. As each person shuffled within, they disappeared into the darkness like ragged bits of flesh into the maw of a gargantuan beast.

In turn I stepped up to the sailor.

"How are you paying?" he asked.

I laughed, incredulous. "What's the charge?"

He looked over my shoulder. "Don't insult me."

I dug into my pockets and pulled out what was stuffed there—credit card, Cashstop, ten dollars. Did most soldiers carry such things? I held them up. He took the bill and then laid hold of my watch, pulling it off my wrist.

"What else do you have?" he asked, and then repeated it. "What else do you have?"

"I don't have anything else," I cried, flipping open my wallet to show him.

"What's there, in your wallet?"

He'd seen the white edge, yellowed by then, of Katherine's picture that I'd taken in Yoho Valley. It was in rough shape. The image was faded; the paper was worn and beginning to get tattered. I withdrew it, certain that he'd have no interest in such a thing, but his eyes flashed, and he snatched it from my fingers. At first I was too shocked to react. A heartbeat later, when my anger rose, and I advanced on him, he quickly brandished a gun and levelled it at my chest.

"You can't have it," I hissed.

"This is your fare. It's this or you stay."

Logic told me to surrender it, but my emotions were raging. It was a horrible moment. In the end, I let it go, reasoning that the desire to hold her image wasn't worth keeping me from reaching her in person. I hated him though. I've hated others since, but never with the terrible, murderous intensity of that moment.

I stepped on board and entered into that dark cavern. When I'd taken the ferry before, the cargo area had always been filled with vehicles, cars, R.V.s, semi-trailers, whatever. It was empty now. I walked along the central space, found the stairs leading to the upper decks and made my way to the top of the ship.

The same vague aura of desertion and neglect that had been so prevalent along the coast was equally powerful within the metal bulkheads of the ferry. The galley, which had always smelled of grease-fried dishes, was now cold and dark. I walked along the stainless steel counter and glass displays, searching for left over food. There was nothing to be found. On other journeys, everything had been wiped clean; now it was sullied by a shroud of dust that lay in an even, almost perfect sheath upon the steel. I ran my fingertip along it, exposing a strip of bright metal. There was nothing in the kitchen, but the taps still ran with water. I bent my head under the cool stream to drink my fill. It had a slight iron taste. I wiped the moisture from my lips and set out to explore the rest of the deck.

Out on the streets, those few people I encountered had maintained a safe, almost comfortable distance from one another. In the passenger lounge, there was all too little space. Where strangers had been able to circle without having to acknowledge the other's humanity, now circumstances forced either an averted face, a terrified nod or a hostile glare. It was all too much for me. I left the shelter of the viewing compartments and escaped onto the outer deck.

The night was cool with a strong wind coming off the mainland. There was the distinct smell of salt water and with it that clammy moisture which the ocean air leaves on you at night. I climbed to the top observation deck and sat upon one of the lifeboats that lined the side of the ship.

I was utterly alone. The faint, dark, withdrawing silhouette of the Island was still visible. On other passages, in days gone by, the Island used to be sprinkled with light. Not so now. It wasn't hard to imagine that that entire mass of rock was now devoid of life. Why had they chosen the Island for such a fate? Aside from the initial fighting, in every other part of the country, the revolution had been fought more on idealistic and ethical battlegrounds. It was true that the New Christian Army met any armed resistance with a deadly force, but it most often gave civilians every possible opportunity to avoid violence by converting. Of course, this didn't always happen, there had been instances of great bloodshed; but that didn't seem to be the intent of the Coalition. They obviously realized that whatever was destroyed in their rampage would then have to be rebuilt.

So what about the Island? The utter desolation demanded a reason, but no answer was forthcoming from the night.

I spent most of the trip sitting in that one spot, then restless, I made my way up to the front of the boat, wanting a better view of our destination. As soon as I circled around from the cover of the cabin, the wind grew so intense that I was forced to grab hold of the handrails to keep myself from being swept off my feet. In all my life on the prairies, I'd never experienced a wind such as that. I wondered how fast the ship travelled; there was nothing to use as a reference point, just the moon and the sea. Gasping, I plodded forward until I stood at the centre of the front deck. I let go of the rail and stepped back. The wind pushed me against the metal of the ship. Feet tight together, I let my arms fly wide and then stood there trapped by its invisible force. It seemed so futile to fight it anymore.

There was little to see; we were still too far out from the coast. My gaze shifted upward to where I noticed a faint light emanating from the ship's bridge. I wondered about the man who piloted us across that dark expanse. There was a story as tragic as my own; I was sure of that. Weary of being pressed so remorselessly by the wind, I made up my mind to return to my perch upon the lifeboat, thinking even to seek out the captain.

I had scarcely settled upon my seat, when I was joined on the upper deck. So quietly he approached, or so loud was the rush of the ship, that I didn't immediately realize I was no longer alone. It was a man, dressed in the same uniform of the ticket taker, only dirtier and more threadbare. He climbed atop of the lifeboat beside me and stood, somewhat unsteadily, staring out at the black sea. He was mostly in silhouette, but enough light came down from the moon so I could faintly discern his features.

He had the face of an ascetic, long, lean, with a few days of rough growth. His hair was shoulder length, dark, and flipped about in the wind. He wore glasses, which I watched him remove and let fall to his side. Something about that gesture, that simple gesture of letting his fingers relax so the glasses dropped to crack on the walkway, spoke of such despondency that a soft cry escaped my lips. He lifted his arms before him, palms upward, as if expecting some gift from the night.

I moved closer, crouched at the edge of my perch.

"Who's the captain on this ship?" I cried out to him.

He was silent, then as I prepared to speak again, he replied, "Why are you here?"

I swung my legs down to the deck and stood at his side. "I'm looking for a friend."

"The coast is burning." He sounded like a prophet for the apocalypse, but too melodramatic to be convincing.

"How do you know? Where have you been?"

"North."

"What about Vancouver?"

"We've seen the sky alight with fires."

"You don't know," I said and repeated to myself, *He knows nothing.*

I wondered what his job had been and why he now stood upon that deck. As I watched, he lifted his arms to his side and tilted his head back, mouth opening, as if to catch rain. An odd sound rose from out his throat. I had struck a deer once on the highway, and as it lay dying, it too had made such a sound.

"You know nothing," I said and turned away.

The sound stopped, punctuated by a rush of air. When I glanced back, he was gone. Had he jumped? I looked about, startled, half suspecting that he hadn't been there at all. I leaned forward to look over the railing at the black sea until a rising sense of vertigo drove me back.

I decided that I would see the pilot if pilot there was, thinking that surely someone had to be guiding that ship. I trod with purpose upon the mist-moistened deck and a little too quickly came to look up at the dimly lit bridge.

Midway up the metal stairs I paused, suddenly frightened of what I would find. Frightened of what I might not find. Maybe there was no pilot at all. The ship could simply have been speeding unguided through the black night. What was I to do then? If I leapt in desperation into that dark ocean then surely I would die and the journey would just as surely have been without meaning. If I stayed on board, I would also die when the ship finally reached the invisible shoreline. I concluded that the only true option left for me was to accept that he was there in that cabin. Without that limited faith, the journey itself would be unbearable.

I ascended the remaining steps to the bridge then paused again, hand clutching at the frigid handle of the entrance. Even if the pilot stood at his post, what would he be? What kind of man would set out on a night like this? There was nothing for it; I opened the door and stepped within. Except for the lights of the instrumentation, the room was dark, but that was just enough for me to see him.

The pilot was there, with full uniform, pressed and clean; he stood behind the wheel, eyes fixed on our impossible destination. My gaze swept over him, and I was surprised to see that he wore no shoes. I pulled the door closed behind me. There was an audible click, but his concentration never wavered. He stood staring straight ahead.

Somewhat shaken, I moved closer. Cast in that eerie illumination, his face was unearthly pale. He seemed other than human, the image of a man, but not a man. "Excuse me," I said. "Hello." There came no response.

Just a little frantic, I tapped at the back of his shoulder and spoke again, louder now, certain to be over the sound of the ship's engines. "Captain, are you all right?" Under the circumstances,

I suppose it was a ridiculous question, but I really didn't think it mattered what I said. I gripped at his shoulder, and he twisted suddenly in my direction. I jumped back, startled. He hadn't really turned, for his feet remained planted, but his right shoulder pointed at me now, and I could see the profile of his face. He said something inaudible or inarticulate. His face was hideous. He motioned with his head, perhaps signalling me to move closer that I may hear what he had to say.

I ignored the gesture, suddenly preferring ignorance.

He motioned again, then shifted his feet so that he faced me. Now I regarded a silhouette, an animated darkness. He spoke more loudly this time, yet I could just make out his words. "I know thy works, and where thou dwellest," he said.

Those words, so out of joint with the present time, set me trembling as nothing else could have done. I backed swiftly to the door, fearing that I would hear him speak again. As I wrenched the handle and exited, his final comment boomed behind me: "Write the things which thou hast seen." I slammed the door and descended unsteadily back into the night.

So that was it.

The ship had a pilot, but the pilot was insane.

I had left the smoldering waste of the Island and put my faith in the white clad figure that stared straight into the pitiless dark and saw visions there that none of us could share or even understand. I sat once again upon the lifeboat mistakenly comforted by the thought that whatever misfortune befell us, it would allow me an avenue of escape—that I could find my own way across that black sea.

Where I sat, protected from the worst of the wind, the night air was cool and pleasant; it feathered my clothing. At some point, the lights of the ship had gone out, so I rested upon a swiftly moving husk of steel and black glass. The moon was full, and directly above me the grand brush stroke of the Milky Way swept across the sky. Even with the moonlight, the heavens were alive in a great mosaic of constellations, planets and stars. Things that were familiar, such as the dippers and Cassiopeia, were hardly discernible, lost as they were in the brilliant cluster about them. Though I knew where it should be, I couldn't find the North Star. Is it possible to lose your way if there is too much light? I thought to myself: *With this vision above me, why do I care if the pilot's insane?*

Is it enough that there's beauty, or do we need something more?

The ship drew closer to the coast, and I was able to discern a dark mass of land that reached south of us and out into the sea. Though darker than the water and sky, it was sprinkled with lights, and I felt comforted by this small sign of civilization. Whatever had happened, there was someone there to send out those tiny rays. Some inglorious Prometheus lived still. Above that dark arm, the moon hovered. Its light flattened that part of the sky, but below and nearer to me, the waters of the Pacific rippled with its illumination. Looking down and watching the swift waves pass, I finally realized the speed at which the ship was travelling.

The land mass grew ever larger, abruptly rising into mountains as my vision followed it inland. Heavy clouds hid the mountaintops, coloured an eerie amber by the city lights. A particular sense of unease troubled my thoughts: something seemed wrong—the coastline was different than it should have been. I realized with a start that the ferry was heading directly into Vancouver instead of docking kilometres north of the city. Worse still, that image that lay before me was not the Vancouver that I knew. I'd seen it by night before, and what I saw then was wholly unfamiliar to me. A growing unease urged me to withdraw from the deck, to seek safety and warmth inside.

I was about to do so when a bright light burst upon the night, momentarily blinding me. I lifted my hands to my eyes, startled; then I was tossed from my perch as a monstrous shudder tore at the ship. I thumped upon the deck, slid toward the railing and stopped with one leg hanging out above the cold sea. We had slowed, I could sense that, and when I scrambled to my feet, I realized with horror that the deck was no longer level.

I had no idea what had happened. A rocket from the shore, another ship, a mine, all those possibilities raced through my head. I hadn't heard anything. The ship was listing and with a mad pilot at the helm there was little chance that we would make it to safety. The ship would sink and pull me with it into the abyss or carry us all to thunderous oblivion against the docks. *This is really how the world ends*, I thought, *not with a whimper, but a bang*. I glanced quickly to the black horizon, cursed the Pilot, and then, forgetting the lifeboat, scrambled over the railing and dropped into the darkness.

It was a long fall, seconds, and when I hit the water it felt like I had come down on concrete. Sudden, terrible cold, confusion, searching in what direction lay life, where lay death, then in desperation kicking with heavy legs to get away from the wounded leviathan. The ship passed by, and its wake overwhelmed me. Coughing, choking at bitter water, I flailed with my numbing arms and suddenly frozen fingers. It was so hard to breathe. I clawed at the water until a rhythm found me, then kept it and prayed that it would lead me to land.

The coast was not so distant. I had little concept of time, but before the ocean overcame me, the features of a rough shore came clear to my sight. I had come to Vancouver for a final time.

The tide swept me fifty metres before I found a bank upon which I could scramble to shore. As I drifted along, even through my fear, I witnessed the lurid panorama of a dying city. Vancouver was burning—those were the lights that I had seen. Everything was desolation. I had stopped shivering, and drifted in the black waters almost complacently. A part of me screamed, knowing that I was hypothermic. Death was close, and the thought of drowning in that lonely place horrified me.

The port was once framed by a cluster of towering structures and architectural wonders—billion-dollar real estate that glistened in the sun, reaching like the Tower of Babel to touch the footpaths of angels, but the Coalition had brought it down, righteous in their belief that no human artifact should threaten the sanctity of God.

The towers still glistened, but did so now by moonlight, made lively through the thousand fires set by the revolution and still smoldering after it passed. While on the ferry, I had thought that the dark mass of a thunderstorm hovered above the city. I realized then that what I'd seen were clouds of smoke marking the storm that had already passed. The brilliant stars, which had seemed to guide us across the waters, were now hidden from view.

Then the bank dropped low, and I saw a stretch of debris-darkened beach. I kicked with my heavy, numb legs and thrashed my trembling hands at the water. I hardly seemed to move but shortly came upon a log floating close to the shore. Choking, warmed by my exertion and now shivering, I clutched at the wood, desperate to catch my breath.

The log was pale against the sea. I moaned as it proved soft and rolled beneath my hand. It was a naked body. Vacant eyes flashed upward. I think I retched, kicking violently back from the corpse that rolled again, turning cold eyes to stare once more at the depth of the dark and silent sea. I swallowed a mouthful of bitter water. Frozen and gasping, yet so close to safety, I almost went under.

When I finally scrambled ashore, the heat of the dying city warmed me. The death of such a Titan is not instantaneous; its gargantuan heart struggles with a fading rhythm equal to the labour of its creation. It dies slowly and the cremation of its flesh darkens the globe.

III

I had used to enjoy coming to Vancouver. There was a particular part of the city, English Bay, which had an open market and clusters of little shops selling anything from New Age literature to Nike running shoes. My ritual was to browse for several hours then buy a cup of coffee and sit in a street café watching the people pass by. I'd make notes in my journal—reflections on what I was seeing, things I could write about later. Those afternoons allowed me an odd combination of solitude and companionship.

On that particular night, walking amid the ruins of a city I once loved, my passage illuminated by the lurid light of the smoldering ruins, something drove me to once again seek out English Bay. I should have known it was a bad idea. Already despondent, the destruction of my treasured memory shook me deeply, even though by that time there was little left to be shaken.

I won't tell you of my walk to English Bay. The bodies in the streets, the fear of disease. The fetid stench of the thick, moist air and the buzz of black flies, more bloated than the corpses they fed upon.

At some point, I found a rucksack and also a rifle to replace the one I had left in that kitchen on the Island. The ammunition clip for the rifle was all but spent, yet it gave me a sense of security. I'd knelt upon the asphalt to pick it up, when I straightened, the side of a building caught my sight. Upon it, with a deep red paint, though hardly discernible in the smoke masked moonlight and inconstant flames, someone had written "The Rapture." I stood staring at it, more startled than I should have been. The sight of it triggered a rapid succession of images and associations beginning with Oppenheimer's quoting from the Bhagavad-Gita to Kurtz's harshly whispered self-damnation. I trembled. I checked the clip once again. I turned slowly in the deserted, cluttered street looking, seeing everything and seeing nothing. The only sound was the scuff of my shoes upon the road. That, and the flies, always the flies. Since when did flies feed in the night?

When I reached English Bay, I saw that many of the stores had been burned; why the flames didn't engulf everything, I don't know, but the fires and the arsonists had been selective. Perhaps arbitrary would be a more accurate description. Some buildings had only been touched by the flames; others were gutted.

How did it happen? Had an officer stood in the street centre and directed the demolition? Were orders given to smash this door, that window, to set fire to this shop and then just as quickly douse the flames? Or was it nothing more than anarchy? Perhaps the devastation had been caused by citizens looting and not by the army at all. If so, it was a populace that had gone mad, for the destruction was a testament to a desperation that had found its voice in a terrible rage.

The scene was almost incomprehensible to me. Fires would have lit the sky with an inconstant diabolical light, and in that light, aglow, the maniacal face of the Coalition, manifest in several thousand tormented countenances, must have swept through the streets swinging the heavy-handed sickle of oblivion. Fire after fire would have been lit to cauterize the wound of the west coast, already infected with sin, and Vancouver became the hell that the Coalition believed it to be. I wonder what Christ thought to see the ruin that was created in his honour.

I walked down that street, sickened by the smell. The air was still, the stench of wet ash and decaying refuse was thick about me. Death drifted like a midnight mist. Quite a few people would have resided in that part of town, so the area must have been evacuated when the Coalition finally arrived. Unlike the places I had passed getting there, blessedly, English Bay was free of bodies. The pavement, however, was littered with other debris. There wasn't a single shop that didn't have its front doors and windows smashed in. Glass was everywhere and to avoid it, I strode down the centre of the road. The New Christians must have laid hold of every one of those shops and scattered its contents out onto the street. A whirlwind had swept through my little refuge as it had swept through my life.

Strangely, many of the items on the road were still intact, and as I walked I paused to lift something from the hard asphalt, the similarity between that action and the manner in which I used to walk and browse suddenly struck me. Deeply disturbed, I left the past to lie where it had been thrown.

I decided to leave the city, thinking to search the first residential area for a bike or a motorcycle, anything that would hasten my escape from that titanic sepulcher. Lifting my gaze from the cluttered street and ignoring the broken façades of those stores frozen in mid-cry, I turned my back to the memories and began walking eastward. *Perhaps,* I had thought, *if I can find a place just a little untouched by the violence, I might try to rest a little.*

Having seen so much, I felt that I was immune to further shock, but I encountered the one thing I least expected. Sitting outside what had once been a coffee shop, a man sat quietly watching my approach. Across the street from him, a smoldering fire cast illumination upon his despondent countenance. Was he to be my Virgil, my guide through that lurid Inferno? He had righted two chairs and a table, upon which rested a half full bottle of red wine. There was an empty glass beside the bottle, another he held cradled in his fingers. He sipped from this as he watched me approach.

He wore no uniform, but as I came near, more curious than cautious, I noticed the white on black armband of the N.C.A.— the very thing I'd sought for so tragically upon the girl whom I'd murdered on the Island. And he had something else; something I'd never seen before; tattooed upon his left temple, there was a tiny cross. I also noticed the handgun that lay upon the tabletop. A rifle was propped against the wall of the shop to which he had turned the back of his chair. My own weapon was heavy on its strap, slung back behind my left shoulder. I judged that he could reach his faster than I could reach mine; however, he made no motion, save to study my approach.

Finally, he said, "Join me. There's an extra chair."

I sat opposite him; the rifle slung over my shoulder pressed into my back, so I took it off and leaned it against the side of my seat.

"N.C.A.?" he asked.

I shook my head. "Are you going to use that?" I said, motioning toward the handgun.

"I intend to," he said, "once I build up the nerve." He looked me straight in the eye then hefted the gun and popped the clip. He studied and then replaced it. "Not to worry. I've only got one bullet left."

I didn't understand what he meant. Then the same hand that had held the gun clasped the bottle and poured me a glass.

"For some reason," he said, "I thought that I'd have company tonight."

"When did the city fall?"

"You weren't here?"

"No."

"Regular army?"

"Emac."

"Deserter?" he asked, but I said nothing. Then he added, "Welcome to the crusades." He nodded, as though surrendering to a thought, then he set his wine down and fingered the armband upon his jacket. Abruptly he tore it off, tossing it upon the street. "As for me, I'm a civilian," he choked.

"Why is it so bad here? Why did...?" How could I sum up all that I had seen? "Why did it have to be so bad?"

"You mean the coast?"

The coast? Good God, I thought, *the whole coast.* "It's all like this?"

"All of it. You should leave here and not turn back." He stared at his hands, then nodded slowly, saying, "I can quote you word and phrase from *Bethlehem*, I've whole passages of the Bible committed to memory." I didn't understand his point. He took a drink and refilled his glass. "Somehow none of them seem to apply." He glanced at me sharply, studied me for a long moment, then grunted. "I was a theologian, you know."

"I taught university. So what are we doing with these guns?" I didn't understand what he was getting at.

His eyes brimmed with tears, then he looked away and shrugged, muttering, "'Things fall apart.'"

The centre cannot hold, I thought. *Why do we have these guns?*

"Well then," he said, "let's have a toast."

"A toast?" I didn't see much worth toasting.

He spoke slowly, raising his glass, "To 'the sun that is young once only.'" We both drank. "I expected company, but I never dreamed it would be you." Then I understood; he had recognized me. It was shocking, but it made the most sense that, if anyone should recognize my face, it would be a theologian. "It seems so fitting that you're here."

"Fuck you," I rasped, disregarding his loaded weapon. "I only came through here because I'm looking for someone I love."

"I was looking for a loved one too, or at least that's what I believed. Somehow that purpose got confused in all the rhetoric. Why did you write those things?"

I hesitated, considering. I'd been asked that question many times but never by someone so apparently desperate. Still, the response was the same. "Because I loved Man."

He nodded. "I guess I just loved God more. You asked why it had to be like this?" I grew uncomfortable under his stare. "It was you, Dr. Harris. It was your book." I'd heard it all before, and there was nothing I could say. People believe what they want to believe. He sat staring at me, wanting something, but there was nothing for me to give him. After a moment he spoke again, repeating words that I had written long before, quoting from *Bethlehem*: "'The flotsam and jetsam that pollute the shoreline of this sea must be cleansed before we can embark upon our new journey.'"

Bile choked me. *That's it?* I thought. *That simple line set fire to an entire coastline. They don't even understand.* I let my head sink low, eyes fluttering shut. I felt so weary that nothing short of death could have given me the rest that I desired.

He apparently had the same idea. He emptied his glass then picked up the gun. "Would you mind leaving me now?"

I had an intimation of his purpose. "You could come with me," I said.

He flicked off the safety. The sound of it was loud in the gloom, "There's nowhere left for me to go; there's nothing else I can be."

I arose, and, for a second time, left my weapon behind. I turned my back on that lonely image. Maybe his way was better. God knows, I wasn't one to pass judgment.

"You were right, you know?"

I glanced back, regarding him a final time. "How is that?"

"About the Second Coming."

Either his words or the terrible empty look in his eyes chilled me. I whispered, "God forgive you," and left him. I hadn't gone more than ten metres when the shot echoed in the ruined street. It was strangely muffled. Curiosity tugged at me savagely, but I wouldn't let myself look back.

He had lied. That last bullet *was* for me. The sound of it tore through me as if he'd fired straight into my chest. I remember that I cried aloud and stumbled clumsily away, my eyes blurred with tears.

It overwhelmed me then, all of it. The ferry, now certainly crippled at the mouth of the bay, the bodies in the water, the smoldering city and Kathy lost. Finally this, one more death,

I fell to my knees and gave voice to the horror that had been growing inside of me.

I hardly remember where I slept that night.

The next day, I walked away from Vancouver. I thought that I'd seen the worst of what people could do to one another. Before this all started, even just the idea of a civil war within this country was inconceivable. That was something that happened in Eastern Europe or Central America, never here. The image of people in the streets carrying guns was beyond me. Or at least, at one time, I thought it was beyond me.

And then I saw the worst of it.

They say that the road to Rome was lined with the bodies of the conquered. The road leading from Vancouver was no different. You know when you drive along the highway, on one side of the road there's always a row of power lines? For some reason they remind me of crosses. I would always get a macabre sensation when I'd see three of them spread out on the top of a hill. It's an image out of Golgotha. Evidently someone from the Coalition made the same association.

When I left the ruins of Vancouver, I found that the power poles supported a burden other than that for which they had been erected. They were hung with corpses. Some were strapped on, some nailed. Some of them…well. I had noticed the cry of birds when I'd left the city, gulls and ravens; they seemed more numerous than usual, but…. At the first body, I collapsed on the roadside and needed to struggle for my breath. I was dizzy, but worse than that, a general, I don't know, confusion overwhelmed me. The world was spinning, and I thought I heard voices crying out. My heart hammered at my chest, and the heavy drum of blood throbbed at my temples. It passed in moments, how long I wasn't sure. I regretted leaving behind my gun. As it was, I could only wring my hands and fight to keep my eyes closed to sight.

But, even blind, I could not have escaped the horror. I could hear the birds feed. Once again, the air was thick with flies. Once I strode past the first body, I realized with a sick stomach, that the stench of death would accompany me until Vancouver was just a ghastly memory.

After a time, I crawled to my feet and continued on my way. My shoes shuffled and scraped upon the dusty road. I was torn between watching for N.C.A. and keeping the row of corpses from my sight. I shouldn't have been out in the open in the first place, but the experiences of the last few days had made me reckless. I hardly cared. I hardly cared at all.

I couldn't comprehend the rationale behind what I was seeing, what I refused to see. It seemed such a parody of the crucifixion, how could the New Christians have done it? I didn't understand then that there was no logical reason. Consider what the Coalition had done up until that point: on the basis of one small book, actually on the misinterpretation of one small book, they'd brought the Apocalypse to an entire city, no, more than that, to the entire coast, and they'd done all of this in the name of Christ. I was looking for logic? I understand now that it doesn't exist in the world of religion.

I'd walked perhaps a half kilometre when I heard a sound. At first I thought that I was becoming feverish, sun stroke perhaps, a touch of delirium. I was certain that what I had heard was a human voice, weak, but near. I stopped and looked about me. In each direction, the road was clear. Back westward, I hadn't noticed it as I had passed, but upon a sign that had once introduced visitors to Vancouver, the name of the city was covered by spray-paint, and another name was written in: Gomorrah. Beyond that, there was the illusion of water on the road and then nothing. I was alone. Myself, the burning sun, and Christ upon that flat black road—a thousand times over. When I heard the voice again, the tiny kernel in my brain that still maintained some semblance of lucidity understood immediately from where the sound originated.

It came from one of the crosses.

I continued walking, praying that silence would see fit to bless me. It wasn't to be so. That rasping sound came again. Did it say "please"? It was too muffled to tell, and I sought to deny it.

"Please. Kill me."

So I stopped and listened.

"Kill me."

I had walked past but looked up and saw a woman's broken body stretched upon the cross. The rucksack came off my back. I stepped slowly up to the base of the crucifix. The power pole wasn't that high, her feet were only a little above my head. They hadn't forced spikes through her hands or feet, just tied her to the wood and left her to die. Was that more humane? Less pain to begin with, but the dying would take longer.

"Please," she begged.

Ghastly thin, wasted arms and legs thrust out from t-shirt and cut-offs. Her skin had been tormented by the sun; her lips were swollen and cracked. Dried blood formed vertical slits upon them. Something seemed wrong with her shoulders. There was nothing I could do. There was nothing that I had to do. She would die. She would die without me. I stepped away.

"Please."

I slipped the knife from my belt and held it before me. After a moment's deliberation, I dragged my backpack to the base of the pole and propped it against the wood. Then I climbed upon it, my left hand clutching the far side of the wood. My head was at the level of her thighs. I lifted the knife and pressed the tip against her ribs, thinking to sink the blade into her lungs, her heart and give her an early release. She whispered, "Thank you," her voice choking. I looked into her face, seeking resolve from her suffering, but I saw instead the face of the woman who had killed Stephan Low, the woman I had killed.

I couldn't do it again. I pulled the knife away, seeing that my shaking hand had accidentally pressed the tip of the blade through her skin and caused blood to flow from her side. She uttered something inaudible, her voice rising. I used my shoulder to rub away the sweat that was stinging my eyes. I brandished the knife again and, stretching out far, cut the weathered ropes that bound her wrists. She fell forward upon my shoulder. I could hardly feel it. She weighed so little. I cut the bindings from her ankles and then stepped down to the road.

Her panting was loud in my ears as I gently laid her upon the hard earth.

"Thirsty," she rasped.

I fumbled in my pack, finding a small bottle of wine that I'd scavenged in the city. I used the knife and then my finger to push down the cork. Tilting her head, I lifted the bottle to her lips and held it there that she might drink. The liquid passed between her lips, and she turned her head away, choking. The spilt wine upon her shirt was a dark red, contrasting to the bright hue of the fresh blood coming from her side.

"Go slowly," I whispered, but she refused to accept more. I brought the wine to my own lips, but the first taste of it was bitter. It had turned on me. I'd given her vinegar. The bottle slipped from my hand and shattered upon the pavement. Unable to comfort her, unable to kill her, I cradled her head in my hands and waited.

Sometime after nightfall, she died.

* * *

I stopped speaking. To have finally told it, to have finally released all that suffering was a panacea that left me utterly spent. I looked at Simon's tranquil face and felt thankful for his sightless eyes that could express no judgment. God, I wished Katherine was there.

"I had no idea," Simon said eventually.

His hand was upon my arm. It felt moist, and I realized that I wept once again.

"At least, at the end, that soldier saw the truth of what he'd done," Simon offered.

"He didn't see the truth at all. He looked into his own heart and saw the very thing he'd come to the Island to fight." I pulled from Simon's grasp. "He died as confused as when he lived, and it was my words that did it to him."

"You're not so important that you can claim responsibility for anyone else's actions," Simon said. "The least any of us can do is speak our own truth. No one can blame you for that."

I wondered what he was really talking about. "You weren't there, Simon," I said.

"No, I wasn't there."

There was still some distance to go, but the two of us were silent for the remainder of the walk. After everything I had told him, what was there left to say?

As we approached the hospital, one of the few other patients left there was sitting on the front steps when we arrived. He regarded us as we neared, took a long, last drag of his cigarette, then flicked it onto the sidewalk. It rolled off the curb and came to rest amongst dead leaves and tattered bits of paper. I watched its ember burn out, leaving a thin wisp of smoke in the still air. "Hey, Simon," he called.

"Is that you, Matt?"

"In the flesh." The man stepped down to take Simon off my arm. I hadn't met this person before. No doubt there were many people Simon knew whom I'd never seen. I had intended going into the building, hoping to speak with Christina, but for some reason then the idea seemed out of place. Perhaps I was jealous of Simon somehow. Jealous of his friendship, that is. I had just bared my soul to him, and he was to be suddenly stolen from my company. Yet again, what was there to say? What could be said that wouldn't ring like a platitude, wouldn't insult the stark truth of what I had experienced? Still, I needed to know what he thought. I needed for him to tell me that nothing was really different between us.

Simon paused and turned back to me. "Goodnight…Jacob. If you're up to it tomorrow night, I'd still like to go to the poetry reading."

"Sure, Simon, I'll come by. Tell Christina."

His friend escorted him inside.
That was all. That would have to be enough.

IV

I left as well, but I didn't head straight home. Returning to an empty apartment didn't appeal to me right then. My thoughts were racing. Relating the story of the coast had physically exhausted me, but for some reason my mind would not keep quiet. So much had happened. So much had yet to pass. None of us could know why we had ended up there together or where it would all lead.

I let my feet take me, and they strayed from the main thoroughfare down a deserted side street to a destination I wasn't aware of. Having just relived that night in Vancouver, I couldn't help looking at Regina with the same eyes that had regarded the ruin of that coastal city. What would Regina look like in a few weeks? Certainly it wouldn't take longer than that. The city would serve as some sort of symbol, a final lesson for all those under the sway of Joseph Adams. The question on everyone's minds had already been asked by Simon: what type of message would the new Messiah prefer—that of the lion or the lamb?

I walked a dozen blocks before taking note of my surroundings and recognizing that I'd made my way into a less than desirable area of town, somewhere I would never normally go. Before discretion replaced my valour, however, I spotted the sign of the Salvation Army Mission building that had caught my eye so powerfully the day Simon guessed my identity. There was a light on inside. I tugged at the front door. It was locked. I knocked, thinking that perhaps street people used this place as a refuge from the cold of the night as well as from their hunger. No answer came. I saw no movement inside.

So what had drawn me there? I stepped back from the doorway, studying the front of the building in the weak light. Nothing caught my eye. Actually, the place had a cold, dead feel to it, not at all like the impression it had made upon me the first time I'd seen it. Still, I had an intimation of something; I knew not what. Whatever it was that I had been seeking, it was no longer here. I turned and shuffled away.

As I came back onto Albert Street, I realized that my walk had taken me close to the Free House. Seeing the Mission had made me think of food, and I realized that I hadn't eaten since lunchtime. I decided to stop in and grab a bite before going the distance home.

The café was almost empty, which seemed odd to me, even being as late as it was. I took a seat far from the door, asked for whiskey from the waitress who sat smoking at the bar. She brought it, and I ordered food.

The condensation on the curved sides of the glass had barely begun to form when I heard the door of the café open and glanced up to see William enter. He was alone. He didn't see me at first, and I sat back in the cover of the dimly lit room to study him. I had the fleeting suspicion that he was following me. In that dim light, he looked tired…and dangerous. That was an adjective that I'd have never thought to associate with him. He was no longer the youthful, manic poet whom I had met so many years ago. An exhaustion, or desperation, dragged down his shoulders and marked heavy lines on his face. I wondered if I had undergone such a transformation myself.

He stood in the entrance, searching over the room. I got the impression that he was looking for someone, or avoiding someone. A smile flashed across his features when he finally saw me watching him. He came over and sat down.

"I've been looking for you."

"Where's your buddy?" I asked.

"Huh? Oh, Braxton. Planning the resistance, I guess." Fool that I was, I thought he was joking. "We haven't been moving around in the same circles as of late."

The tone of his voice warned me to leave that well enough alone. I reached back to a topic that had once occupied most of our conversations, "How's your story?"

He looked a little confused, then nodded. "Not so well. It's been a busy day. There was a meeting tonight."

"What's up?"

"Believe me, this is something Samuel Harris doesn't want to get involved in." The waitress shuffled over, and he ordered a drink. She brought it a moment later.

"Well, what's going on?" I insisted.

"There was some sort of, I don't know, 'happening' at the encampment today. It looked like someone important arrived." He didn't need to tell me who that would most likely be. "We think the Coalition is through with waiting."

I had a flash of déjà vu. Was he to always be the bearer of bad news? "Is that what the meeting was about?"

"Partially. There's some argument as to how it should be dealt with."

I tried not to, but barked a short laugh. "Don't kid yourself, Will. There's nothing to be done. We either capitulate or run. Tell your scheming pals that that's all there is to it. I've seen the results of people who tried to 'deal with' the Coalition."

"Yeah, well, that's what I said, but I don't think I made much of an impression."

"Why don't you let me speak to them? My words should carry some weight."

"Not if you're dead they won't, and Sam, two steps into a room with these guys, you'd be dead. Joseph Adams isn't number one on their hit list; you are." I had been leaning forward, speaking close to a whisper, but Will's comment pushed me back into my seat. I felt a chill. I'd grown complacent over the last few weeks, thinking my alias as more of an affectation than a necessity. It was startling to receive another such reminder on the same day. "Have you thought anymore about my offer?"

I realized that was his reason for seeking me out, but it took a moment before I could collect myself enough to reply. "Yes, but I have two friends I can't leave behind."

He nodded, considering, then abruptly finished his drink. "Let me talk to Roland about that. I know that he's spoken to others about joining this little expedition, so I can't guarantee that he'll have enough room. Christina?"

"And Simon."

"He's blind, Jake. That's going to make things difficult."

"He wouldn't survive under the occupation."

"Who would?" He stood up, reaching into his pocket to fish out money for his drink. "I'll get back to you soon as I can."

"Poetry reading tomorrow?"

He grunted. "I have to take a short trip, so not likely, but keep an eye for me." He began to walk off, then hesitated. "Actually, Jake," he said pointedly, "just keep an eye open period. Okay?"

I attempted a flippant remark, but my voice caught in my throat. I nodded instead.

He gave a half-hearted wave and left the café. I remained only a little while after that, then made my lonely way home.

It was a lengthy stroll from the Free House back to my apartment. Often I enjoyed the solitude and time to think that it offered me. That night, as you might expect, was very different. I tried not to admit it to myself, but Will's comments had frightened me, and I walked through the Regina night fearful of doorway shadows and alley entrances. I encountered no one.

Near home, I passed through Victoria Park, where the obligatory gatherings of teenagers sat half-hidden and hunched by clumps of bushes where they smoked drugs and spoke of God knows what. They took on a particularly sinister aspect that day. Subconsciously reacting to that perception, I found that, instead of walking upon the grass and listening to the wind in the trees above, I walked on the concrete path where park lights illuminated my way.

Like spokes in a wheel, all paths in that park lead to a central monument—a cenotaph erected for those who gave their lives in The Great War and World War II. I paused there, considering how those efforts seemed so wasted that evening. It's ironic that the freedom they fought so hard to preserve would be lost, not to enemies from without, but from within.

At home, in bed, sleep came only begrudgingly. When I dreamed, I dreamed dreams of violence.

V

The morrow came, and nothing happened. After the paranoia of the night before, I'd expected the Second Coming, but apparently Christ, or Lucifer or Joseph Adams was too busy to make it. I spent the day writing in my journal, wandering around the city and listening for news on the street. Rumours and rumours, no one knew anything. Some time in the early afternoon, I caught a carriage to the south end, near the city limits and tried to catch a glimpse of the rough beast that lay in wait beyond the confines of my little sanctuary. There was little to be seen. I grunted with dark amusement, thinking: *If I can watch a dog running away for three days, I sure as Hell should be able to see an invading army.* But the day was overcast and the afternoon light weak. If they were out there, nature conspired to conceal them.

Most of the afternoon had passed before I recalled my agreement to take Simon to the poetry reading at The Thirteen Avenue Coffee House. Throughout the day, I had kept an open eye for Will, and it was thinking of him that reminded me of the reading. At sometime around eight that evening, I decided to walk to the hospital and collect my charge. It was a funny thing; had the phones been working, we would have arranged a specific time to meet; as it was, we had all learned to operate on a loose schedule where an hour, give or take, didn't seem to matter all that much. If this lifestyle had been created under different circumstances, it could have been very relaxing.

When I arrived at the hospital, I found Christina sitting on the front steps waiting for me. She'd pulled her hair back and tied it. It was a good look for her. The lines of her face appeared almost striking.

"Hi, Jacob." She frowned at the misnomer then shrugged. I shrugged back.

"Where's our literary doppelganger?"

"What?"

"Simon, where's Simon?"

"He says he's not up to going out."

At first, I felt the rapid slip-wire of a snare, albeit not an unpleasant one, then the apprehension came that Simon was avoiding me, had judged me after what I'd told him. I felt sick. "Oh," I said, and pulled her to her feet. "Let's get a move on or we may not get in. Peter's isn't that big of a place."

"Lead, and I'll follow." I paused, uncomfortable. That was the kind of thing Katherine would have said. "Are you okay?" Christina asked.

I pushed aside the sensation and forced a smile. "Just a thought. I'm fine."

We turned from the hospital. I wondered if Simon had someone watching us as we set out down the street. We didn't talk for a time; I knew that she was thinking something out, deciding what to say. There were things that I needed to say as well, or needed to hear. We hadn't really spoken since Simon had pulled back the veil obscuring my identity.

"I don't blame you, you know," she said finally.

How many people would have said that? She had looked past her own reactions and concerns, questions, and sought to understand what it was that I needed the most to hear. Then she had said it. "Thank you," I whispered.

"But I do worry about you."

"You should worry for all of us."

"Even the Coalition will need doctors, and I can take care of Simon."

"Are you sure of that?"

"We've already discussed it. When the hospital closes, and there isn't the money or supplies to keep it open much longer, he's going to come stay in my place. I've got room and can look after him."

"Someone like Simon," I was shaking my head, "how can you look after him? I mean, I know you can look after him, but his words, his thoughts; if they ever discover him, what he says will get him crucified."

"They won't. I'll make sure of that."

Her mind was set. I let that thought go. "Do you want to stay in Regina?"

"Want to? I don't want any of this. I want things back the way they were, but that's not going to happen. The Coalition will get here, and we'll just have to adapt."

I wrestled with the idea of telling her about William's plan but wanted to wait until I knew for sure that Roland would allow them to go. At that moment, I wasn't sure that I could convince her that I really wanted to leave myself. I had, by then, begun to consider an alternate plan—one I knew she would not agree with.

"What do you think it will be like?"

She stopped walking and squared off to look me in the face. "I think for you it will be deadly. You have to get out of Regina before it's too late."

"Don't you think I know that?" I continued walking. "Whatever they have in mind for me, I'm not going to like it, but I'm just so tired of running. I've been running since before the war."

"Don't give up because you're tired."

"Where is there to go, really, where they won't come to eventually?"

"Oh, this isn't really such a big thing; we just think so because we're in the middle of it. Half this world probably doesn't even know who Joseph Adams is. Or Samuel J. Harris, for that matter."

"Maybe not, but like you said, we're the ones in the middle of it. The rest of the world doesn't matter."

"What I meant was, if you could get out of Regina before it was too late, then you could go to those places. It doesn't have to end here."

No, I thought, *it doesn't. I just wish it would.* Without Katherine, there hardly seemed any point.

The Coffee House was absolutely full. Once again, I was struck by the surreal nature of life in Regina. As the Coalition hunched sniffing outside our door, people ventured out to the café to share poetry. I understood that their only other option was to stay indoors and dwell upon the desperate circumstances of our lives, but it still struck me as odd.

On the pretense that we already had seats, we squeezed our way through the crowd outside the door. Once inside, I cast about for Will, hoping he'd be there and have a table. He wasn't. Instead, I caught sight of Adam sitting at a table with three young women. He saw me and waved us over. Finding him there was a coincidence, but it wasn't a surprise. I assumed that, like myself, his life within the city was limited to a relatively small area. On a daily basis, I hardly ventured beyond a five-block radius, and until I volunteered with Simon, I hadn't gone that far north in the city. William and I rarely made plans to meet because we ran into each other almost every day. The fact that neither one of us enjoyed eating alone in our apartments made our impromptu rendezvous all the more likely. Now that I had expanded my wanderings to include the Thirteenth Avenue Coffee Shop, I expected that I would be seeing Adam a lot more frequently.

He had his foot on a chair and pushed it out as we came up.

"Are you saving it?"

He grinned, "Yes, for you. Sit down." I let Christina sit and moved around the table to put my back against a wall. I'd never seen the place so full of people. Some blues was playing over the stereo, and people struggled to be heard above the music. The overall effect was cacophonic, not at all the Peter's that I was used to. It took me a moment to realize that I knew all three of the women with Adam. One was Moe; she smiled at me mindlessly, waving. I waved back, fairly certain from her actions that she was operating under the influence of something other than a love for poetry. I grinned, happy to see the Moe who I'd grown to know in Tofino. She was never so much fun as when she was less than entirely lucid. I was surprised to see that the other two were her friends whom I'd met before on the Island—Maude and some name I couldn't even begin to pronounce. They didn't speak English, and I didn't speak French. We all smiled and waved, which was the full extent of every conversation we'd ever had anyway. I decided to quiz Adam about it later and find out how they had come to Regina.

I asked Christina what she would like to drink and then struggled through the maze of chairs to the self-serve bar, finally returning with two drinks for us. One of the girls had left, up to the washroom I supposed, and I appropriated her seat.

Moe hugged me and gave me a kiss on each cheek. The French are all too demonstrative for my liking. Christina raised an eyebrow. I'm sure I blushed, but the dim light would have hidden that. Moe then lifted her drink, gulped it back, rattled the ice cubes then thumped the glass down on the table, all the time smiling at me. I just laughed. Whatever was going through her mind, I had no chance of figuring it out.

"Hey," she said.

"What?"

She turned her head sideways, still grinning and through closed teeth, said, "What am I?"

I could barely hear her and knew from experience how futile it was to engage in conversation with her when she displayed such theatrics. At such a stage in an evening, it was much better to just sit back and watch her interact with others. "Shut up, Moe," I said.

"What am I?" she insisted.

"You're an idiot; that's what you are," I said, laughing.

"What am I?"

Adam was watching us. "'E doesn't know. What are you?"

"I'm a cat. Cats can't talk." She kept grinning, took another drink, still staring at me. The other girl made a remark, and they both giggled.

I looked at Adam, leaned toward him, "Is she on something?"

He shrugged, "Of course. You are not?"

Christina leaned toward me. "It's packed in here," she said.

"I guess people are starved for distraction."

A half hour passed consumed by small talk. It seemed that, by silent consensus, no one there desired to talk of the war or even mention the Coalition. For a time, we immersed ourselves in the fantasy that the world was sane and reasonable and just.

The crown thickened. Finally, Christina leaned over to me and asked, "Would you mind going outside for awhile? I'm already getting claustrophobic."

I shrugged. "Sure." I asked Adam to save our seats, and he warned me that the reading would start in less than a half hour.

We arose and made our way out the front door. Once outside, we took a seat on a bench near the sidewalk. "I'm glad we came," I said. "I need some diversion."

"I'm starved for entertainment too, but do you mind sitting out here for awhile?"

"No, it's a beautiful evening."

She leaned back on the bench, stretching an arm behind me. "Look at that sky."

I did. It was a clear, magnificent night. During the time that I'd spent on the coast, I'd forgotten the wonder of the prairie sky. From habit, I sought out the Big Dipper, followed the line of its cup to the northern star and then to Cassiopeia, a bit further. "Look," I pointed, "it's clear enough to see M31."

"What's that?" she said, leaning into me to sight along my arm. My pulse quickened; I shifted uncomfortably.

"That's Andromeda, at least I think that's Andromeda, the galaxy closest to ours."

"Really? That little smudge there?"

"Yeah, that's it."

"What else do you know?"

I shook my head. "That's all. Oh, Orion's belt, but I can't see it now."

She leaned against my shoulder and sat quietly for a time.

We heard an oddly familiar sound come echoing down the street. Christina twisted and looked up at me, her eyebrows furrowing. It grew quickly louder, and I suddenly realized that a car approached us. It rounded a corner a block away then turned in our direction. The sudden glare of the lights made me flinch like some animal startled on a midnight road.

"Relax, Samuel. It's just a car." It sped by as she spoke. Echoes rattled. "Someone out for a joyride."

"I wonder where they got the gas."

"Oh, I'm sure people have it stockpiled all over. I doubt there isn't a car in this city that couldn't get you out to the mountains."

It seemed to me a fortuitous thing to say, and I considered again telling her about William's plan.

"Christ, it would feel good to go for a ride right now. I'm sick to death of walking."

She watched me for a time, finally saying, "You're so tense."

"Aren't you? It seems so odd to be sitting here waiting for poetry when the N.C.s are just one kilometre from the city."

"When they come, they come."

"I wish it would be that easy."

She nodded, "Me too." Her head rolled back once again, and she stared at the night sky. "Look at the lights on the cathedral." Two sets of red floodlights were trained on the spires of the church. With star speckled darkness as a backdrop, the building created a dramatic image. Between the ruby fingers pointing up to God, and illuminated by light from the street, there stood Christ with his arms outstretched. Did he gesture in blessing or supplication? *What will the N.C. do with such a statue? Does Christ have a place in the new religion?* Stupid question. I searched my memory for any passage *in Slouching Toward Bethlehem* that would in some way justify his immolation, but nothing came to mind. In all probability, it would become a moot point; the cathedral itself was destined for destruction. There was no way the Coalition would allow such a monument to survive. Samuel J. Harris had said to burn the churches, and this church would make such a flame as to warm the feet of angels.

"What are you thinking about?"

"Nothing. We probably should get back to our seats."

As we stood and entered the coffee shop, I realized that at some time she had taken hold of my hand and had not let go.

"What's that girl's name again?"

"It's Moe." They grinned at us with blank faces as we pushed our way through the crowd.

"I have an inkling that she's on drugs."

I grinned. "No, do you think?"

I was beginning to suspect that we wouldn't be able to hear any of the poetry when the music stopped and a voice came over the loudspeakers, asking everyone to be quiet. In the far corner of the room, near the window to the kitchen, a woman stepped upon a small platform and stood restlessly before a microphone. It was a makeshift podium, but as much as was allowed for by the cramped conditions. Except for those sitting just before her, I could see over the heads of most of the other customers, so I had a pretty good view of her reading. She was nervous, that much was evident. She clutched a few scraps of paper in her hand. The way that she twisted it, I doubted that there would be anything left for her to read.

One of the waiters, who was doubling as M.C., stepped up to the mike, introduced her, then disappeared into the crowd. She glanced about, unsure of herself, then selected a sheet, straightened it, and began to speak. Totally belied by her appearance, her voice was steady and strong.

"These are some short works that I wrote while hiking in the Rockies." I let go of Christina's hand. She folded it in her lap, looking at me questioningly. I concentrated on the speaker.

"White river froths under granite mountain. Knees bent, silently broods. Witness eternity."

There was silence for a moment until people realized that she was done then they clapped politely. She waited until they were still and began another poem.

"Sitting in the small shelter of my tent with flaps open to the gentle night, I sit cross legged reading by candlelight. A quick wind shakes the trees. My lantern is blown out."

The response of the crowd was more immediate and a little louder. Moe leaned across the table to say, "I wonder if these pieces are titled."

"Ask her."

"I have one more to read for you. It's called 'Rain.'"

Moe giggled. The room was once again quiet.

"Swift, light pastel steaks of gray, rapidly fading, one following the other until the canvas seems smeared with soft translucence, and the dark background green of swaying pines is smoothed away."

She folded the papers, jammed them into her back pocket and left the little platform. Applause followed her, and I could see friends meet and congratulate her. She finally smiled and heaved a sigh of relief.

Adam had his eyes closed as the woman was reading. He opened them and looked at Moe. "Ryokan?"

She nodded, "Same understatement. I liked them. I wonder why she did so few." Adam shrugged. I shrugged too, trying to appear knowledgeable but having no idea what Ryokan was.

The waiter returned to introduce the next reader, a man in his late thirties. He was wearing a jean jacket with a ball cap turned backward. He seemed a lot more relaxed in front of the gathering. When the waiter gave him the stage, he stepped up and took hold of the microphone, lifting it from its stand.

I remarked to Adam, "Doesn't look like your typical poet."

"Maybe he writes sport poems," Moe said.

I sniped, "There's no such thing."

Christina rolled her eyes, "Aren't we all just so Bohemian?"

"About a year ago," the poet said, "I lost my mother to cancer. Up until that time, I'd never considered myself much of a writer, but the experience brought out something that I didn't know was there." He'd caught the attention of the crowd, and the room became very quiet.

I wished that we had sat closer to the doorway so that I could leave without being noticed. His circumstance was too similar to what I'd experienced with my own family, and I didn't need to relive it through his eyes. I looked toward the exit, but it was too crowded. I couldn't get away without causing a disturbance. I suppose my discomfort showed in my face, for Christina leaned close to me and asked if I was okay.

"I'm fine. I just don't need to hear this."

"I'll go out with you."

"No, it doesn't look like we can get away."

The poet began.

"Simple wishes…to have known her when she was young, to sit together in a field of rainbow blossoms sprinkled by summer winds, to make her smile, to hear her breathe and, for a moment, hold back this cancer, this death."

One man at the table next to us began to clap, but ceased when he realized he was alone. Any response would have seemed gauche. I lifted my head with closed eyes and fought back the tightness in my chest and throat. Christina's hand smoothed my shoulder. She didn't even know why I was upset. How could she know about a mother and father who had died from cancer years before the war? I wondered what Katherine would have done.

"In every time of sadness," the poet spoke softly, "there are always moments of beauty and grace. This was true for me. Up until my mother got sick, I'd never really looked at her and my father objectively, never really understood through the eyes of a stranger what a couple they made. I wrote this after watching him care for her in those final days. It's called 'This Quiet Love.'

"In this coil bound journal, my silent companion, I scratch in ink those moments of beauty that have coloured my life: The dance of fireflies on the red clay cliffs beneath the silver cast silhouette of the Devil's Tower; A fire born mist clothing the time battered ruins of sacred Delphi; The frail lights of Tofino sprinkled against the dark mass of Vancouver Island while moonbeams sparkle off the high waters of the Pacific Ocean.

"Of all these things I've seen, where the deliberate brush of antiquity and the grand sweep of this great artist Earth have made images of such magnificent scale, none surpasses the beauty of the quiet love between this aging man and his dying wife."

That time there was an immediate and spirited response. Under cover of the noise, I rose quickly and left the café.

The night had turned cool. I hurried past the people sitting on the plastic chairs outside and set off down the street. I knew that my suffering wasn't special; everyone there had lost someone they loved sometime during the war, but the associations that had been rekindled by the poet's words opened a floodgate of emotion that was threatening to overwhelm me. I had to get away from his voice and gain some composure from the night. There came the sound of footsteps behind me, and I paused to look back. It was Christina.

"Are you all right?"

"Yes."

"I don't mean to…. If you want to be alone, just say so. I only wanted to see if you were okay."

Here is another problem, I thought. *What am I to do with this beautiful, gentle woman?* "Thanks; I'm fine. It's okay if you want to walk with me, but I'm going back downtown. I don't want to hear any more."

"I can leave now."

We began walking. Funny, but we kept to the sidewalk, even though the streets were empty of vehicles. Old habits. We passed several couples. Some smiled. Some looked away, nervous with strangers, I supposed. As always, I looked about to locate the moon, but couldn't find it. Perhaps it was too early. There was a thin layer of cirrus, dark below the stars. *New weather on the way*, I thought.

"Sad memories?"

"Are you kidding me?" I could feel her stiffen. "I'm sorry. It wasn't supposed to come out like that."

"I thought his poems made you remember something."

"They did, but I don't want to talk about it."

"Sammy," she said, "you can't keep it all inside."

I strangled a bitter laugh. She had called me "Sammy." It was an obvious, and I wondered, conscious, expression of intimacy. How could I react to that? It wasn't just the memory of Katherine, who had also called me that, but by allowing that name, I was also allowing emotions that I was unable to return.

"You shouldn't call me that, Christina."

"Oh," was what she said.

We walked on in silence. It occurred to me that she had never revealed her own story. In truth though, I don't think I ever asked her. I wondered if Simon knew. I sought to break the silence, "What do you think Simon's up to?"

"Reading of course, well, being read to."

"What's he into now?"

"You don't know? I thought you talked about those things."

"We do, but I can never keep up with him. He consumes books like I eat food."

"You don't know the half of it. Everyone on staff and in the wards tries to avoid him now just so they won't be asked to read."

"You don't approve, do you?"

"Does it matter?"

"Honestly? Yes."

"It's too late now anyway. He's moving with his own momentum."

"You're right. When we started these visits, it was exhausting to have to explain everything to him. Now I ask the questions. He's got a brilliant mind, you know? I can't help but wonder what he did before his accident."

"He hasn't remembered anything, has he?"

"No. Nothing."

"It's funny, but that doesn't seem so important anymore."

"Certainly not to him."

"What do you mean?"

"He picked this up from the Tao, but he put his own spin on it. He has this idea that nothing exists except for the present. He says he was born right now, and before this moment nothing mattered. He calls it the Infinite Now—I think. Maybe it's the Eternal Moment. I really can't remember. You've heard him talk about it haven't you?"

Christina nodded, "Now that you mention it, yes, but I had no idea what he was talking about."

"It has a certain logic."

"I wonder how the New Christians will react to that?"

"Yeah, philosophy is fine, but it doesn't stop bullets."

What would Simon have said at that point? I could hear his voice. *No, Samuel, you don't understand. I'm not saying there is no future or past; my point is that both exist in the now. Everything is one. What can the Coalition do to me when I'm really already dead? How can I be afraid?*

I didn't feel like explaining his theory to Christina so we just walked quietly on.

After a short time, Christina stopped walking and said to me, "You don't need to walk me all the way home. I know it's out of your way."

I was about to offer anyway, it being the chivalrous thing to do, but realized that what she said wasn't what she had said at all. She wanted to be alone. I worried about her walking home on her own, but the look in her eyes precluded an argument. "Perhaps I should go home," I replied.

She nodded, and leaned forward to kiss me lightly upon the cheek. "Goodnight, Samuel…Jacob. Sleep well." Then she walked away beneath the streetlights, and she was gone. I set off to my own bed, more tormented than ever. It was a terrible thing to admit to myself, but a part of me wanted to go with Christina—to be with her. I was so alone, and she suffered as much as I did. Rationally, I accepted that Katherine was dead, but I just couldn't let her go. As if it were a talisman to give me strength, I pulled the hopelessly tattered piece of paper that I'd not let from my grasp since finding it in Edmonton. I unfolded it, smoothed it flat and looked at the single word written upon its surface: Regina.

When finally at home and in bed, sleep did not arrive at once. I spent hours of unrest, semi-lucid, with fragments of conversations and arrant thoughts flashing through my awareness. My greatest concern was for William. I recognized at some level that he had become immersed with the Regina underground, such as it was, and feared that his failure to arrive at The Thirteen Avenue Coffee House bespoke of some tragedy. The image of him, shot and dying, left in some night-shrouded field, kept clicking in my dreams like the battered footage from a World War II documentary. At last, sleep blessed me.

BOOK THREE: SLOUCHING TOWARD BETHLEHEM

"Christ didn't die for our sins; he died because of them."
- *Slouching Toward Bethlehem*

I

When the next morning arrived, the first clue I had that it would be no ordinary day came in the form of what I thought was far off thunder. The morning was overcast, with a very dark northern sky. I awoke early, thinking to try the markets and see what kind of produce was available. The arrival of the Coalition outside the city limits had sent people into shock and a kind of siege mentality was beginning to manifest itself. There was still food to be had in the restaurants, as expensive as it was, but the grocery stores had mostly been picked clean. Perhaps the Coalition had shut down supply lines—just flexing a bit of muscle. In any case, I thought it was worth searching for food.

As I neared Victoria Park, I realized something was afoot. It was only shortly after ten, but the park was crowded. My heart sank. I hoped vainly that an activity had been planned to raise the morale of the people, but as I neared the gathering, I realized the inevitable truth—the Coalition had finally entered Regina. On Victoria Avenue, just south of the park, there was a line of five vehicles, four tanks and in between them an armoured car with a loudspeaker mounted on the roof. Something was being broadcast, but the noise of the crowd made it impossible to hear.

I remembered the sound of thunder that had drawn me from my dreams. Had Braxton's resistance already occurred? Was it the sound of gunfire, cannon fire that I'd heard? Had people died? I felt cold, experiencing an almost overpowering impulse to turn my back and run, but with the N.C.A. in Regina, there was nowhere else to go. Hopelessness washed through me. Sluggish with despair, I moved closer to discover what fate had been determined for us. I watched a man push his way in my direction, evidently having heard enough. As he passed by, I caught hold of his arm and asked him what he knew.

Eyes hostile, he pulled loose. "They're coming," was all he said.

I fought my way forward. People on the perimeter of the crowd were anxious and struggled against my advances, but as I drew within hearing distance, the crowd grew more and more passive, as if the life had been drained out of them. After twenty metres, I could finally make out the broadcast. It had the flat sound of a recording, "... true Christians who believe in the words of the holy prophet," the loudspeaker declared, "will be given a chance to freely express their faith and swear their loyalty to the church of the New Christianity. Locations for this ceremony will be posted throughout the city on the twenty-fourth of August."

Then there was silence. I realized that I'd just heard the tail end of the recording. The crowd loosened a bit as people, apparently having listened long enough, began to leave. Others came forward to take the empty places. Some thirty seconds passed before the recording began anew.

"Citizens of Regina, this is the voice of Joseph Adams, your saviour." I found myself trembling. "Your day of liberation is at hand. As the birthplace of Samuel Harris, the holy prophet of the New Christianity, your city has been extended an honour reserved for you alone." My mind reeled at the disclosure. Was I at once to be responsible for the respite given Regina yet at the same time carry the blame for its inevitable invasion? "The great revolution experienced its birth in this very city, in the mind of one of your sons. It is only fitting then that Regina should be the final city to be united under the flag of the new order."

I almost laughed, hardly believing what I was hearing. Would they ever leave me out of it? It was such a final, bitter irony that I was actually there to witness their arrival.

"In recognition of your important role in history, the New Christian Army has allowed Regina to exist unmolested, and it will continue to do so until the twenty-sixth of August when the New Christian Army will enter your streets and usher in a new age of love and faith." Bile sickened me. I'd seen their idea of love and faith. "For those who do not wish to await the arrival of the army of liberation, true Christians who believe in the words of the holy prophet...."

I listened to the recording once more, hardly believing my ears. It had finally come. The twenty-sixth, so little time remained. I left the park and wandered, a little dazed, back in the direction of my apartment. All thoughts of hunting for food were lost.

In my anxiousness to discover the source of the gathering crowd, I had taken little note of the people whom I passed on the street. I saw them now, and the despondency within those vacant faces startled me. That the Coalition would come had been an inevitability, but the echoes of Joseph Adam's metallic voice reverberated with a finality too uncompromising for acceptance. Warm blooded zombies, people reeled away stiff-legged from Victoria Park and stood in the adjoining streets stunned and without hope, struggling to apprehend the incomprehensible nature of the truth that had been thrust upon them.

I was near home when I came upon William apparently leaving my place.

"This is lucky. I left you a note."

"When did you get back?"

"Early in the morning."

"So you've heard?" I asked.

"Yeah, I heard. Beautiful isn't it?"

"They've probably got the whole city surrounded now."

"No, they don't. We have people keeping a watch; the north roads are clear."

"Except for a few hundred thousand troops waiting to march into Regina."

"They're all South. The Coalition doesn't seem to care much about closing off the city, and why should they?"

"How do you know they aren't monitoring the roads?"

"People have been leaving Regina for days, Jake, and we'll stick to the grid roads. It's all prepared."

I nodded, struck by the utter hopelessness of my situation. No matter who discovered me first—the Emac or the N.C.A., my fate was as good as sealed. Whatever happened though, I was done with running. My time had reached its end. All that concerned me were Simon and Christina. "What about my friends?" I asked.

"Roland wants to meet them. The N.C.s have given us a few days, but the sooner the better. I'll arrange something for tomorrow evening. I'll let you know."

"Alright."

He started off, then stopped and called back. "Jake! Get your stuff together and start gathering supplies. It's going to be a long drive."

I nodded and gave a half-hearted wave.

II

I immediately set off for the hospital, thinking that I could no longer afford to be separated from Christina and Simon. It was useless and dangerous for Simon to continue living where he was when we might at any time be forced to act. Though neither one of my friends wanted to leave Regina, I was determined to engineer their escape.

As I neared the hospital, the same sickening feeling began in the pit of my stomach that I had experienced upon returning to my home in Edmonton. Luther College had the look of a place deserted. I began running a half block away, and as I came up to the front of the building, my horrible dread was realized—the hospital was closed. Christina had said it would happen, but....

I groaned, mounted the deserted steps and tugged frantically at the locked doors. Hopelessly, I made my way around the building, searching, checking windows and doors—nothing. I came full circle, back to where I had started, coming to realize that once again I'd let those that I love slip from my grasp. I immediately decided to go to Christina's house, but just as quickly realized that I didn't know where she lived, and she didn't have a land-line so I wouldn't be able to get her address from the phonebook. How was I to find them in that city? I had a vague recollection of where I'd left Christina the night before, but she'd walked off alone, and my thoughts had been elsewhere. I cursed my egotism.

In retrospect, I can see how badly I overreacted. All Christina would have had to do was spend an afternoon wandering around downtown, and I would almost certainly have run into her. At that time, however, I was not in the most lucid state of mind.

Weakened legs bent beneath me, and I slipped down to sit lost upon the front steps of the school. What could I do, I wondered, other than begin a futile search through the city streets? How much time was left me? A sense of déjà vu made the situation worse; I'd been through all this before....

* * *

It had taken over a week to get from Vancouver to the outskirts of Edmonton, my home. It was a dark quest, full of fear and paranoia, kept alive only by the light of a faint hope—that Katherine would await me back in the city where we had lived together.

I travelled most of the way on a motorcycle I'd found outside of Vancouver, driving on logging roads and in ditches, stealing gas at night. There were only a few roadblocks, and I had managed to avoid them.

I won't ever make an effort to hang on to those memories. It was a lonely and painful journey. Of course, I longed for Katherine—the image of her hung before me like some vision of the grail—yet there was more; the things I'd witnessed upon the coast refused to relinquish their macabre hold upon my imagination. They shadowed my tracks, and I fled before them fearing quite literally that if I looked back the way I'd come, I'd see once more that sad, limp body upon its cross and hear again the thick buzzing of bloated flies.

The highway curved through dense forests, wrapped itself around mountainsides. The sound of the bike was thunderous and troublesome; only in the occasional clearing did its echo flash away and leave me in relative silence. I saw almost no one. Sometimes I passed buildings and caught glimpses of half-hidden faces peering out from the shadows. Once, alone by the roadside, a man stood and stared at my passing. An object I could not identify dangled from his left hand. His lips worked as I passed, forming words lost in the cacophony of the motorcycle. I shook my head, attempting to laugh off the incident, but somehow it troubled me. What had he been holding? How long had he stood there and had that been a message for me alone? I was frightened by it.

Shortly after that, perhaps only the next day, a light rain was falling and as I drove white-knuckled upon the slick asphalt, I came upon a car that had been abandoned by the side of the road. I don't suppose that ordinarily I would have taken much note of it, but in my cautious approach, I saw that its driver's door had been left open. On impulse, I slowed down and then also pulled over to the shoulder of the road. I got off the cycle, removed my helmet and lifted my head momentarily to the drizzle. The vehicle was empty. Keys were hanging from the ignition. A pair of sunglasses and a wallet had been left upon the passenger seat. I stepped back from the door and looked around. Although I half expected to see another traveller suddenly emerge from the trees, there was no one near.

I can't really recall how long I stood there, but the rain had ceased by the time I drove off. It's the reason why I stayed that makes this moment stick in my mind, for there was really nothing of it that was of any consequence. You see, nothing happened, but as I turned from the car I was quite unexpectedly seized by a sense of responsibility. I thought that if I left things the way they were, someone else would come along and steal the wallet. It was a dilemma. I considered a number of options: taking it myself and mailing it to whatever address I found within; locking the door and hiding the keys; pushing the car further off the road. In the end, I did nothing but wait for what seemed like an incredibly long time hoping against reason that the owner would return. I left finally in disgust, my throat hoarse from shouting and foot sore from giving the door a final kick shut.

I often wonder what interrupted that journey.

By the time I escaped the claustrophobic valleys of the mountains, I had almost forgotten the overwhelming, simplistic beauty of the prairies. At times, I paused in my journey to let the immensity of that sky lighten my spirit. In one place, well into the great plains, I stopped the motorcycle and regarded the magnificence of a wheat field edging close to the side of the road. I drank deeply from that simple world of blue and gold. Even with all that had transpired over the last months, at least one farmer had still kept care of his land. It reassured me that some fundamental things would not change. Away from the politics of the city, life could remain the same.

I propped the cycle on its stand and wandered out into the nearly knee-high wheat. There was such a profound magnificence to that landscape. Near to where I stood, the brilliant sun glistened gold off a circular bale of wheat that rested in a stubble field rising ever so slightly to touch the horizon. The sky, an incredible dome of soft blue, swept in an arch that strained my perception. Tufts of white floated one beyond the other, sinking gradually lower and lower until they fell beneath the earth a hundred kilometres from where I stood.

How distant was that cumulus that touched the flat prairie?

After so much time in the mountains, I felt at last that I could breathe again. My heart welled inside me, and the sky seemed so eternal that it misted my vision. There was the minimalist's vision of beauty—a few unbroken lines washed with gold, blue and white, left pure of jagged detail.

The serenity of that setting was difficult to relinquish. I whiled away an hour in that field. At one point, I heard the sharp cry of an eagle and searched the sky to discern its distant form high in the ether, circling in slow sweeps above me. *How would Laocoon have interpreted this sign from the gods?* It was a foolish thought. I was no Priam. The fate of Ilium did not rest upon my shoulders. It didn't matter anyway; having come that far, I wasn't going to turn back.

Reluctantly, I mounted my cycle. Time was pressing, and I wanted to reach Edmonton while the sun was still shining. There was another thing I loved, and it would not release its hold on me. I pulled out onto the deserted road and once again drove toward home. Soon, I came within sight of my destination, and that time upon the open prairies came to an end. Seeing the city from a distance gave me a sense of security. I was exposed on the prairie, but I could also see anything that approached me. When I saw Edmonton with its glass faced buildings reflecting back the light of the sun, I knew that at least the city hadn't found its destiny in flames. That gave me hope that Katherine might still be there. Little else mattered.

My original plan had been to scout Edmonton from a distance during the light of day and then use the cover of darkness to go within and seek Katherine out. After skulking at the city limits, however, I decided not to wait. I'd seen nothing to indicate that my approach would place me in danger. There were no patrols, no posted guards, nothing. Edmonton seemed free.

I drove into the city. The normality of the scene disturbed me almost as much as the ruins of the coast had done. Certainly the Coalition had been there—was still there, yet cars drove past, and I could see people walking upon the streets, seemingly without care. At the very least, I'd expected and was prepared to avoid stop checks set up at entry points from the highway, yet there was nothing.

Apprehensive, my skin peppered by goose bumps, I came home.

The house that Katherine and I had shared was located in the northwestern part of the city. I stayed off the main roads, making my way through a tangled combination of side streets until I reached the avenue that would take me home. I felt trapped within the script of a *Twilight Zone* episode. There was a change in Edmonton; I sensed it in everything I passed, but I couldn't isolate exactly what it was.

Midway through the city I took the chance of travelling a short distance along one of the major thoroughfares. It was instantly unnerving. In the past, taking the street that I'd chosen, I always looked to see the high spire of a local Bible college rising above the surrounding urban sprawl. Well, I saw it once again, a skeletal finger of fire scorched metal girders. The rest of the college had been given to flames as well. I wondered about the teachers and students. Had they fought, capitulated, or did the N.C.s simply find an empty building when they marched upon the college?

I know that it has happened throughout history, but the image of Christians fighting Christians strikes me as absurd. Thou shalt not kill and all that sort of thing. Too bad I hadn't included that quotation in *Bethlehem*. Who was I kidding? It wouldn't have made any difference. Do you think God picks sides, or does he just stand back shaking his head? It's an interesting theological question. I wondered if the Coalition made allowances for conscientious objectors.

Strangely enough, the sight of the college calmed me down. I was familiar with that kind of destruction. I slowed as I passed the blackened spire, studying the remnants of its fiery immolation.

Beyond the college, I bent forward and gunned the cycle, only to immediately squeeze full into the brakes and almost dump on the side of the road. There was a checkpoint little more than a block ahead of me. I wasn't sure if I'd been seen, but I spun the cycle around and cut my way through the ditch, leaning dangerously into the first right turn that I came upon. Following that, I raced through an alley, across a schoolyard and down several side streets. When I was certain I was no longer followed, if indeed I had been followed, I once again made my way north toward home. This time I stayed on side streets and alleys.

I was glad for the helmet I wore. Its use invited no inquiry and allowed me the relative safety of anonymity. It was with some trepidation then that I decided to park the bike a block from our home and go the rest of the way on foot. I reasoned that the motorcycle was too loud for me to approach the house unnoticed, and when walking, I could quietly pass by our place if what I found seemed suspicious. I slipped from the bike and without thinking, checked for my house key. It was such a gesture of habit, so out of place in my present circumstance, that I actually laughed. I had no idea where or when I had lost the keys to our house. If I couldn't find the extra key we hid outside, I would have to break in.

Walking down that street, I couldn't help but grapple with an unsettling sense of déjà vu. It felt too much like a reenactment of the day I'd returned to my childhood home only to find the heart of my memory gutted. My breath was shallow, and my hands trembled.

Because of its position on the street, the house is visible from nearly a block away. Although somewhat unkempt, the place looked pretty much as I remembered it. The flowers that Katherine had always planted in the spring were there, albeit now choked by weeds. The windows were closed and dusty. The lawn, patchy and dry. There was no vehicle in the driveway.

From the house's appearance, she could have been living there, just too worn with worry to care for the place, or she could have left a week before, a month before. I had prayed for a definite sign that she was waiting for me, but that image gave no hope.

The front door was locked. Looking in the windows, there was no movement, but I could see everything was as it had always been. I went around the back, only to find it locked as well. Searching the shed at the corner of the house, under the red brick on the left side of the French doors, I found the spare key and let myself in.

The door creaked from lack of use, and my heart sank. The house had the smell of neglect. A thin layer of dust covered everything. No answer came in return to my calls, but I already understood that I was alone. She was gone. She hadn't waited for me. What fate had befallen her? Had she actually left, or had the N.C.A. come knocking one night? *The door was locked,* I assured myself. *If they'd taken her, they wouldn't have bothered to lock the door when they left.* I had to believe that she had gotten out before the occupation. It was passing strange that the Coalition hadn't ransacked the house, but perhaps they'd had it watched and, realizing it was deserted, just let it be. Maybe they *had* locked the door behind them. I realized it was impossible to attempt to make sense of anything those fanatics did.

I wandered the house, eventually returning to the living room to collapse onto the couch and just stare into space. *Where do I go now?* Her parents lived in Ottawa. Certainly that was too far and too dangerous of a journey. My parents were dead, brothers and sisters also too far away. I had tried to contact them, but…. What was left for me? The silent house had no answer. I thought that I could stay there, but to what end? No, I would be recognized too quickly, and then it was only a matter of time until the N.C.s found me out. The house was probably watched, and I had to leave. It had the same feel as the rest of the city—still the same place, but it wasn't still the same place. The sense of loneliness it conveyed was wretched. There was no way I could have stayed there.

It's funny how even in the worst of circumstances, prosaic concerns find a way of asserting themselves. In spite of every reason that I had for leaving, I realized that I was hungry and decided to cook myself a meal. I suppose I was just too tired of running to care anymore.

Searching the cupboards, I found a container of pasta and a can of sauce. When I tried the oven, I found that the power was still turned on. Katherine hadn't been gone too long; it appeared. The realization brought a dull pain to my chest, or perhaps simply made me cognizant of an aching already there. I cooked myself a meal, and in a gesture of mind-numbing banality, ate it while watching television.

It was such a common thing, such an everyday thing, that it took a moment before I realized that I was actually watching television. With a slowly dawning and then suddenly abrupt awareness, I sat bold upright and began flicking through the channels on the set. My amazement was short-lived. All I could receive were the local stations, and when the commercial break arrived, I realized what was happening. The first advertisement was for a car rental agency. Following that, the screen went momentarily black then the propaganda for the Coalition began. I hit the mute button and watched the polished façade of the N.C. announcer speak her nothingness. Words, words, words. Orwell would have loved it. No, most likely hated it. What's that line? "Religion is the opium of the masses?" Or is it television? In that particular instance, I suppose the difference was moot.

I hadn't been cognizant of nodding off, but some time later, I awoke. Night had fallen. The television was still on, its hypnotic light flickering in the darkened room. I shut it off and arose, spilling the unfinished portion of my meal and almost breaking the plate that was resting forgotten on my lap. Without thinking, I went to the kitchen to find something with which to clean it up. I paused midway through the action, and after a moment's hesitation, decided to leave it where it was. It would serve as a symbol of my departure forever from that life.

Still tired, emotionally exhausted, I climbed the stairs to our bedroom and slept in that house for a final time.

Morning came. My major concern after cooking breakfast was money. I'd managed to survive off stolen cash and supplies all the time while travelling through the waste of the coastal war zone, but since reaching the prairies, it had become increasingly more difficult to come upon essentials surreptitiously. While I was on the road, I had avoided the cities, and it hadn't occurred to me that things could seem so untouched by the war. I'd just seen so much, and there had been so much destruction. I thought, maybe, just maybe, I could simply access my account and withdraw funds. There was an outside chance that the N.C.A. had left the banking infrastructure untouched.

Before venturing outside, however, I thought to search the house a final time. Katherine and I had always kept some extra money hidden away, and in a small compartment at the back of my desk drawer, I kept a wallet with an extra credit card, Cashstop and I.D. Katherine considered me paranoid, but I liked to have a back up system whenever I travelled out of country. I knew it would come in useful sometime. Returning upstairs, I searched in my little hiding place and pulled out the folded leather of my wallet. Everything was as I had left it. I reached in again and found my cheque book. So far, so good.

I went down to the storage room and dug out my old backpack, trading it for the one I had carried from the coast, then I loaded it with fresh clothing. When I left for the coast, it had been in a hurry. I'd travelled light, expecting to return fairly quickly, so most of my wardrobe was still hanging in the closet where I had left it. I looked in Katherine's closet and saw that only her favourite items were gone. I thought it odd that she hadn't taken our store of cash: perhaps she had been in too much of a rush herself. Or maybe….

When I'd gone through the house the afternoon before, I'd been looking for Katherine herself, not for signs of her leaving. I'd been too tired to take note of details. It occurred to me then that she may have expected me to return and left something, a message for me to find. I felt a new sense of purpose.

It was a given that of any of the houses the Coalition would search, mine would be one of the first, so if Katherine were to leave me a note, a sign, it would have had to be in some place where no one else would stumble upon it. Perhaps it had been found. No, I couldn't accept that. I had to assume that that wasn't true; otherwise, I'd be lost again.

I began a room by room search and room by room found nothing. There was nothing on my desk, nothing written on our little message board. I picked through the leftovers of our life together and discovered only the melancholic remnants of a banquet we once shared. It had all passed.

I'm one of those who like to stick pictures of family and places on the front of the refrigerator. Some were missing, leaving bare spots, but still others remained, and a mosaic of forsaken relationships stared out at me. The revolution had cost me the woman I loved, but it also stole a lifetime of close friends. As I stood looking at these, I suddenly noticed a picture of Katherine that hadn't been there when I left. Startled, I plucked it off the metal door and flipped it over to see if anything was on the back. She'd written there, "I love you, Sammy." My breath caught in my throat, and I was unable to fight back the tears. I could hear her voice as I read it. I felt certain then that she was all right. She'd left it for me, and if she'd done that, there could be something more within the house.

After a fruitless hour of searching, more than half of it combing through files on the computer, I sat back down in the living room to think. Nothing, nothing, nothing. It just couldn't happen like that. My final inspiration was to check messages on the answering machine. Again, nothing. I played the recording, but it was still my voice. She had kept it on. I imagined the times that she must have listened to it just to hear the sound of my words. I'd have done the same.

Eventually, with more despair than I care to admit now, I made ready to leave. I went into the shed to find extra straps with which to fasten my pack to the motorcycle. I replaced the key under the little red brick. Returning to the house, I swung the pack over my shoulders and stepped out the front door, but then I stopped, and, for reasons I'm not even sure of now, returned inside, dumped the pack, moistened a cloth, dabbed it with soap and cleaned the mess spilt on the living room carpet.

In twenty minutes, I was ready to leave. I gave the place a final look. As an impulse, I felt my pocket for the wallet and cheque book. Again, I considered the oddity of Katherine leaving those things behind. *She expected me to come back. She expected me to come back. She left them for me.* As I stood, unable to leave, the realization stuck me.

I tossed the pack down a second time and scrambled upstairs to the den. I yanked out the desk drawer where I'd reached in to find the wallet. Stuck back there, folded between some other documents was a single piece of paper. It was neatly folded. I didn't remember ever putting it there. I lifted it delicately out and flipped it open. Upon it, written in Katherine's own hand, was the single word: Regina.

Regina.

That was her message to me.

I read it over several times, imagining her hand touching that paper, her body close to it. Regina.

It was only eight hours distant on a straight highway that stretched southeast. What could that message mean except that she had gone there, and I was to follow her? My heart soared. Hope was reborn, and the future broke clear like the startling prairie sky. With shaking hands, I folded the note and placed it safely into my pocket. Strengthened, yet struggling with tears, I hoisted my belongings onto my back and set out to find her.

Before leaving the city I knew I would need to pick up a lot more cash and get fuel for the motorcycle. I pulled into a gas station and went inside to try the Interact. It fed me five hundred dollars and an account balance that was no different from when I'd last accessed it. The ease of it, the normalcy, was stunning.

It felt odd to use money that I'd received from the sales of *Bethlehem*, but necessity dictated my actions more than ethics did. Katherine had her own account, so whatever she had done, I couldn't get a record. I filled the tank and used the credit card to pay. It worked too. I really shouldn't have been surprised; the Coalition certainly had greater things to worry about other than my finances.

I strode out under the warm prairie sun feeling elated but a little mystified. Perhaps I had worried too much about the influence of the Coalition. I had gotten into Edmonton, found what I needed and was well on my way out of town without speaking to an N.C. soldier. It never dawned on me until later that by using my card I had just sent up a flare marking my position for any Coalition who may have been instructed to keep an eye out for me.

As I adjusted the strap of my helmet, I heard someone quietly call out my name. I hate to use a cliché, but my blood ran cold. I considered hopping on the cycle and making a run for it, yet something about the voice held me back. I turned to see a friend of mine from the days before the revolution.

"Danny." I smiled with relief. "Long time no see."

His face was pallid. "You're not dead. Man, I was sure you were dead. There were rumours."

"I know."

"Are you crazy coming back here? They'll kill you for sure."

"Who? There's no one around."

"Oh Christ, they're around. They're everywhere. If you haven't seen anyone, you've just been lucky. I get checked twice a day. If you're not tattooed or don't have your papers, then you disappear. Some people disappear anyway."

"I've been driving around all afternoon."

"Then someone's looking over you. Listen, we have to get off the street. Do you remember where I live?" I nodded. "Go there. I'll meet you."

He hurried off. I wasn't certain what to do. The wisest thing would have been to leave, but I felt like I was operating in a vacuum and needed information. Still, I was uneasy. Danny was very nervous, understandably of course, but was it that he feared to get caught with me, or because he had something to hide? I watched him climb into his car and drive away. He still had that old beater that he'd bought his first year out of university. When he sped out of the parking lot, he spun his tires and threw bits of gravel to where I was standing. Not too smooth, but sincere. That about summed up Danny. I decided that if he really had been hiding something, I would have sensed it. I got on my cycle and followed him home.

When I got there his garage door was open; he was standing in the shadow signaling me to come in. He shut the door and hid our vehicles from sight. It felt like the closing of a trap. We entered the house through the garage door.

He opened me a beer, and we sat at the kitchen table.

"Where have you been?"

I shook my head. "Don't ask."

"You left Katherine?"

That simply declaration struck deeply. "Yeah, I left Katherine. We thought it was dangerous for me to stick around, and too dangerous for her to go with me."

"You were on the coast?" I wondered how he knew that. "Was it really so bad out there?"

"Worse."

"It's been so hard to tell what's true. The New Christians have control over everything—T.V., radio. There were newscasts about the fighting in Vancouver, but no one knew if any of it really happened. Some people said it was all just staged, so that when they came for us, people would be too afraid to resist."

"It looks like it worked. There was no fighting here at all?"

"Not really. Before the army came, they sent in a group, priests or something, and people had the chance to swear over. By the time of the occupation, half the city was converted. Those people who tried to stir up some sort of resistance, and there weren't many of them, disappeared in the night. There was a bit of fighting, but it was mostly between different groups within the city."

My throat tasted bitter. "So they just marched in and took things over?"

"What there was left to take over, yeah. Edmonton was pretty much all theirs by that time anyway. Compared to what we saw on the news, giving up seemed a good idea."

"When did you do it?"

"Swear over? Me? You mean did I wait? For what it's worth, I did, but the end result was still the same." He brushed back his long hair and showed me the tattoo on his temple. A little cross.

"I guess that makes you the enemy."

"Yeah, I suppose it does." I couldn't identify his expression.

"When did Katherine leave?"

He sighed. "You don't know? It was a couple of weeks ago, just before the occupation. We all hoped that she left to meet with you. You have no idea?"

"No, she didn't leave any messages anywhere."

"I'm really sorry, Sam."

"Did she say anything to you?" He shook his head. "How was she before she left? How did she look?"

"She looked like Katherine. You know how she was; if she was suffering, it was all on the inside. She even planted flowers in the springtime. A lot of us thought the Coalition would never get here. Watching it on television, none of it seemed real."

I didn't want to know about anyone else. "She didn't say anything?"

"No, nobody saw her go. She must have left during the night. One morning we noticed that your car was gone."

Even though I knew it wasn't true, and it made me shudder to even consider it, I wanted to read his reaction. "Are you sure she left, she wasn't taken?"

"She left on her own. When they come to get you, you don't take your car along."

Or leave a note, or lock the door behind you, I thought. "Any idea where?"

He heaved a sigh. "Where else is there to go? They came and searched your house."

"I thought as much. They hardly left a trace. Do you…?" I paused. A noise had come from outside. "Is there someone else here?"

Danny rose to his feet.

Why is he getting up? I was instantly alert.

"There's no one home but us."

I rose too, beginning to move to the back door. Before I had really committed myself to running, the front door opened, and Dan's daughter stepped in.

"Good Christ," I said, laughing and dropping back on the couch, yet the tense expression on Danny's face hardly altered; just something more wretched seemed to wash over it. His daughter, in her mid teens, stopped when she saw me and set down the package she was carrying. I noticed, even from that distance, that her hair was pulled back on one side to expose the small tattoo that she bore. It was on display. I hadn't expected that the mark of the Coalition could become some kind of fashion statement.

"Hello, Susan," I said.

"Hello, Dr. Harris."

"You should get going, Sammy. It's gonna take you six hours at least to get down to the border."

The border? What's going on here? He'd intentionally lied to his daughter; I hadn't told him where I was going. I set down my beer and stood once again, this time more frightened than the last. We went out to the garage. Susan stood unmoving, watching us go.

Danny answered my questioning gaze with a pained look. "Young Christian. It's a kind of rebellion, I guess. You'd better hurry."

My chest tightened. "What's the safest way to get out of town?"

He shook his head. "Don't ask me and don't tell me anything. I can't say what I don't know." Beads of sweat were starting on his forehead, and I realized that he was terrified. As I stared, sickened by the pain I had brought his way, I saw a different expression darken his features. His hands clenched into fists. "I'll buy you some time," he whispered, "but get out of here fast."

I got on the motorcycle. He extended his hand, and I shook it. It was clammy, unsteady. He walked over and opened the garage door.

"I hope you make it all right," he said. I pulled the helmet over my head and gave him a thumbs up. He said something else. I saw his lips move, but couldn't hear his words. It didn't matter so much. I was leaving Edmonton with the intention of never returning.

I drove the cycle out of the shadows and into the brilliant glare of the sun. An hour later, I was out of town, racing precariously on loose gravel and heading east to connect with the highway to Regina. If I had faith, I would have prayed that Katherine awaited me there. As it was, I just held tightly onto the handlebars and kept my eyes fixed on the uncertain road ahead.

* * *

A prairie wind came searching down the street. A discarded newspaper was lifted, tossed at my feet. It brought me back to the present, and I regarded it dispassionately. News, news was what I needed. *Why didn't I walk Christina home?* The paper rustled and wandered on. I could hear the sound of it going and then could hear the sound of it still. I looked up, curious at the noise and realized that what I heard was a paper flapping in the wind. There was a sheet hanging from the glass of one of the front doors, but it had blown partially loose and was hanging upside down. I hadn't noticed it before. When I tore it from the window, I recognized the handwriting as being the same as was on the poster that had drawn me to the hospital in the first place—Christina's. She had written only my name and an address: Samuel, 12 Ave., #6. I thrust the paper into my pocket and hurried off.

A half hour later, after a moment of desperate knocking, the door to the apartment opened, and Christina stood breathless before me, misted eyes and trembling. I had an apprehension then of what she'd experienced believing that we had been lost to each other.

I was moved when I saw her, but when I think back on it now, I find that the memory has become altered, and I put Katherine in her place, imagining the woman I love when she first heard the news of the war and knew, without uncertainty or hesitation, that the two of us had been torn apart—separated by half a continent and all the malevolence of the New Christian Jihad.

But…there was Christina standing before me. I stepped within, and she came into my arms. "We waited for so long. I would have stayed, but Simon…." She wept, briefly, and I made a clumsy attempt to comfort her. Afterward, she ushered me into the room and closed the door. I glanced around at her apartment as we crossed through the foyer. It was spacious and expensive, incongruous with the impression of her that I'd formed in the hospital. Florence Nightingale didn't belong in those trappings.

"Nice place," I quipped, attempting a façade.

"I don't spend much time here."

But she had; I could tell. Once you looked past the affluence, the place pronounced character at every turn. I saw framed posters of shows in New York, pictures of sites in Europe that I recognized: Venice, the Parthenon and Stonehenge. In several, Christina stood arm in arm with a man—obviously intimate. *An old boyfriend? Husband? Where is he now?* There was something; was this the loss that had left her so marked with pain? Seeing evidence of her suffering, I despised my own self-indulgence.

"Where's Simon?" I asked.

"Sleeping."

I sat in the living room on the leather couch. She asked and then went to pour me a drink. "What are we going to do, Christina?"

She sat beside me. "I don't know."

"I'm worried about you two."

"About us? It's you, Jacob…sorry."

"Forget it."

"You're the one they want, Samuel. Simon and I will be fine."

"No one will be fine, Christina." The memory of Danny flashed before me. When his tattooed daughter came home to discover us, the expression on his face had been terrible to see.

"Even the Coalition will need doctors."

"What about Simon?"

"It's like I said. He'll stay here with me. We've decided that. The question is: what are we going to do about you?"

I disregarded the question. "Are you willing to swear over?"

She shrugged. "It means nothing to me, and Simon already said he would."

"It won't end there; you'll have to live under them as well. You might be able to deal with that, but Simon won't. He just doesn't know enough to keep quiet. You know what he's like, Christina. A newborn child has more social sense. The first Christian he meets, he'll try to argue theology, and it'll get him killed."

She was silent. She knew it was true. Simon was just too pure and good for the Coalition to let him live.

"It won't last forever," she finally answered.

"What if something happens to you?"

"Nothing is going to...."

"Christina, people disappear. Do you get that? People disappear. Anything could happen."

She sat back regarding me. "What have you planned?"

"I know a place where we can go."

"Escape from Regina?

"Yes."

"This is my home."

Tears welled. I felt like a bastard, but everything I was saying was true, and she had to be convinced.

"You've got to do it for Simon."

She broke down and cried, and I knew then that she would go. Poor Christina, it probably never even occurred to her to ask me to go with Simon. Perhaps it did, perhaps, but she would never ask it.

After a moment, she gathered herself and asked me to explain. As best as I could, I told her of William's plan.

III

"I won't do it," I said. "I almost died fighting the N.C.A. If I swear over now, then there's no purpose to that."

"What would it mean," Moe asked, "if I did swear over? It's still Christian. What's the difference?"

"I'd like to know what they make you say," I said.

"But that's the point," Braxton interjected. "They *make* you say it. That's what's important. It doesn't matter what it is you have to say."

Why Braxton had joined us, I wasn't sure. I didn't know if being in my company made him feel superior in some way, or if he was so hard up for friends he'd latch on to any familiar face in a crowd. Christina had no food in her apartment, so the three of us had been forced to go out for lunch; we happened upon Adam and Moe on Thirteenth Avenue and found a table at Dante's. Braxton had been sitting on his own and made eye contact with me. He'd come over and joined us. Whatever his justification, he didn't fit in, and the topic of conversation was such that I feared he'd get violent.

It was the same day as the public proclamation by the Coalition. In the time I'd spent there before the coming of the N.C.A., the mood in Regina had been tense enough. People had been waiting—expectant. Now the end was nigh, and the city felt ready to explode.

When I'd first arrived from Edmonton, I'd been fascinated by the high concentration of artists and intellects who'd found their last place of refuge in Regina. They were the free thinkers who anticipated persecution by the Coalition or believed that they would be unable to exist under such a neo-Fascist regime. Now that there was nowhere left to flee, they tended to discuss the only option given them by the Coalition, the chance to swear over, and they did this openly and without the witch-hunt mentality that had marked the general public's first reaction to the rise of the New Christians.

During the weeks I'd been in Regina, however, more and more displaced members of the Emac and regular army had arrived. These were people who had risked their lives and dealt hand to hand with death, all in a vain attempt to stem the inexorable advance of the N.C.A. They had failed and been driven to that place. With the Coalition once again growling at the doorstep, they were not inclined to regard their imminent occupation in so philosophical a vein. Soldiers and poets—it was like mixing gasoline with fire.

The table where I sat in the café was a microcosm of the contrasting peoples within Regina, and, as I stated earlier, the more the option of swearing over was discussed, the more likely it seemed that my good friend Braxton would express his growing frustration through violence.

I worried over that, and worse, I worried that Simon or Christina would somehow slip-up, unintentionally revealing my identity and present Braxton with an appropriate target for his anger. I prayed that Will would show up and lead his erstwhile friend away from us.

"Why would one have meaning when the other doesn't?" Simon said. He was particularly gregarious that day and just a little pedantic. "It's a difficult decision whether to surrender of your own free will and live, or to fight for what you believe is right, and die; but that's not the case here. So what if you lie? If they have you proclaim your loyalty to their concept of God, but you don't believe, then you've given your word to nothing. Would you rather fight and kill and then have that on your conscience?

It's nothing more than words, and if you truly believe, then God will certainly know what's in your heart."

Braxton spoke, "It's a matter of honour."

"What does honour have to do with spirituality?"

Braxton frowned. I didn't think he quite understood what was being asked. Simon repeated the question. Finally Braxton answered, "What meaning does your life have without honour?"

Simon nodded, "Exactly."

I almost laughed; the expression on Braxton's face was so comical.

Christina finally entered the conversation, "I don't understand."

Simon's blind eyes studied the space above our heads. "Braxton," he said, "you've fought the New Christians. Wasn't their cause an honourable one?"

It was risky to say such a thing in Regina. The image of Simon being dragged out onto the street and beaten to death flashed quickly through my mind.

I've never witnessed someone suffering from a cerebral hemorrhage, but I was certain Braxton was close to one. He couldn't even answer. Adam, who had been silent for most of the discussion, spoke in his place, "No, it is not. Dey are robbing ot'ers of deir freedom to t'ink, freedom of belief. Dere is no 'onour in dat."

"They're fighting for God; you're fighting for freedom of religion. In reality, neither one of you is right." Simon paused to sip his drink, seemingly oblivious to the crackling tension. "No, let me rephrase that: both of you are right, neither one of you is true. How can anyone justify fighting for either of those two beliefs? The idea's absurd. Even putting the obvious moral reasons aside, God has no need for the Coalition to fight on his behalf, and God doesn't care what you say to the Coalition. If you believe something in your heart, words have no meaning. Just *say* whatever you need to say and *live* by what you believe is true."

"And if they won't let you live it?" Moe asked.

"Then believe it in your heart."

It was an odd thing to sit on the sidelines and disagree yet agree with both sides of an argument. Obviously, if Braxton were asked to express his need to fight against the N.C.A. he wouldn't be able to do so, yet he was justified, and he was sincere. It was just that he couldn't understand the concepts involved; he was thinking with his gut. Simon was attempting to intellectualize human desire. Logically, he made sense, but he really didn't get it. In a way, he was as stupid as Braxton.

Braxton shook his head violently, a meaningless gesture before Simon. "That's bullshit. If I say what they want, then they've won."

"Won what?"

Braxton spread his hands in frustration. Once again, Adam spoke in his support. "Do you not see, Simon? It would mean dat dey 'ave beaten us. It would be admitting defeat, saying dat day are stronger dan us."

"So we should go out and fight them?"

"That'd be suicide," Braxton exclaimed.

Simon just tilted his head.

At this, I did actually chuckle. They all turned to look at me. "You know it's not the same thing, Simon."

"I don't know that at all."

"Listen, we all admit that they're stronger than us. That's a given, but what everyone here is saying is that if we swear over then they haven't only beaten us...physically, they've also won spiritually. You've gotta see what I mean? Maybe spiritually isn't the word I want, but you must see the difference."

"If you're truly worried about your spirit, then march out there and let them kill you," Simon said. The statement was met with silence. He continued, "Obviously, no one is going to do that, but if you resist them when they get here, it's pretty much the same thing isn't it? What's the use in being a martyr? It's very noble to have something worth dying for. It is much more noble to have something worth living for."

An hour later, I walked with Simon through the city streets, taking the long way back to Christina's. She had tarried with us for a time in Victoria Park but insisted that she needed some rest and, after agreeing to meet again later in the day, set off for her apartment. I was unwilling to escort Simon home. We'd begun a discussion that I was loathe to cut short and knew Christina would have little interest in.

That particular discourse had been precipitated by my warning to Simon that he would have to exercise more caution in his arguments.

He countered with, "I don't see why I shouldn't just say what I think. If we don't speak our ideas freely, how can we possibly arrive at the truth?"

"People aren't trying to find the truth. Not most of them, anyway. They're interested in what's right and wrong, and those concepts are dictated by the ethics of whatever society you happen to be in at the time. In this specific place and at this specific time, people like Braxton will beat the crap out you if you don't spout the acceptable rhetoric."

"He didn't do anything today."

"You didn't see how red his face was. Try pushing him when you two are alone and see what happens."

"I don't understand."

"Just be careful who you talk to."

"Did what I said make sense to you?"

"Some of it."

"It must seem odd to know what you know and not be able to say anything about it."

"Sometimes. I was never one to unmuzzle my wisdom anyway."

"Except in your writing."

"Except in my writing, and look where that got me."

"What do you believe in, Samuel?"

"Haven't we hashed this out already?"

"Ha, I've hashed it out. You've never really said much of anything."

I was silent for a moment, reflecting over the veracity of that comment. I supposed that it was true. Before Simon discovered who I really was, naturally, I thought it best to be evasive. Once he was aware that I'd written *Bethlehem*, I assumed he knew full well what I stood for. Then again, I'd learned some things since then.

"I don't stand for anything, Simon. Nada."

"That's very sad."

"It's better to be deluded?"

"Is it delusion to believe in something beautiful? Isn't that really what faith is all about?"

"I don't know what faith is, but over the last few months I've seen what it can do. From where I stand beauty and faith have nothing to do with each other."

Simon nodded, "Touché."

"What do you believe in?"

"How can I tell you? I feel like I've just been born again, innocent as a lamb. I haven't decided what I believe."

I actually laughed. "That's such a cop-out. What about your—what do you call it—the Infinite Now?"

"What about it?"

"You believe in that."

"It's not faith; it's just the way things are. There's no deity or mythos involved in that; I'm simply recognizing the nature of our existence."

"So it's philosophy rather than theology."

"I guess."

"You're splitting hairs."

"And you're fishing for a red herring."

"What happens when you die? Does your...Eternal Moment continue?" I wasn't attempting to mock him, but I really couldn't remember the details of his theory.

"I've already told you: in a very literal sense, each of us is already dead; it's predetermined, Samuel. Not by some higher power, but because that's just the way things are."

"Now *you're* being evasive. What happens when you die?"

"Okay." He shrugged. "Then I die."

"And?"

"And you live on. That's what you should be concerned with."

"You're still avoiding the question," I said.

"Not really, it's just a ridiculous question. Who can answer it? Christina was right. No one knows. Why concern yourself with a mystery?"

"You're talking in circles. You just said that I should have faith."

He looked surprised. "No, I didn't, but even if I did, why is it that faith must be about the afterlife? Can't we have faith in something now? Wouldn't that serve us a lot better?"

"Like faith in other people?"

"Or in beauty," he said, "maybe in love. Faith in yourself."

"Sure, that's a beautiful thought. Tell it to the Coalition."

"I can believe in those things, even with all that's happened. Maybe you're just blind to the world around you."

"That's me, the Blind Prophet." He didn't laugh, so I continued, "Whatever you sense right now, it won't last. Nothing does, and the N.C.A. will see to that."

"Maybe in the future, but not now, and what is there besides the Now?"

"Yesterday and tomorrow, Simon, and neither one of them looks all that good."

IV

A quiet knocking came at the door, and I hurried to respond. I was much more nervous than I had expected to be. Some of William's paranoia was rubbing off on me.

Evening had come. Simon and I had picked up Christina and eaten at my apartment hoping that, sooner or later, William would arrive. It was unnerving. When last we spoke, we had agreed to meet, but hadn't planned further than that. I not only feared we might not get together but also that something had happened to him. Obviously, he was involved in some type of underground network, and I had no idea what degree of danger that might expose him to.

But evening had come, and there was a knocking at the door. I opened it to see William and a man I supposed to be Roland. He was a little shorter than me, about six feet, and he had muscular arms folded across a thick chest. His cropped brown hair made him look like he was military, but he had kind eyes. Both stood crowded by the entrance and looked the length of the hallway before they entered.

"Just a little cloak and dagger, don't you think?" I asked.

"You're not cautious enough, Jacob. You know how they work. For all we know, this city could be half N.C.s already."

He was right. I closed the door behind them and flipped the deadbolt. Will introduced us; Roland and I shook hands. He kept my grip for a moment longer than he should have, studying my face. I thought I saw surprise flash across his features. We walked into the front room, and I made the necessary introductions.

Roland nodded at Christina and stepped forward to shake Simon's hand. There was an uncomfortable moment, then he let his hand drop. "So, you're the blind one."

"It doesn't matter to me whether I stay or go."

I decided to interpose, speaking to Roland, "Just listen to me before you make any decisions. All right?" He took a seat. I couldn't read his reaction; his face was impassive. *He's really got nothing to lose. If he doesn't like what happens here, he just leaves us all behind.*

"I'm listening," he said.

I sat on the couch across from him, leaning forward for emphasis. "Christina is a doctor. If we're going to go back into the mountains and stay there without being detected, we'll need someone with her training. Even if you haven't got the room, you need to make it. Her presence will guarantee our survival. Plus, she can get us medical supplies before we leave." Hoping she'd back me, I glanced at Christina as if for confirmation. She nodded with her best poker face.

Roland allowed himself a slight grin. "It's not as rustic as you think." He looked at Simon. "I can see her usefulness, but, excuse me, Simon is it? How could you possibly help out?"

Simon shrugged, "Honestly?"

"He's my brother," Christina said. "If he doesn't go, I won't go."

"Are you willing to sacrifice your place for him?" Roland asked me.

I nodded. "I am." From the corner of my eye, I caught the odd tilt of Christina's head. Did she suspect something?

Will spoke out, "Roland, if you need…."

But Roland raised his hand. "It's all right." He sank back in his chair. "The truth is, it's a big ranch. My parents have lost a handful of workers to the Emac and to their own families, so there's lots of room. That's not the issue. The issue is trust. We all know how the Coalition operates, and I don't know these two people. I'm willing to take Will's word for Jacob, but…."

I didn't know what to say. How do you go about proving you're not a spy for the Coalition?

"They're not N.C., Rolly. If they were, Jake wouldn't be here right now."

"Why is that?"

Will's mouth snapped shut. *Yeah*, I thought, *why is that?* I knew what he was considering, and it was a dangerous card to play, dangerous for me. Momently, he said, "Tell him who you are."

I stared at Will in stunned silence, slowly coming to recognize the desperation in his expression. I realized then that Roland had made up his mind before arriving at my apartment: Simon and Christina were not coming with us. But William knew that I would not leave without them, and he must have decided that this was the only way to have Roland accept us all. *And if I tell him, what happens to me?* I realized though, that it was a fair trade: Roland had as much at stake as I did. More, actually, his family was involved. *Even if I tell him, how can I make him believe?* "I'm Samuel J. Harris," I rasped.

Roland grinned once again. I'd expected a number of reactions, but that wasn't one of them. Simon was swinging his head back and forth, trying to figure out what was going on. "Well," Roland finally said, "the way I look at it, if anyone's got the guts to publicly denounce the Coalition, then I'll believe pretty much anything they tell me."

Technically, he wasn't quite accurate: the Coalition formed after I'd gone public, but I was a little too anxious to point that out. "So, you believe me?" I finally said.

The grin widened. "I'm kind of a history buff. I thought it was news in the making when you made your public address, so I recorded it." He paused to let us absorb what he was saying. "I recognized your face when I came in." I laughed, and the others laughed with me, albeit nervously. It was the first time that being the writer of *Bethlehem* had actually done me some good. "I don't agree with a lot of what people say, and I appreciated what you tried to do before the war. You and your friends are welcome to come with us."

William and Roland stayed for an hour after that, and the two of them gave us the details, such as they were, regarding our flight from Regina. The plan was a simple one. We were to collect supplies and, in two days time, on the eve of the occupation, wait outside the Cathedral at sunset. William would meet with us, and we'd leave the city at dusk to rendezvous with the rest of the group at a farm just outside Regina. The way into the mountains was clear. We'd travel by night, and the underground had set up places for us to stay where we'd be out of sight during the day. It was a simple enough plan; by the time we had shaken hands once more and they'd left, I felt fairly confident it would succeed.

It was too bad that I wouldn't be with them. I was done with running and had decided that I'd come to that city for a final time. Without Katherine, I no longer had the will to carry on. I didn't like to deceive William, let alone Simon and Christina, but if my assurance was all that guaranteed their passage, I would have to live with the lie. I wouldn't tell them until everything was packed and everyone was ready to leave. I was sure that at that time I could convince them all it was the best thing: with the true Blind Prophet in their midst, their chances of success were drastically reduced. It was better for everyone concerned that I stay behind.

V

I hardly slept the night before the N.C. officials arrived to begin the swearing over. I doubt that I was alone. Who could have found rest when the morning would bring about such an irrevocable change? I wondered if others were like myself and had, somehow, entertained a delusion that this final city would be overlooked—that the home of the so-called Blind Prophet would be granted amnesty. That secret hope had alleviated my guilt somewhat, but waiting in the dark for the gray morning and the sound of approaching tanks, I could entertain the delusion no longer. The future came swift upon us. We were left with few options: capitulate, flee or die. Had I made the right decision? Even if I changed my mind and set out to the mountains, the plan could easily fail. We'd be caught and sent to camps. Would I be allowed to swear over if I stayed, or would they have me killed? I rubbed the webbed scars upon my wrists; I'd evaded death for so long.

Turning, falling, spiraling out of control…giving in to nightmares more vivid than waking. I rose from my sweat-moistened bed. It really wasn't that warm of an evening. Where was Katherine? Where was Christina? Did Simon sleep, or did he also stare sightless into the same pall of darkness and fear that I did?

This is the way of all philosophy, I realized. *When the time of action comes, words mean nothing.* But then, I knew that wasn't really true. That particular time of action within which I found myself had been the result of words. I could smother myself with bitter reprisals and think that all people like me were fools for hiding in our cocoons of language, but the destiny of nations has been and always will be determined by words.

Sometime before sunrise, I found comfort on my sofa and finally drifted off to sleep....

Then I had the strangest dream. It was odd enough in that I actually remembered it, still remember it; I rarely recall my dreams. Of itself, the dream made no sense. It had several phases to it. My first recollection is that I was a fighter pilot in the middle of a battle, a dogfight, and I was surrounded. I was clutching the controls of this bullet of a plane, tearing through the heavens while all around me the sky flashed in darkness with the flak of exploding shells. Enemy planes were everywhere, but they didn't fly like jets at all. They circled around and above me as scavengers would, and.... I realized with a terrible start that they weren't fighter planes at all—they were angels.

Still locked within my dream, suddenly I was suffocating. My hand grasped at the oxygen mask covering my face and tore it off. I looked down at my body to see that I was naked and covered with a film of translucent, sticky fluid. A thick cord protruded from the middle of my abdomen and connected to the console of the aircraft. When I reached down to touch it, I could feel the movement of fluid within.

At that moment, my aircraft was hit, and I lurched forward to stare into the face of a stewardess who was shaking me by the shoulders.

"Put your seatbelt on, Samuel!" she cried, then rushed away. I reached down to do what she had said, but there was no seat belt. The plane was flying as roughly as the fighter had, and I looked outside to see that the dogfight had become a terrific thunderstorm. Savage winds tossed the aircraft, and flashes of lightening blinded me. I was sitting in the emergency exit seats at the centre of the plane. On one side of me was a little boy who smiled and reached to shake my hand. "Happy birthday,

Sammy," he grinned. I turned away from him. On my other side, my left side, there sat an old nun, praying and fingering the beads on her rosary. The plane plummeted. I became obsessed with the thought that there was no pilot to steer the craft. I scrambled from my seat and rushed up the aisle to the cockpit of the plane. I thrust open the door and looked upon the silhouettes of two people sitting at the controls of the plane. I cried out, but they didn't turn to listen to me. They didn't answer. I grabbed the pilot by the shoulder and spun him around to face me.

It was the captain from the ferry that had taken me to the ruins of Vancouver. "There's no auto-pilot," he whispered. I backed away and looked to the copilot. He was a young man, barefoot and dressed in dusty rags, looking as if he had just returned from the desert. A gag had been stuffed into his mouth. I saw that his bloodied hands were strapped to the arms of his seat. His eyes turned upon me pleadingly.

I fled the cabin and returned to my seat. The nun's rosary had become a length of heavy link chain that she rattled threateningly as I approached. Then I noticed the tattoo of the cross upon her temple. The boy was standing, still smiling, and as I watched helplessly, kept from interfering by the nun, he lay hold of the handles on the exit door and lifted. There was a sound like gunfire. "For you," he cried and was sucked out of the plane. Half of the interior of the cabin went with him: chairs, passengers, stewardesses, but I just stood there and watched, unaffected by the abrupt loss of pressure.

When it was all finished, I was alone in the plane, staring out of the exit door onto the smooth surface of the wing. The storm had dissipated and the air was calm. I stepped quietly outside and stood waiting. After a moment, the sun came through the clouds and sent a stream of light to illuminate the far tip of the wing. Though brilliant, the light hurt my eyes not at all.

And that was the dream.

When I drifted back into awareness, the sun was already high in the sky. Unbelievably, I'd slept in. Suddenly alert, I could hear, faintly, the alarm beeping in my bedroom. It must had been doing so for some time. I stumbled in to shut it off, then threw on clothing. Christina and Simon would be waiting for me in the park. They'd left the night before, shortly after Will and Roland. Now that we had a clear plan, Christina thought it would be more efficient if we separated that morning and each covered a different area of the city searching for supplies. My sleeping in was not part of the plan. She also needed time to prepare herself to leave Regina. It was far easier for Simon: he had nothing to leave behind. Nor did I.

I felt apprehensive, sick, thinking about what the day was to bring, and of how I would face it all. For so long now, since I had fled to the island, my life had been controlled by the desires and actions of others. I wanted somehow to grab hold of things and keep them from spinning away from me, but at the same time knew that I couldn't. Like the events of my dream, my life simply unfolded before my eyes, and I seemed powerless to effect any change.

Out onto the street, where throngs of people crowded toward Victoria Park. Even with the noise, the morning seemed timeless, like a hesitant breath, a pause before exhaling. No doubt that scene was being duplicated at other locations throughout the city. Following the proclamation, the N.C.s had placed posters all over Regina indicating locations where citizens could willingly come to swear over.

Near the Victoria Park I passed an oddly compelling figure of a teenager sitting by the side of the road. He was disheveled and slumped on the curb with head down, arms forward and draped over his knees. That in itself was in no way extraordinary, but he caught my eye, for among the action of the street, only he was static. He stood out by doing nothing.

Despite my haste, I stopped and regarded him for a moment. I almost touched his shoulder, bent to speak with him, but as I drew nearer, he glanced up and transfixed my eyes with his own. His expression—it startled me. Surely I had never before witnessed such a look of utter despair. Without thinking, drawn by an unidentifiable impulse, I knelt down to the asphalt beside him.

He mumbled, hardly audible, "Leave me alone."

"Are you all right?"

"What? Do I know you, man?"

"No, I just…."

"Wait a minute; I do know you." He scrambled to his feet, clutching at my shirt as I backed away. "It's you. You're the one." He shook his head in disbelief. "That just so figures. How much money did you make?"

"You don't know what you're talking about. This wasn't my fault." I had broken out into a sweat, frightened he'd cry out; after weeks in Regina, I'd been recognized twice in less than twenty-four hours.

"Yeah, tell my mother that. Do you know they have camps?"

I'd heard that, and I believed it. He tightened his grasp, holding my shirt with both hands. I couldn't pull away. A couple stopped to watch us. In desperation, I punched him. I startled myself, but it was a weak effort, and he didn't let go. More determined, I hit him a second time, and he fell back to the sidewalk. No one helped him. I fled into the crowd, thinking that Regina had gone mad.

I can hardly explain the impact of that brief meeting. Somehow that teenager was a catalyst that released a cascade of emotions and perceptions tumbling through me. Up until that point, I had somewhat successfully struggled to fend off an increasing sense of guilt for everything that I saw about me, but looking into his eyes and seeing the accusation there, I found that I no longer had the power to do so. My hand throbbed, and looking about at all of those gathered there, I knew without doubt where the responsibility lay. Where was the justice in that? After witnessing all the suffering and destruction that had come as a result of my words, why was I allowed to walk free?

"Jacob!"

It was Adam. I turned and spotted him in the crowd. Moe and the two other girls stood at his side. I walked over; we met and moved up beside a building to get out of the current of people.

"Where is your ticket?"

"What?"

"Your ticket. Dis is going to be a show." *What a time to joke.* Adam asked me if I was going to swear over. Nervously, I laughed, then realized that he wasn't joking.

"Man, if you go up there," I said, "people will kill you. You're not in the free world anymore."

"Oh, don't worry; I will not give in to dese Fascists."

"Good, I thou…."

Moe cut me off, speaking to Adam. "You're not? What happened to all that brave talk last night."

"It is morning."

"What?" Her cheeks turned scarlet. She barked something in French, and he snapped back a reply. One of the other girls joined in. Almost immediately the four of them were shouting at each other.

"English! English. I can't understand a word you're saying."

Adam broke off, making an abrupt gesture and turning his side to them. "Damn kids. Why am I wasting time wit' dese children?" Moe punched his shoulder, cursing in French.

"They're not going to do it are they?" I asked.

"Dey decide last night."

I pleaded with Moe. "You can't go up there. I'm not telling you what to believe, but there are enough Emac and army regulars gathered here that if you swear over willingly, you'll never leave Victoria Park in one piece."

"No one is going to try anything with the N.C.A. here."

"What about when they leave? Don't do it. It's suicide."

"I never thought you'd say such a thing. If I believe something, shouldn't I stand by it?"

"But you don't believe the same thing that they do. You've told me that."

"I think what Samuel Harris wrote was true." She waved her hand to include her two friends. "We all do. This is our way of proving our faith."

"Oh Christ, Moe. Harris wasn't talking about religion at all. If you go up there, people will hate you. No one will care about what you really believe. It'll be a political thing. It won't have anything to do with God."

She didn't answer for a moment, instead translating for her friends; then she turned her attention back to me, and, somewhat calmer, finally said, "Didn't you listen to Simon the other day? You're missing the point. It doesn't matter what it means to anyone else; what's important is what it means to me…to us."

I wanted to slap some sense into her or lock her up until the day was over. How could someone who had done so much at such a young age still be so naïve? "Sure," I said, "that's beautiful, but it will get you killed. People won't understand. Look at Adam; even he doesn't get it. Think about that. If it's something you have to do, at least wait until the occupation. It'll be different then." I thought of my friend Danny back in Edmonton.

She had no response, just stared at me for a moment. As she was about to speak, Adam interrupted. "Is dat your friend?" I looked to where he pointed and saw Christina cautiously leading Simon toward the park. "You will lose dem in de crowd. Go. We will meet wit' you later."

I looked straight at Moe and spoke to Adam, "Don't let her do anything."

"Do not worry."

The two had already disappeared, but it only took me a moment to catch sight of them again. I caught up, half expecting Christina to reprimand me for being late. Instead she looked concerned. "I was worried," she said.

"Don't let Will's paranoia get to you."

"It's hard not to. The city felt so strange last night. I was afraid going home."

I frowned, "The carriage took you right to your doorstep, didn't it?"

She smiled and touched my arm, "Yes. I'm sorry. Don't worry."

"You should have stayed at my apartment."

"It doesn't matter now."

The scene in the park was like nothing I'd ever experienced. The faces I glimpsed were frightened and desperate. There was such a tension in the air that it worried me just to breathe too heavily. It stank of a nervous sweat. For all the cacophony, it felt somehow that we were walking on eggshells. Regina was collecting its breath for a final, prolonged scream.

We had stopped moving and were now in Victoria Park, standing under the shade of a birch tree. The park was full of people. On its south side was Victoria Avenue, which posters had identified as the site of the downtown swearing in.

Nothing was in sight yet. No tanks, no trucks, no Jeeps. I wondered where everyone would go once the vehicles began to roll into the park.

"What can you see?"

"Nothing yet, Simon, just the crowd, waiting."

"Describe it to me."

Christina glanced around, apparently not sure where she should begin. "Well, we're standing in the north east corner of the park. People are everywhere. The streets are full, every window has a face in it, and I can even see some people standing on the rooftops. If there was a fire, we'd be dead for sure."

"That's a comforting thought."

"Do you remember how I described the park to you, with the cenotaph at the centre?"

"I remember."

"There are people climbing all over it. I can't imagine how they got up there, but someone's on the very top." She was interrupted by some shouting, but we couldn't see where it came from. A kind of ripple went through the mass of people. We found ourselves pushed two metres to one side. Simon almost fell, and I realized suddenly how vulnerable we were. It wasn't a fire that could so easily kill us there; it was the crowd. If people panicked, there would be deaths, Simon among one of the first.

It was for those people that I had written *Bethlehem*. For them, and then I watched as they milled about like cattle awaiting their butcher. It was all such a colossal waste of time. I grew certain then that there was no hope for any of us.

"I think we should get out of here. This is just way too dangerous."

Christina realized it too. "You're right. This crowd is starting to worry me."

"But I don't want to miss this."

"You can't see it anyway, Simon. What's the difference if someone tells us about it later?" I knew it was a little harsh, but I was also worried for all of us and didn't much care to stay for the sake of his curiosity.

The sea of people had calmed momentarily. We clasped hands and began to make our way out of the crowd. When people realized that we were leaving, they made room for us and pressed forward to fill our spots. We made our way to Scarth Street and soon were able to walk freely.

There I sensed a different sort of danger. When we had been squeezed together, the peoples of Regina seemed one collective mass, now I could see the divisions within that unit. The first to catch my eye, mainly because of their attire—fatigues—was a group of a dozen army regulars who were gathered near the end of the street closest to the park. A lot of them sported crew cuts that made them look like skinheads. They seemed to be waiting. Moe came to my mind, and I felt sickened by the thought of what they would do to her. As I watched, another group joined them. They weren't in uniform, but I thought them Emac for sure. *Here's Regina's standing army. They've switched roles with the*

N.C. Now they're the revolutionaries. Is this William's underground? Somehow I doubted it. A short while before, those people had fought to save the lives of their countrymen, yet as I looked at them, I couldn't for the life of me see how they were any different from the Coalition.

There were other parties that were less distinct, but the subtle shifting of people in the street made them discernible to anyone watching carefully. None of them seemed to have the same obvious bond that the military did, and I found myself wondering what forces would cause people in a doomed city to create such divisions amongst themselves.

As I watched, I noticed a small number of teenage hipsters shuffling our way, walking past the army regulars, who studied the ragtag and multicoloured clothing that passed by them with so intense a hatred that I actually shivered. I had just begun to tell Christina that we had better leave, when a face in the group of Emac caught my eye. It was Braxton. Beside him was another man whom I thought for certain I knew. After a moment of bewilderment, recognition came in a terrifying flash—it was Ben Hallings, the man I'd served with in the Emac. Somehow he'd gotten off Vancouver Island and made it to Regina. My heart started pounding.

I grabbed both Simon's and Christina's arms and hauled them away. She pulled back her arm, exclaiming, "What are you doing?"

"I've just spotted an old acquaintance; we have to get out of here, now. I'll explain later."

We left in a hurry, putting some distance between us and that strange scene that awaited the coming of the swearing over. I realized that I'd now have to be much more careful moving around the city.

It wasn't too long afterwards that we learned what had happened in the park. Christina and I escorted Simon back to her place where he stopped to rest. He hadn't slept the night before either. Then the doctor and I set off to try a cautious search and gather more supplies for their journey—what they thought was our journey. It bothered me a little to spend time alone with Christina. I found myself in the odd circumstance of thinking about her when we were apart and then thinking of Katherine when we were together. It's amazing how great a capacity for unhappiness and guilt we humans possess.

Ironically, though they had been scarce just the day before, provisions were no longer difficult to come by. I suspected that certain businesses had created artificial shortages so that they could hold back stock and then sell it at an increased profit. It appeared now that the jig was up, and they were trying to make what money they could before the N.C.s came up with their own restrictions. People can be such bastards to one another.

After several hours gathering what we could carry and not wanting to disturb Simon if he slept, Christine suggested that we stop by the Free House and eat. It was suitably distant from Scarth Street and the skinheads for me to agree. As usual, the place was full and buzzed with animated conversation. I know I've commented on this before, but in retrospect, the images of those crowded bars and cafés still strikes me as odd. In that time of chaos, it just seemed that there was nothing else to do but wait, and it was much less painful waiting in the company of others.

I paused at the entrance and studied the crowd carefully for Ben Hallings' face or any other kind of threat, but I saw nothing. Thinking of Ben and Braxton together made me shudder. While I searched for danger, Christina spotted an old friend. I hadn't seen her for some time, but when Christina pointed into the crowd, I immediately recognized Samantha, the doctor from the hospital whom I'd first met in Dante's wine bar. She was sitting at a bench by the bar nursing her drink. I hesitated just inside the door, but Christina led me forward, and we joined her. Samantha stood and the two of them hugged. She and I waved at each other. Something about her seemed changed. The cynical edge I'd noticed the first time we'd met was gone, replaced by a more sincere exhaustion. When Samantha sat back down, her spine hunched forward as if she'd been beaten. There was an empty chair in which Christina sat. I stood, keeping an eye open for anyone leaving or, more importantly, entering the bar.

"How have you been, Sam?" Christina asked.

"You have to ask? As well as can be expected, I guess." She smiled at me. "I see you two are still together. Good. How's Simon?"

"He's fine—no change, yet."

"No, I wouldn't have suspected that. Not the way things are. Were you in Victoria Park today? That was quite the performance, wasn't it?"

"How do you mean?"

"Mayor Burke. Where's he been all this time? That's what I'd like to know. Probably holed up in a cottage somewhere in the mountains waiting to see how things would turn out."

"I have no idea what you're talking about."

"You didn't see it?"

"We were there, but we left before the Coalition arrived. It wasn't very safe for Simon."

"You missed a real show. Did you even see them pull in?"

"Not a thing."

"Oh, this you've got to hear." She took a long draught from her glass, and then ordered drinks for the three of us. I found myself a chair and settled down to hear her story, still keeping an eye on the entrance to the bar.

"They didn't get here until around two o'clock, two hours later than they were supposed to. People were getting really restless. I thought there'd be a riot, but everything stayed under control. Then the tanks rolled in. It was nuts. From what I was told...."

Our drinks arrived. She took a break to wet her lips. Christina took hold of her wine, tipped back the glass and finished it. She lifted an eyebrow, giving me a mock startled look and then gestured to the waiter to bring her another. Samantha continued with her account.

"A friend of mine went to the south end of the city to watch them come in. He said that there must have been fifteen tanks and just as many trucks carrying troops. During the night, someone had re-erected the barricade that used to block the entrance into town. I guess the Coalition didn't even slow down. They went over the cars and other crap like they weren't even there. The soldiers in the trucks had to hang on as they went over what the tanks left unflattened."

"How many were at Victoria Park?"

"Four of them, and there were three trucks packed with soldiers. The one in the middle of the whole procession had the N.C. officials. Everyone was armed to the teeth."

"What's this bullshit about 'officials'?" I asked. "Why don't they just call them priests and get it over with."

She gave me a funny look. "What about the Mayor?" Christina said.

"Hang on. I'll get to that. When they turned off Albert Street and came up Victoria, everyone went crazy. People were screaming and shaking their fists. I thought that the soldiers would open fire, but they didn't. The tanks just kept coming, and people finally scrambled out of their way." She paused. "Some didn't make it."

"Jesus Christ."

"That settled the crowd; I'll tell you that. After they straightened out and stopped on Victoria, the soldiers unloaded and drove the crowd back at gunpoint. Some workmen set up a kind of prefabricated stage. It only took ten minutes. They also had a P.A. system which started playing a recording about the greater glory of God and the holiness of their Messiah, Joseph Adams."

"Their Messiah?"

"That's what they said."

"I remember when this thing first started, he was just going to prepare the way for the Second Coming, not be it."

Christina looked incredulous, "But how could people forget something like that?"

"Perhaps he got ambitious," Samantha quipped. "Maybe he had a vision. Isn't that how it happens?"

"Never underestimate the collective stupidity of the human race," I said to Christina.

Suddenly serious again, Samantha shook her head at my comment. "It's not that. I don't doubt that half of the New Christians are as afraid of him as we are. He's just gotten too powerful."

"I wonder if he believes all that himself," Christina said.

"How could this not go to his head?" I asked her.

"Oh, it's gone to his head, all right. I don't doubt that he'll be here on the twenty-sixth. I can't imagine that he'd miss the final conquest."

"The city of the Blind Prophet," I said bitterly.

"If it hadn't been for that," Christina said, "we would have been New Christian recruits ages ago."

"You really think Adams will come to Regina?" I asked.

"How could he not?"

"Yeah, but even then, he'd wait for things to cool down a little. He'd be an idiot to show up for the occupation."

Samantha shook her head once again, "I don't know about that. This Messiah thing may not just be a power grab. He might actually believe it. If that's the case, why wouldn't he show up? I imagine a lot of people would really like to see him in person." It wasn't what Samantha was thinking, but I was reminded of the comment Braxton had made to William and myself.

"I could live with the disappointment if he didn't," Christina said.

"So…go on."

"The P.A. was blaring and these workers constructed a stage right in the middle of Victoria Avenue. They covered the whole thing with an immense purple cloth, and set up some tables and other equipment. Then these officials," she paused for emphasis, "these officials came out and took their places on the stage."

"What were the soldiers doing?" I asked.

"I was watching the stage and the crowd for the most part, so I didn't notice much, but when the tanks swung their turrets around to face the park, that caught my attention. That caught everyone's attention. The soldiers were all standing in a ready position with their rifles covering the crowd, but when you have a tank staring you down, you hardly pay much attention to men carrying guns."

"They can kill you just as dead."

"Yeah, anyway. So these officials, there were four of them, they were dressed in long, golden, well, kinda robes, like judges wear, and two of them had hoods. They looked a lot like Klansmen to me."

"Not too far from it."

"The Coalition for Ethnic Purity."

It was an old joke and not a funny one.

Samantha snorted and took another drink; I saw an echo of her past cynicism. "There were two tables, and the two priests with the hoods stood at the sides of each of them. It turns out that they were the operators of the branding irons."

Christina was disgusted. "It's really a brand?"

"I wasn't close enough to really tell."

"What does that have to do with spirituality?"

"This whole thing is a sham," I told her. "It's all just a guise for power."

"I don't understand why they bother to keep up the pretense," she said. "Who's left to oppose them? Why not just come out with the truth, instead of staging this elaborate show?"

"The show isn't for us, Christina. It's for the converted. If Adams dropped the façade, there'd be another revolution. It's easy for people to justify bowing down to the will of God. It's not so easy to capitulate if you're doing it for a man. He's just supplying them with a reason to live as slaves."

"Anyway, the others sat facing north into the crowd. I couldn't really see, but I think they had Bibles set out before them."

"Maybe they had copies of *Bethlehem*," Christina said.

"Could be, couldn't tell. Then the message on the P.A. changed and announced that anyone who wished to renounce their beliefs in favour of the New Christian Order were to come forward and do so. It sounded more official than that, but you get the idea.

"You wouldn't have believed the tension. It was just charged. Everyone turned their attention from the stage and looked around, just waiting to see who would be the first to move. Some guy made a noise; I think he sneezed or coughed and a thousand people turned their heads to stare at him. Then everyone else looked over to see what was going on. For a second, I thought people were going to jump him, just to relieve the stress. It was awful."

"So who went first?"

"Like I said before, it was Mayor Burke."

"Who's that? I've never heard of him."

Christina said. "He was elected a couple of years ago, but after the revolution began, he disappeared. I think he went into hiding."

"And now he shows up?"

"He made his way slowly through the crowd, drawing almost no attention to himself. Then when he was under the protection of their guns, he spoke out and said that as mayor of the city he would find it an honour to be the first to swear his loyalty."

"What a bastard," I said. "There's your true politician for you."

"How could you hear what he said?"

"At first, the park was absolutely quiet. You could have heard someone whispering on Albert Street. A murmur went up after he spoke, and some people shouted at him. It got gradually louder, until one of the tank turrets moved slightly and then it was silent again."

"So what was the process?" I asked.

"Not much. He stood at the table, placed his hand on the Bible, *Bethlehem* or whatever, repeated something the priest read out to him. Once he reached the stage, it was all on the microphones, so everyone could hear what was said. When he was done that, the hooded guy stepped forward and marked his temple. I don't know if it's really a brand, but everyone who got it, seemed pretty shaken. Whatever it is, it obviously hurts like hell.

"When he was done, some of his aides, I guess that's what they were, climbed on the stage and helped him down. Then they escorted him through the crowd."

"Did anyone do anything?"

"With those tanks staring down at us? Nobody did a thing.

"After him, a slow stream of people approached the stage, got branded, then climbed down and disappeared into the crowd. Some people fainted and were carried off by soldiers. I didn't see what they did to them, probably just threw them on the side of the street."

I was struck by a sudden thought and raised my hand to interrupt her. "Oh Christ, what about Moe?"

"Uh, who's Moe?"

"The little French girl?" Christina asked.

I nodded, "Yeah, she said she was going to swear over today."

Christina breathed in a heavy sigh, "I hope she stays out of sight."

Samantha leaned toward me, "No one was forced to go up there. If she did, it was her decision, Jacob. There was nothing anyone could do about it."

But there was. Samuel J. Harris could have talked her out of it. He was just too much of a coward to tell her what she really needed to know.

"In a few days it won't matter anyway," Christina said. "What else happened?"

"After awhile, the crowd just began to thin out as people drifted away. It was anticlimactic, as though everyone had expected some sort of…well, I don't know. Something big and nothing happened."

"I left around three."

"How many got branded?"

"In the time I was there? Maybe thirty."

"When did they pull out?"

"I'm not sure they have."

"So that was it?" Christina asked.

"Mostly. There were rumours of people fighting, but I didn't hear much. How late are you guys out for tonight?"

"Not late," I told her. "We're going to eat, then head home."

"'Home?"

I didn't understand, but Christina blushed and said, "No."

"Well, that's too bad." She finished her drink and stood. "Listen, this day has beaten the hell out of me. I need to go home, turn off the lights and sit in the dark for awhile. You have my address?" Christina nodded. "When things settle, we have to spend some time together." She reached to take Christina's hand, and they smiled sadly at one another. Then she gave me a quick hug, whispering in my ear, "Take care of her. She deserves it."

She pulled away and waved at us both, "See you at the occupation." She was being flippant, I knew, and I guess that was as valid a way of dealing with things as any other reaction, but I was too heavy and too sad to answer in kind.

"Alright, Sammy. Take it easy," Christina said quietly. We watched her leave, fairly certain that neither one of us would ever see her again.

The crowd at the café thinned out eventually, and we ate. After another hour, we left and I escorted Christina home. I thought then that it would have been wiser to stay together, but I could not allow myself to sleep at the doctor's place. I'd suggested the night before that she and Simon stay at my apartment, and I'd realized almost immediately what a mistake that could have been. I didn't want to compound that error in judgment. We said goodnight, and I left her.

VI

As I walked home from Christina's, I realized that returning to the loneliness of my apartment was something I could not do that early in the night, and certainly not that sober. The silence of the place frightened me, and the thought of sitting within those walls awaiting sleep, surrounded by the dark and stillness of the night, only deepened my terror. Was I afraid to be alone? Certainly. At least walking on the streets of Regina, I could, to some degree, sense the life of the city, and that was preferable to the lifeless monotone of where I lived.

So I walked the night for a time, thinking darkly of what the morning would bring. Tomorrow, we would go together to the cathedral and wait in its shadow for William to come with Roland and lead us out of the city. At that point I would surrender Christina and Simon to William's protection.

The deception troubled me. I remember at that time thinking on Conrad's *Heart of Darkness*. I felt an affinity to the tale, although I was uncertain as to whom I identified with—Marlow or Kurtz. One of them, I didn't bother to recollect who, had commented on how he hated a lie. Each lie, he said, was like a little death. I had become immersed in lies, and they sickened me. Even those who knew who I was didn't know what I thought or was planning to do. What type of epitaph is engraved for the dissembler? Written by those who knew me not, that too would be a lie.

I already knew of how I would refute their arguments. If I left with them, the Coalition would not rest until it had tracked down the Blind Prophet. I would doom everyone by riding out into the mountains with them. If that were not enough, I could insist that I needed to stay and continue to hope for Katherine. Neither reason was valid. The N.C.s hadn't bothered to freeze my accounts, unless they were using that information to track me. Even so, I was sure that our party would be one of a hundred fleeing Regina, any one of which could have me among them. The Coalition could never even be sure I had left the city. Whether I went with William or not, it would make no difference to their safety. Nor did I believe that Katherine still lived. I trusted enough in fate that had she been in Regina, I would have received some sign, some impression that she was here. I'd received none and believed then that I never would.

So the question remained, why did I stay? It was a question that I couldn't answer directly. I had a feeling, an emptiness that I knew wouldn't be fulfilled by leaving. What would fill it I didn't know, but I was willing to wait and find out. I was tired and refused to run anymore. It was better to stay in place and let Fate deal my hand.

All of that was an area of my subconscious that I was willing to examine, yet there was something else there, an old companion hidden from the light; Robert E. Howard had called it "The Temper." I didn't care to stare once again into its feral eyes.

God, I was lonely.

I continued to wander, in time coming upon the creek and sitting near its sloped edge. The current had slowed during the time that I'd been in Regina, but it was hard to tell now, under the stars. There sounded in my ears the low rustle of its passage. I glanced around at the silhouettes and shadows of Wascana Park, its areas of midnight blackness that belied my recollections of the day. This place was man-made, sculpted upon the bank of the creek, and it would decay as all things in Regina would decay. The creek itself, though, it would not pass. It was an eternal thing, eternal enough, and after the Coalition came in two days time and after it left years hence, the creek would remain essentially the same. It had diminished since I arrived in Regina, but this winter the prairies would be heavy with snow once again.

As I sat lost in my thoughts, the moon made its slow way up above the trees of the park, and the world became progressively more visible, washed with an empty light. Beneath me and a short distance to my left, I noticed a pale smear near the edge of the water. At first I had thought it a rock, but as the light increased, the form grew distinct. My mind was distant, wandering in the mountains, yet my eyes continued to piece together the image. Then, altogether, I realized what I had been seeing. I think I grunted with shock, then scrambled down the bank to clutch at the naked body floating in the water. My memory flashed back to that night on the shoreline of Vancouver when I thought I had taken hold of a log.

It was cold in my hands, and I knew that I dragged a corpse from the creek. How long it had been there, I had no idea, but it was beyond me to leave it where it was. The skin was firm beneath my grip, and there was no bloating. I remember thinking that these things meant the body hadn't been there long. I dragged her—I could see it was a woman—face down up the side of the bank, and then set her gently upon the grass at the top of the incline. I turned her over, brushed the leaves and dirt from face and then stepped from the pale light to regard the face before me.

It was Moe.

Oh God, it was Moe.

Touching her porcelain flesh, I felt my life ebb from my fingertips and leave me empty. One more death that I could add to my list.

There was the dangerous and misguided nature of idealism—hers and my own. In that little book of mine, with a towering disdain, I had thrown out my doctrine of irresponsibility and enticed this cold purist to her death. She was the best of us.

Sweet little Moe. She had believed in my words; she'd believed in me, and when she most needed the truth to save her from that terrible decision to proclaim a mistaken theology, I had failed her, utterly failed her and remained hidden in my deceptions. I was a coward, not at all worthy of one such as her. Lies upon lies upon lies. More and more, there was only one way to cleanse myself of it all.

Brushing back a strand of hair, I exposed the small cross that I knew had been branded there. She'd picked the wrong time to be an idealist.

"She was murdered, Sammy," I whispered. "Murdered for you." My voice was barely audible. They'd beaten her, stripped her, and then threw her body into the creek. Who was it? The Army, Emac? Was this William's underground?

I stepped further back, wrapped my arms around myself but couldn't turn my face from the sad sight of that innocent teenager.

"This isn't Regina anymore." I didn't know where in Hell I was.

I wanted to leave, to just go and not come back. It was part denial, I knew that, but somehow it seemed that if I just walked away, I could sleep that night remembering seeing Moe as a dream that I had had—a delusion brought on by the madness of the day. What other choice did I have? To bury her? Alone? I could hardly think it, but I knew that I couldn't go for help. It just wasn't Regina anymore. If a small bit of ink staining your temple could kill, there would be no more theological discussions under the summer sun. What we said now would be done so in shadows, lest violence hearken to our words.

I felt the stirring of a pathos that I'd long thought dead since leaving the city limits of Vancouver. "How can this ever end?"

"It can't. It's the way of things now," I answered myself, and then realized that I was speaking aloud.

Yet it didn't have to be the way of things with me. Moe had believed in me. I owed her something for that. It didn't have to be deep, just deep enough.

I covered her with the sweater I wore, then picked her up from the ground. She was so light—no weight at all. A short ways away, distant from the creek, in the darkness of the park, I set her upon a bed of dew-moistened grasses. The trees hid her. I bent to the ground and begun to dig a grave.

The soft surface soil slipped away, turning easily, though buried rocks cut my fingertips. I swept it back in cupped palms, fingers like talons—fingers that had touched and briefly held Moe—then swept it behind me. Beyond that, the dirt grew stiff, and in her makeshift grave I left remnants of myself and of my grief. Small clumps of soil mingled with my blood and my tears.

After a time, I was done, and placed her gently to rest. Covered her finally. She was in the earth, yet gone from the earth.

Afterward, I stood, thinking that something needed to be said, but not knowing what to say. I sighed, wishing that such a task had not fallen to me. She had believed in my words, and, for a second time, my words failed me. Instead, I used those of another. I grasped a fist full of moist dirt and flung it on the grave, whispering, "'Flights of angels sing thee to thy rest.'" Then, as Shakespeare had written, the rest was silence.

With my hands I had dug into the earth and fashioned a final bed for Moe. She lay under the cold ground accompanied by all the emotions it had cost me to put her there: hope, faith, beauty, truth, a love that had never died but been lost and grown cold nonetheless. Hands dirty and bloodied from the digging, it couldn't have been more appropriate. It was too much; it was, at last, enough. At that moment, a timeless moment, I realized ultimately that there was nowhere to go and nothing to be done.

Nothing.

The allure of suicide, the comfort of suicide, the certainty of suicide. There would be no blade this time. I had no desire to carry a second set of scars. Back in my apartment, I kept a gun that, upon my arrival at Regina, had been given to me by William. I'd kept it for self-defense, and now, in a way, it would serve just that purpose, not against a human foe, but against a witless universe devoid of meaning, justice and love. The shot fired by the N.C.A. soldier would finally find its mark.

Having attained resolve, a cold, cleansing rush of stillness washed through me. My breath slowed, and my heart calmed. At last, the voices in my head grew quiet. This then was to be my coda—the perfection of silence. I couldn't have asked for anything better.

I walked back home through the twilight city. The night had grown late, and I encountered no one. When I reached the downtown, here and there I came upon the figures of other fugitives in the night. It was so much like the east coast of the Island that I experienced an occasional uncanny rush of déjà-vu. Ordinarily perhaps, it would have amused me, but not on that night, certainly not on that night.

The lights of Victoria Park were working, and they floated like disembodied spirits amongst the trees, piteous in their attempt to overcome the darkness. The N.C.A. were gone. At the centre of the park, the cenotaph was fully illuminated. Someone stood before it, a silhouette in the lights, with head down as though praying. For some reason the image attracted me; the sense of loneliness and isolation spoke to me, I suppose, and I made my way to the monument.

The cenotaph was lit by four floodlights, each set fifteen metres from its corners. As I approached, three of these sent shadows sliding away from me, half shadows, really, weakened as each was by the illumination cast by the opposing lights. As I came before the monument, one of the shadows moved onto its surface. I experienced the odd sensation that I had been split in three. One third of me stood upon the marble, the other two parts lay flat beside it and stretched from my feet out into the night. As if engraved into the stone, the shadow of the person who had drawn me there was motionless upon the monument surface. As I took my final step, our shadows crossed, joined and formed one figure darker than before, gaining substance from one another and becoming complete.

I regarded the mute figure of the soldier carved in relief upon the surface of the cenotaph. I noticed for the first time that the eyes of the soldier were closed. In sleep? In death? One could not be sure. Then I read the caption beneath, "For all those who died in the great war, for the glory of God." Perhaps those eyes were clamped tight in horror. I couldn't remember when I'd become so cynical, but somehow that emotion had seeped its way into the very core of my being. I turned from the cenotaph and took the first of the final steps to my apartment.

An almost inaudible gasp arose from the dark figure that I passed. It was a woman's voice. Hearing it arrested my movement, and I stood there, frozen in a moment of startled disbelief. That sound, that tiny sound had reverberated down to my very essence.

Then I heard her magnificent voice speak out, "Samuel?"

My breath caught in my throat. It was a memory from out the peopled throng of my past, a voice I had believed lost forever. I was too terrified to turn. It came again, "Samuel," and then I spun about to face her. With the light illuminating her hair, I could scarcely discern the features of her frantic, disheveled, beautiful face, but I could see enough to know.

It was Katherine.

Book Four:
The Second Coming

"Perfect wisdom is silence."
- Slouching Toward Bethlehem

I

She stood trembling and speechless. As I stared, barely able to control the deluge of emotions, she slowly lifted her hands to her face and began to sob. She seemed to fall toward me, and I realized that I also moved to her. Was I laughing? I couldn't tell for the tears that rushed at my eyes. My whole being flushed with sensations: the cool night air on my cheeks, the scent of the newly fallen dew, the sound of scraping feet, my outstretched hands and at last the thundering drum of my heart, her heart, as she was in my arms. I kissed her; I covered her face with kisses then crushed her once more to my chest. I kissed her still. The flesh of her neck was sweet. I could feel her warm, lithe body pressing against me, trembling.

Finally, the wordlessness of passion faded, and I pushed her to arms length, still clutching at her.

"Katie...."

She laughed and lifted her face once again to my own, stopping my breath with a long, slow kiss. I surrendered to her, then, panting, she pushed me back.

"Don't you ever, ever leave me again."

"Not for the devil himself. Not for death, not for life." I searched her eyes for the betrayal that I feared would be there, but she looked back at me with a clear, white love.

"I'd given up on you, Sammy." Quietly, guiltily.

I nodded, "Yes, but...." During all the time that I had travelled eastward to Edmonton, I had practiced what to say when we were reunited, but with her in my arms, I forgot it all. I said again, "Yes, but...," then finished my thought with an expression so much more sincere than words could ever be. When I finally gasped for another breath, we stood beneath the blind eyes of the soldier and held each other until our hearts calmed and began to beat as one. I vowed to myself, over and over, that they would never beat apart again.

In the early, early morning, I lay in the dark listening to Katherine breathe. Curled into one another, emotionally, physically exhausted, her smooth back warmed my chest. I could not understand how I had ever left her. Each contented pulse and echo of my heart repeated the tiny refrain, *I love you, I love you, I love you.*

Katherine stirred. *How did I ever leave you?*

Before making love, we had talked for hours, and I felt all the horror, the sorrow and the despair of the previous months escape from me like a slow, deep sigh. What I had been willing to do to myself only hours before, what I had almost done, frightened me and seemed part of a resolve so distant as to belong to another lifetime. In effect, I guess it really did. The absurdity of it smacked of a bitter jest.

We told of what we'd done: my long, sad story of the coast and of coming to Regina, her months of desolation and loneliness in Edmonton. Katherine had waited, faithful to my promise that I would return. After war broke out, she tried her best to get word to me, no longer caring about discovery. It was a futile effort, as my own attempts had been. She came to hear of Regina, however, and that knowledge gave her a destination when the Coalition marched upon Edmonton.

She had been forced to flee three weeks before my arrival, leaving the picture and note in hopes that I would finally make it home. She'd left other clues—ones that I'd missed, but she hadn't dared leave anything obvious, fearing that the Coalition would find it first and somehow use it to trap me.

I interrupted her as she told me this, digging from my pocket the worn and tattered note I found in my desk. I carried it with me always; I still have it now, though the writing is hardly legible anymore. She cried when I showed it to her, and she wept when I described how her picture had been taken from me.

Since I'd been in Regina, Katherine and I had lived in the city almost side by side yet never knowing of each other. Finding herself bored, as I had, she'd sought out something to occupy her time while she spent the long days waiting and hoping that I'd come to find her. She eventually happened upon the Salvation Army Mission that I first noticed while riding in the carriage with Simon and Christina. She spent her time there serving food to the homeless and doing whatever else she could to administer to those whose hearts and souls hungered more than their bodies. In doing so she'd eased her own suffering somewhat. I understood now why the place held such a fascination for me and cursed myself for not paying more attention to my intuition.

We had gone to the same places, sometimes, missing each other by a day, or by hours. Mostly, though, because she had found a place to stay in the northern part of the city, she rarely came downtown. Because of the density of the crowd it was unlikely that I would have seen her anyway, but she was present at the swearing in. Still, I wonder how things would have changed had we met when I'd first come to Regina. Those long moments spent with Simon would have certainly been lost. I would regret that; although, certainly then, the events of that day we last saw each other would also never have occurred. I suppose, however, that is left to the realm of wishes, rather than regrets. I'm getting ahead of my story.

It was such a thing of coincidence for Katherine and me to be at the cenotaph at the same time. Was God working to finally bring us together, or had he conspired to do the opposite and only at that last moment lost interest? Perhaps he just enjoyed the irony of the two of us meeting at the foot of a war monument. Maybe he wasn't quits with me yet, and my resolve for suicide had come too early. With the two of us together once again, the potential for further tragedy was so much more interesting.

Such thoughts, however, did not run through my head in the morning as I lay beside the woman I loved and savoured the feeling of a world recently plucked from the crumbling edge of self-immolation. No, not then.

Still, contented as I was, the faint, but harsh strains of reality were beginning to be audible through the protective confines of the bedroom that we shared. Our love hadn't protected us before; I wasn't about to trust to it again. Yet what was there for us to do? My plans, all the preparations had gone to seeing Simon and Christina out of Regina. I was to stay, yet that intention was unknown to everyone but me, and it wouldn't be difficult to convince Roland to bring Katherine along. We hadn't the supplies, that was true, but William wouldn't come for us till near the fall of darkness, and that gave us an entire day to prepare. We could do that, and Katherine and I could travel free into the mountains. I explained it all to her the evening before, and we'd made plans for the morning.

Tired as I was, for some reason I feared surrendering myself to sleep. I lay awake, listening to her breathing, her shoulder tucked under my chin, my arm wrapped about her side. After a long time of thinking myself alone, she whispered, "Are you awake?"

"Only just," I answered quietly, wondering why we were whispering, except that it felt right.

"I'm afraid that if I fall sleep, I'll wake up and find that I'm only dreaming."

"It is just a dream." We were silent for a time. "What sound does love make?" I finally asked her.

"It's just like the beating of your heart."

"But you can't hear that."

"Of course not," she said. "Didn't you know? The sound of perfect love is silence." I chuckled; it was good to be with her once again.

"This isn't going to work, Katie. You've grown far too clever for me."

She twisted back so that the two of us faced one another. "Actually, it's the other way around," she said. "I've lost my edge. Before, I was clever enough never to let it show."

"Ah." I understood. "Perhaps, wise one, you could show me some perfect love."

She did, and afterwards, oblivious to the darkness, I finally fell asleep within her arms.

II

I awoke with a start, then let my head sink back into the pillow. I searched lazily through the somnolent haze of memory and found Katherine—weeping, smiling, in passion. I lay on the bed breathing deeply of her presence. Had there been a thought that troubled me? Vaguely, I could recall something, but in that sweet moment, it didn't seem to matter.

The sun came through the window and bathed me in light. I reached a hand over to touch Katherine, but the sheets lay empty and flat. I was alone.

The bed beneath me shook with an unsettling vibration.

I glanced about my bedroom, attempting once again to catch the tail end of a vagrant thought. There was something… important. The clock read six o'clock, but I wasn't sure if that was A.M. or P.M. And all the time, my bed was shaking.

The window across the room was open. Faintly, I could make out the sound of a vehicle passing by on the street—so unfamiliar now in Regina. Heavy Metal thunder. A truck? I was confused. Sounded more like a train. My befuddled brain wondered at that, a train on the street outside my window?

I had just risen from the bed, driven by my curiosity, when Katherine rushed into the room. She stopped upon seeing me standing, and one hand rose, trembling, to cover her mouth. Even from that distance, I could tell her heart was pounding. My own began to quicken.

"They're here," she said. Then, of course, I knew.

Had we slept an entire day away? Had the moment somehow passed us by? Had the Coalition lied, intending all along to come one day early?

She said to me, "They're here," and everything we'd planned, or hadn't planned but wished to do anyway, slipped from us.

I approached the window and looked down upon a column of tanks rumbling by on the street below. Indeed, they had come. Emotion washed from me, and I felt as dead inside as I had the evening before when I'd decided upon suicide.

"We have to get to your friends," she said.

"Yeah, but let's not go off half-cocked." I backed away from the window, as if afraid that they would see me. "Let's pack what we can first."

"We should go now. They might be closing off the city."

"Kate, if they've got tanks in the streets, the city's already done for. We don't have any way to get out until tonight. We should pack what we can, in case we can't come back."

She calmed visibly, by a feat of will, I was certain. "Okay. Make sure you bring your gun."

We left the apartment less than an hour afterward. I had a loaded pack on my shoulders, and Katherine carried a duffel bag slung over her right side. As we had so often in years past, once again we were heading out to the mountains. For some reason, I didn't experience the same rush of exhilaration that I usually felt.

The decision regarding what to do was a difficult one. I couldn't predict how William or Christina might react when they saw that the Coalition had arrived one day early. It could be that Will would come to my apartment, or that Christina and Simon would do so as well. The chance that we would miss them in transit worried me, but the only thing we all knew for certain was to meet at the cathedral at sunset. Katherine and I decided to go to Christina's, and if her place was empty, we would wait at Peter's coffee shop until the end of the day. I scribbled a hasty note and taped it to the entrance of the apartment. Then we set out.

The streets of Regina were empty. I had expected as much; no doubt, the rumble of tanks often has that effect. It was a harrowing walk; not knowing why the Coalition had come early or what it planned to do, our fear weighed heavy in our steps. If we were stopped, we had no doubt as to what our fates would be. Occasionally we heard the harsh staccato of voices and the rumble of traffic. It tore at me to think that I had gained Katherine back just to risk losing her again.

The sound of activity reached us a few blocks south of Victoria Park where we walked in the relative cover of a tree-shrouded street. Although I didn't know it at the time, a victory celebration was being planned. The Coalition was setting up a national broadcast to commemorate the culmination of their holy revolution. Unbeknownst to us, the new Messiah, Joseph Adams, was then entering Regina and being brought down Albert Street in a triumphant procession that would end at the city centre. Katherine and I walked along quickly in the early sun, afraid even of the terrified voices that came to us from opened windows. I had reached back to take her hand, and then dragged her along, gripping so hard that she cried out once. Every sound we made seemed thunderous.

Several blocks past Victoria Park, Katherine suddenly grabbed my arm and pulled me to a stop. "Listen!"

I did, then without pausing to speak, yanked at her hand and ran for cover into the mouth of an alley we'd just passed. When I jolted her, she dropped the bag she carried, and there wasn't time to pick it up. The sound of a vehicle grew louder. Luckily, the office buildings echoed the noise of the approaching engine, and we had been able to hear it before we were caught in the open of the crossing streets. There was a garbage bin just into the alley, and we crouched behind it, keeping a fearful eye on the pack lying conspicuously in the middle of the sidewalk. I took hold of the handgun in my pocket, handling it nervously. It was a Jeep that turned onto the street where we had come and drove slowly in the direction of my apartment. There came the grounding of stones beneath the tires.

Katherine swore and said, "It's like they're looking for something."

I didn't answer. My heart was drumming so loudly, I could scarcely hear them pass, but they did pass. I had calmed marginally when a rustling sounded behind us. Katherine uttered a soft cry. I turned, fully expecting to face the Messiah himself, only to see a crumpled newspaper rolling with the small breeze and scuttling across the asphalt.

After several moments, we both stood and inched our way back out onto the street. I was afraid that they had noticed the pack and would be waiting just a block away, expecting someone to return and pick it up, but the road was empty. They hadn't noticed, or just hadn't cared. The realization struck me that the war for them was over. The last city was theirs and there would be no more fighting. I envied them that sensation.

It took what seemed a long time to reach Christina's place. So many other things had crowded their way into my considerations that, until we walked up the front entrance, it never occurred to me what her reaction might be to seeing my lost Katherine alive. I hesitated, yet there was nothing for it. Katherine noticed my behaviour but said nothing. I've always wondered what she knew. When finally we knocked, it was Simon who let us in.

He called out and, upon hearing my voice, unlocked the door and pulled it open. There was an odd expression on his face as we walked in. I saw a chair set behind the door.

"You've been sitting here waiting?"

"Christina went to get you; I had to stay in case you missed each other."

"She went to my apartment?"

"Yes, she just left." Katherine and I had entered and closed the door. She had thrown her bag to the floor and was helping me off with my pack. "Who's with you?"

This wasn't the meeting that I had feared, but it made me uneasy nonetheless. As I formed the introduction in my head, Simon cut me off. "This is Katherine," he said.

He'd always seen too much for a blind man.

"Yes, I'm Katherine." From our discussion, she knew almost as much about Simon as I knew myself. My pack thumped on the entrance tiles, and she reached to take his hand in hers. "It's nice to meet you, Simon. Sammy told me all about you."

The smile he flashed was genuine, as I suppose it should have been. I had thought that he would resent her for Christina's sake. Perhaps I only flattered myself.

He invited us in. Christina would be gone for at least two hours, more if she had to travel as cautiously as we did, if she wasn't stopped. I considered going after her but decided that the odds of finding her were too slight balanced against the dangers I might face. More importantly, Katherine would have never let me go alone, and I had no intention of exposing her to any Coalition bullets. The three of us settled down for the wait, and I began to relate to Simon the tale of how Katherine and I had met after searching for so long.

I didn't tell him of little Moe and how I had laid her lost soul under a few forsaken inches of earth. He didn't need to know everything.

We had sat for some time, occasionally hearing traffic in the distance and growing increasingly more anxious as the afternoon wore on. Katherine decided that we should pack all of our provisions and prepare to make our way to the cathedral. Through it all, Simon said little, except to assure Katherine that everything was planned and would be taken care of. I've often wondered what was going through his mind during those hours; I was never able to see into his thoughts, certainly not as he could see into mine.

Midway through our preparations, Simon stood abruptly, raising a hand for silence. He whispered, "My God," and then the windows rattled. "Explosions."

Katherine and I glanced at each other then rushed to look out the window. The glass rattled again, and we stepped back, fearful that it would shatter. Throwing aside caution, I ran out onto the front street. Rumblings echoed back to me from all directions, followed by another deep percussion. Staring downtown, I could see black smoke begin to rise above the nearby rooftops.

"What's happening?" Simon asked, as he stood unsteadily in the doorway, one foot on the front step.

Katherine stepped past him, and then stood in amazement at the columns of ruin that now marked the eastern horizon. "We're in it now," she said.

"We are that."

"What do we do?"

"I don't know, Kate. I really don't know. If we leave now—well, we can't leave now. We can't go until Christina gets here."

"If she's out there, she may not be coming back."

"She's coming back," Simon said.

"We can't leave anyway. Without Will, there's nowhere to go. We could leave the city, I guess, but what happens after that?"

"She's coming back, Samuel."

"He's right, Kate; she's coming back, and we're going to wait for her."

There was nothing to do for it. I looked up and down the street, seeing others who had been drawn out of their homes by the sound of the explosion. People seemed in shock, afraid to make eye contact. I turned my gaze back again at the darkening eastern horizon. There was nothing to do but go back inside and wait. When I mounted the steps, I took Simon's arm and helped him to a seat. He was shaking and clutched at me. I wanted to know what he was feeling, but having shown up there with Katherine, I felt that I'd in some way betrayed our friendship and no longer had a right to ask. Katherine was quiet. I told Simon what we'd seen, and then we sat in the silence and feared what the remainder of the day would bring.

One terrible hour later, Christina slipped in the front door. Unbelievably, I had dozed off, and the sound of the door closing jolted me into awareness. Snapping upright in the chair, I think I cried out.

When she saw that I was there, she rushed forward with her arms outstretched, but then stopped as Katherine came within sight. Christina blinked and brought a hand up, pressing against her lower lip. I wished that I had remained sleeping and not seen the sweep of emotions that crossed her sad face.

"This is Katherine," I said, finally. "We found each other last night."

"Hello, Christina," my lover said as she walked to the doctor and hugged her lightly. What had Katherine guessed? Had I said something the evening before that gave her some apprehension of what had passed between Christina and me while I believed that she was dead? Of course, I couldn't know, and I still don't know now, but what I did understand then was how the two of them met and each extended to the other something of a tenderness that I felt for them both. Christina returned the embrace, and, in the shelter of Katherine's arms, began to weep.

Simon stood and moved hesitantly to the sound of her voice. I approached the two and touched Christina's shoulder. Not understanding, I said, "We're all here, Christina. It's going to be all right."

She raised her head and shook it. "I know, Samuel. I know. I have to sit down."

She seemed to collapse into the cushions and then began to cry again. "It was horrible. Oh, Simon," she took his hand, "it was absolutely horrible."

"What is it?" he asked her.

"They shot him. They killed him, right before my eyes."

"What?" I rushed to her side. "Who?"

"Joseph Adams."

It was a thunderclap, more of a shock than the explosions had been. Braxton had been right.

"Who shot him? How did it happen?"

"I don't know. I couldn't see. Would someone get me a drink of water?"

She sat silently, collecting herself, then gulped back what I brought her.

"I went to your apartment," she said. "On the way there, I stayed on the side streets, and every time I heard the sound of someone or something approaching, I hid. When I couldn't find you, I decided to walk past Dante's and see if I might spot you inside."

"I left you a note."

"I didn't see it." She shook her head. "I was getting frantic and wasn't thinking straight. Then I heard the sound of all the people in Victoria Park. Part of me kept saying just to come back here, but I was so curious, and I felt so lost not knowing what was happening. I thought you might be there too, so I had to be sure.

"As it turned out, I wouldn't have been able to find you anyway. The whole park was full of people, the same as yesterday. They'd erected a platform straight south of the cenotaph, only this was nicely finished and had a single microphone on it. There were half a dozen movie cameras spread throughout the park. After what you guys had said the other day, I thought that it was going to be a podium for Joseph Adams. Several cameras were focused on centre stage, where he would be talking, the others swept back and forth over the crowd.

"On both sides of the platform, not under any camera, there were tanks and armoured cars with their guns pointed at the crowd. The N.C.A. were everywhere. Regina had already fallen without gunfire; I wondered why they thought they needed them now. If Adams felt secure enough to speak in public, why did they need guns?"

"Most likely wasn't his idea," I said. "The guns, I mean. He really probably thinks of himself as the new Messiah and doesn't believe he can be hurt. I'm sure all the hardware was because of someone else's order, not his."

"Well," Christina said, "it didn't make any difference." She shifted in her seat, and hesitated for a moment before continuing. "When he arrived, it was so staged it was almost funny. He was escorted by tanks that just spread into the park. People scattered like pigeons. Then whoever was filming the whole thing had him get driven up a second time without the escort. When that was done, they had to move a camera up closer so that a shot could be taken of him stepping out of the vehicle and walking up onto the platform. It made me sick. The worst of it was that the people nearest him were forced to cheer and clap. Anyone watching the film will think he arrived to free Regina, not conquer it. The cameras will show the cheering crowd, but I'm certain they won't show the soldiers with the guns.

"He was shorter than I expected. Like a little Hitler. If he had a mustache, it would have been perfect. The microphone was at just the right height, though. Obviously someone made sure of that.

"Remember how tense it was at the swearing in? This was a thousand times worse." Christina paused again and closed her eyes, as if recalling the image in her mind. She was terribly shaken, and telling us what she had seen was difficult for her. That was evident. I noticed that my own hands were shaking. Finally, she began to speak again, slowing, reliving the tragedy. "He raised both hands before him and cupped his palms. It looked like he was trying to take hold of the crowd."

"Bad imitation of Christ," I said.

"Whatever effect he was trying for, it didn't work. It looked too phony. Someone shouted something, but I couldn't make out what it was. Adams heard it though. His arms dropped a little, and he frowned. I don't think that it was the reaction he expected.

"He leaned closer to the microphone and said, 'My children of Regina.' And that was all." She paused to look at us. "Then they shot him."

"Christ," I heard Katherine whisper.

Christina looked at me. "I couldn't tell where it came from; I don't think the soldiers could either. There was an echo." Christina frowned.

"So what happened?" Simon asked her. He sat forward in his seat, hands in fists on his knees. His knuckles were white.

The frown deepened, and Christina's expression was pained. "Someone shot him in the head. He fell backwards and didn't get up again. I was stunned." So was I; stunned that he was arrogant enough to stand up there like he did, but also amazed that anyone would have the courage to actually shoot him. Even with Braxton's comments, I hadn't expected that. I imagined that there was more to what she'd seen, but Christina offered no further details.

"I'm not so surprised," Simon said. "I'll bet the gunman came from somewhere else. Whoever it was, they didn't do what they did for the sake of Regina."

The doctor looked at him, bewildered. "What do you mean?"

"For all we know, it could have been one of his own generals. Anyone could be behind this."

Katherine had been sitting quietly and nodding; she finally spoke out. "What were the explosions? We saw columns of smoke."

Christina looked at her for a couple of heartbeats before answering. Was she studying Katherine, or simply framing the image in her mind?

"It was the tanks. There was this terrible moment where nothing happened, and then one of the tanks fired out above the crowd. The turret on the tank didn't move; it didn't look like they aimed, just fired. I thought about that all the way home, and I can almost imagine what the soldier inside was feeling. He, or she, I suppose, would have thought that the war was done, that it was all over, only to see their hopes shattered at the last moment.

"There was this incredible loud *whoosh* and then one of the towers that overlooks the park had its side blown out. The explosion was deafening. I was far enough away, but fire and glass burst all over the people at that corner of the park."

"Was anyone hurt?"

"Hurt?" Her voice broke, and she took a moment to gather herself. Katherine moved to her side on the couch and rested a hand on her shoulder. Christina leaned ever so slightly into the touch. "Oh, it was horrible." Her face lowered into her hands. "I don't know how many people were killed, dozens. Everyone was screaming, and the whole park went crazy. It was chaos. Shouting and running. Soldiers began to shoot into the air; some shot into the crowd. People rushed the stage and swarmed over it. I can't imagine what they did to Adam's body.

"A second tank shot the monument at the centre of the park. There was a hollow boom, and it blew into dust. Concrete went flying everywhere. Some kids had climbed on top of it and….

"I ran. I'd already made my way to the west side of the park. When I finally got over the shock of what was happening, I just turned and ran."

It looked for a moment like she was going to cry again. I didn't at first realize what had forced the tears, but Katherine understood. She said, "There was nothing you could have done for those people. If you had stayed, they would have shot you too." Christina nodded, and leaned more heavily into Katherine's shoulder.

"I know that," Christina said. "I know."

"Were you stopped at all?"

She looked up at me and wiped at her eyes. "No, I didn't see anyone. I heard two more explosions, and that was it. Aside from Victoria Park, Regina looks deserted." Her story done, she seemed to sink back into her seat and grow smaller.

"So, what do we do now?" Simon asked.

I too went and sat down beside Christina. "I think we wait. What option do we have but to go with the original plan?"

"How do you know William will show up?"

"Because he said he would. What choice is there? Nothing's really changed. We just have to be more careful, that's all."

"A lot more careful," Christina said.

Little more than an hour later, perhaps two hours before sunset, we arrived at the cathedral. I wasn't comfortable going so early, but there was the outside chance that Will would arrive sooner than planned. As it turned out, he was nowhere in sight. We sequestered ourselves in the darkness of a clump of shrubbery around the side of the cathedral. From there we were next to invisible yet the position allowed one of us to lay near an edge of the bushes and keep an eye on the street and the Thirteenth Avenue Coffee House across the way. Katherine hadn't seen Will since two summers before and wasn't sure she'd recognize him; Christina was too emotionally drained to keep herself alert, so the job of sentinel fell to me.

Stretched out on my belly, viewing the silent panorama of that doomed city, I found myself reflecting over the past few weeks and wondering at the change that had overcome my life. Strange as it was, all that had befallen us, all the terrible things that brought me to that point of time in Regina, seemed now like pieces in a vast nihilistic puzzle. The night before, after digging that shallow grave for Moe, I had completed assembling all the moments that I'd experienced since leaving Tofino, and I had fit them together, finally, in a clear picture revealing the abysmal nature of Truth. It was a culminating moment, and I thought then that the puzzle of my life was complete. I realize now that it wasn't. There needs to be something to temper the knife edge of Truth or life is too stark to accept. But then, faced with what I knew, those agonizing thoughts of suicide, those comforting thoughts of suicide, had seemed the only appropriate response to what I thought I understood.

Finding Katherine again had changed all that, but even so, the timing of our reunion was critical. Had I not reached the point that I had before seeing her once again, things would not have been the same. I had come to see the harsh and terrible essence of Truth, and because of that, was then able to grasp the equally astonishing nature of love. There was Katherine, with my soul stripped down to a raw and trembling core of fragile luminescence, near to flickering out eternally—there was Katherine. The dark had scraped me clean, had primed me for the pure, remarkable essence of love, and when I needed it most, love was there. I met Katherine in a way that I'd never met her before.

The old one being completed and discarded, this was the beginning of a new puzzle. At its centre, at its core, was the finality of the first puzzle—Truth, and I'd just added a second piece. I was blind to it at the time, but I realize now that everything I was coming to understand had already been explained to me by Simon in those weeks after our first meeting. Simon understood it all; I was just unable to see what he was trying to tell me.

My reverie was interrupted by movement on the street. Someone was walking past. The casualness of it startled me. I called back to the others, and Katherine crawled up along side me. Her hand gripped my shoulder.

"It's just someone walking. God, it looks so strange."

"My thought exactly."

We watched the person turn a corner and disappear from sight. Katherine stayed with me. Ten minutes later a pair of older women approached and entered the coffeehouse.

I almost laughed, "It's open. Do these people have any idea what's going on?"

"They must."

"I don't know. If we hadn't heard the explosions.... Holy shit, look."

"What?"

It was Adam. He stepped from the interior of the shop and sat down on the front steps sipping at the drink that he cupped in his hands. "It's a friend of mine from Tofino," I said. "I've got to go talk to him."

"Sammy, it's not safe."

I hesitated and studied the street; it looked no different than any other afternoon, only more deserted. I wanted to speak to Adam a last time, and I knew that once we left the city I would never see him again. I pressed my gun into Katherine's hand and said, "Keep watch," then was up and in the open before she could protest.

Halfway across the street, the image of Moe flashed before my eyes, and I almost turned around. What would I tell Adam? Before I'd decided what to do, he looked up and spotted me. He almost spit out his last sip. Had the times been different, I might have laughed.

"Jacob! I t'ought you 'ave left by now."

"Almost. Where have you been?'

He hesitated before answering. "Downtown."

"I heard what happened. Christina was there."

"She got out all right?"

"Yeah."

"She was lucky." He shook his head, and his gaze drifted down to stare at the cup he held. It was obvious that whatever he'd seen had shaken him. I thought for a moment that he'd forgotten about me, but then he began talking in a flat voice, "The N.C.s go crazy, honestly. I get out of dere as soon as I can." I sat beside him on the steps.

"I t'ink dey will go on a killing spree, so I look for any type of 'iding place I can find. Dere was shooting and screaming. I was running. Den I pass de entrance of an apartment building wit' its front door 'eld open by a newspaper, I go inside and slam the door be'ind me.

"For awhile I just crouch down and 'ide in de 'allway, but I 'ave to know what is going on. I am not going to go back out on the streets, so I find a stairway and go to de top floor. I look around and come across de door dat open on another flight of stairs leading to the roof. Once I am up dere, I creep to the edge of the building and look back downtown.

"It is like a scene from *De War of de Worlds*. Dark smoke is covering de 'orizon. I see people running t'roughout de streets. Armoured cars and tanks. After awhile, it become too much. I laid down on de roof and just stare at de sky. I am dere for 'ours."

"How did you get home?"

"I 'aven't been 'ome."

"Was it clear after you left downtown?"

"Dere are patrols on Albert Street, but dey are easy to avoid. I do not know what de Coalition is doing, but at least dey decide not to burn de 'ole city down."

"They're probably in as much chaos as everyone else."

"I do not doubt it," he said. "Now everyone fight for de position of Adams."

I thought so myself. People being what they are, the entire New Christian movement was probably little more than another façade employed to obscure the face of ambition.

"What do you do now?" he asked.

I shifted uncomfortably, not sure what to tell him.

Adam shook his head, lifting a hand to silence me. "Do not worry about it. You are better off to keep it secret. Myself, I go to 'ead sout' and see 'ow far down dis madness go. Maybe it is only Canada. Who knows?"

"What then?"

"I do not know. Just live, I guess, or maybe I make my way to the east coast and leave de continent altoget'er. T'ings 'ave got to be better anywhere but 'ere."

"I suppose. Why didn't you leave this morning? The longer you wait, the worse it's going to get."

"I know, but dey were not supposed to be 'ere today. Plus, I been looking for Moe and de girls. We split up yesterday, and I 'ave not seen any of dem since."

So he didn't know about Moe. Of course he didn't know about Moe. I considered keeping silent and sparing him that extra pain, but he had seen the expression on my face, and he knew. "What is it?"

I told him. A silken pallor blanched his features. When I was done, his head tilted almost imperceptibly, and he pursed his lips.

"De ot'er two?"

"I didn't see them."

"Well, t'ank you for taking care of 'er," he said.

What could I say to that? I arose from the step and stood there stupidly, wanting very much to leave that cursed city where such people were killed in the street, yet he wouldn't let me leave just yet. He kept looking at me, misted eyes, his young face lined deeply.

"I did try to stop 'er, you know? I really did, but she will not listen. She 'ad dis pure belief dat I could not touch. She believe in 'im so much, no one short of Samuel J. 'Arris 'imself can change 'er mind."

I don't remember much else of what Adam said. He left shortly after.

I wished him luck, and he hoped the same thing for me. We embraced. I haven't seen him since, but that doesn't mean much. Of course, I'd like to think he made it off the continent, but he did have a long, long way to go.

III

I looked over to the church, knowing that Katherine would be cursing my carelessness. Adam's comment about Moe had shaken me considerably, enforcing my own sense of guilt regarding how I had betrayed and let her down. Suddenly exhausted, I sat once again upon the front steps of Peter's, attempting to stay my dark thoughts. The warmth of the sun's slanted light shone upon my face, so maddeningly incongruous with the maelstrom of emotions within me. As I sat there, a couple walked by the front of the coffeehouse, and I shook my head thinking of the insanity of our situation. *Still, it's almost over*, I thought. *We just need Will to come and lead us away.*

I studied our setting. Dark smoke obscured the eastern sky. The streets were nearly empty. *For awhile at least,* I thought, *we're safe*, and at that moment, Fate decided to prove me wrong. My carelessness became fatal. A Jeep sped past, and the occupants, three of them, a woman and two men, dressed in the new uniform of the N.C.A., looked over and took note of me. I heard the distinctive sound of a worn brake squealing. Tires ground loose stones on the pavement as the vehicle pulled to a stop on the side street bordering the shop. They stepped out, all three carrying rifles.

I considered running but knew that would only force a chase, better to play it cool and walk away, hoping that they wouldn't be interested in me. Surely they'd passed other people on the streets.

Turning my back to them, I set off toward the darkness of the east. My hands shook, heart hammered against my ribs.

A steely voice grated, "Hey you. Hold on."

Oh Christ, I thought, *oh Christ, oh Christ, oh Christ. Don't run. Just stay calm.* I turned to face them. They were much closer. What was Katherine thinking as she watched from the cover of leaves? Why hadn't I carried my gun?

"Where are you going?" the first one who had spoken asked.

I could feel the sweat cooling my palms. My lower lip twitched. For a short moment, we struck an uncomfortable tableau, then the youngest of the three stepped closer to me, staring.

"Holy Shit," he rasped disbelief widening his eyes, "it's him. It's Harris."

My legs grew weak.

"Don't be an idiot," the older man snapped. "Let's get a move on."

The female studied me critically, then her eyes too grew wide. "No, Carl's right. His hair's longer, but it's Harris."

My heart was racing. If Katherine wasn't watching, there was no way of alerting them to what was happening. What if she were watching? The chilling image of Katherine falling before their guns flashed before me, and I knew I had to act before anyone else had a chance to. I cursed my incredible stupidity. *Take me*, I thought. *Take me before anyone comes looking for me.*

"What am I worth to you?" I said.

The youth came at me. He grabbed my arm, and with a slick motion, twisted it behind my back. He couldn't have been older than any of my students had been. "A lot," he snapped. "You're worth a lot."

"Don't hurt him, Carl," the woman cautioned.

"Yeah, Carl, don't bring damaged goods to your Messiah." It was an explosive thing to say, and at the time I wasn't sure why I baited them except that I knew I had to force the issue and push them to act while it was still only me they were interested in. In answer to the comment, my arm suffered a violent wrench, and I could hear thick cursing in my ear.

Then the door to Peter's opened. A pair of older women exited, and one of them cried out at the sight of us. I saw two of the N.C.s snap their heads at the sound; as a reflex, I turned to look as well. Just as I realized that the angle of my twisted shoulder kept me from moving, I was released. A sudden, sticky warmth spattered the back and side of my head.

I'd heard a kind of soft popping sound, but the gunshot itself never registered on my consciousness. It's funny how your senses can deceive you. I never understood that the boy holding me had been shot until I spun around to see his shattered face rolling up at me. He had let go of my arm, but as he slumped down, his weight pressed forward against my leg. I pulled away, horrified, finally understanding that his blood had soaked my hair and neck.

The other two soldiers were momentarily stunned, just long enough for them to go the way of their companion. Whereas a moment before I had resolved to die quickly in order to keep my friends from being discovered, now I was standing alone with three bodies crumpled at my feet. To say I was startled fails to connote even the beginning of my bewilderment. Then I saw William rushing toward me, rifle in hand.

"Are you hit?"

Numbly, I glanced down at myself. My right side was spattered with blood and gray matter, but I didn't think a bullet had touched me. I shook my head silently.

Will grabbed my arm and looked me over. "That was way too close. You're sure you're okay?"

"Yeah, I'm fine. What is going on? How did you…?" I looked down at the N. C. soldiers.

"It's time to get out of here, buddy. Explanations can wait. Where are the others?"

I pointed toward the cathedral, "There. You heard about Adams?"

"Yeah. Our boys were involved. Idiots, they've made it difficult for us now."

"How are we going to get out?"

"Listen, we'd better talk on the run, but first let's drag these three out of sight. Take this one." He gestured at the semi-decapitated youth who had treated me so roughly, and we each bent down to grab a pair of limbs. When I took hold of that boy's arms, felt his weight, my memory flashed back to when I pulled Moe from Wascana Creek. Things had come round full circle, and now I was one of the killers. A desperate sense of preservation kept me from looking into what remained of that teenager's face. I had a strange certainty that his eyes were open and regarding me. Something compelled me to make sure, yet horror kept me from glancing down.

There was a gate at the side of Peter's, and we deposited our limp bundle just out of sight behind it. When we came out, it struck me that I hadn't noticed where the two older women went who had diverted the attention of the N.C.s. For all I knew, they had gone back into the coffee shop and were watching us dispose of the corpses, or they could have been trying to contact the Coalition.

As we took hold of the older male, the one with the metallic voice, I heard a shout from across the street and looked up to see Katherine running toward us. I turned slightly, and she hesitated, startled by all the blood. "It's all right. It's not mine."

"You're okay?"

"It's not my blood."

"Oh Christ, I couldn't...."

"It's okay. Go back and get the others. We've got to go."

She paused for a moment, collecting herself, stared eye to eye with Will, then nodded firmly and dashed off. They too had been friends before the revolution, and up until that moment he had believed her dead. There were no words that could possibly have passed between them.

William and I returned to our grisly task. The last of the three, the woman, groaned as we touched her. Will snapped his hand away. His face had such a look upon it that I thought he would turn his gun upon himself. I was still stunned, and I'd been so rattled about what had almost happened to me, I didn't stop to realize what he had just been forced to do. I have killed, only once, and the thought of it still haunts me today. Will had just gunned down three living, breathing humans. In moving them, the blood that he spilt made slippery his hands. The barely audible cry from the woman whose corpse we had meant to hide behind the fence, appeared almost more than he could handle.

Knowing that he had done it all for me, I told him, "Go help with the gear. I'll finish this."

He either ignored the suggestion, or his mind was so focused on its own wretchedness that he didn't hear what I said. Something akin to a snarl twisted his features. "What are we going to do with this one?" he asked.

"We'll just leave her with the others."

He stood there shaking his head. "God damn it. God damn it."

"You didn't have a choice, Will. They would have killed me."

He shook his head, tears welling in his eyes, then he nodded decisively, "Yeah, nobody invited the bitch. Come on."

We let her fall on top of the others, and then gathered up their weapons. I think she'd stopped breathing by the time we left her.

We met Christina, Simon and Katherine coming back across the street. Christina's face had a hard, professional set to it. She had been shaken badly earlier, and I realized that the only way she could deal with anymore of what we were going through was to force herself into a clinical state of mind. Simon was on her arm, but she walked quickly to me and asked if either of us was hurt.

"We're fine," Will said, "but we won't be for long if we don't get out of this bloody city."

"Where's Roland?" Christina asked.

"We'll meet up with him out of town."

"We walk?"

"No," Will shook his head, "it would take too long. Roland is leaving at midnight, with or without us. I had planned to steal a truck or something." He glanced to the side of the coffee shop where the bodies lay hidden, then he looked to the opposite side of the building where the Jeep was parked on the street. "That's theirs?"

"Yeah."

"We'll take it," he said and then just stood as if transfixed. I looked at the others, a little mystified but suddenly realized why he hesitated. Unless the keys for the vehicle were in the ignition, one of us would have to search through the clothing on the bodies to find them. It was an awkward pause, and I wasn't about to be the one to end it.

I think it took the women a moment to understand what was happening, but after a pause when I began to feel my resolve weakening, Katherine walked over to where she had seen us drag our ghastly burdens. She returned quickly and shouldered her pack. Her hands were darkened. We followed her to the Jeep, heaped our supplies into the back, and climbed aboard. I set the rifle I had picked up on the floorboards in front of me, keeping it in place with the heel of my foot.

William took the driver's seat, and Katherine handed him the keys. The engine sputtered for a moment then leapt to life. We drove quickly off, heading north.

On the northwestern edge of the city, a street named Rochdale runs out toward the setting sun and ends at the beginning of a farmer's field. There's a grid road that intersects it, but for all purposes, the city stops at the far side of its pavement. Will decided to drive to that junction and then head out of town on the grid road. Roland awaited us on a farm twenty kilometres away. He didn't explain how he knew, but Will said the Coalition had only shut off the city's major thoroughfares and that we should be able to slip out of the city undetected if we drove that route.

Crowded into the Jeep with our bags of supplies heaped between us, we were horribly conspicuous, but there were no other options. Every moment that we remained in Regina, the net of the Coalition might tighten and our chances of escaping decrease. I cursed myself for the thought, but it occurred to me that we should have made sure of that woman's death. If she was found and could tell them who she had seen.... We had to leave, and we had to leave quickly.

Such an eerie drive I hope never to experience again. I sat in the front passenger seat and, with one hand clutching the roll bar for stability, watched the panorama of Regina sweep past. The sky was overcast with dark clouds of smoke. It appeared that the downtown was burning, and I found out later that it was. There were no more explosions, although I doubted that we could have heard them anyway. The streets we travelled were devoid of life. I was used to seeing people in the downtown but had never gone out to the suburbs. Had they always been like this, or had people seen the smoke and were afraid of being caught outside? Cars lined the roads, filled the driveways. Unless they had left by foot or horseback, as we had planned to do, it seemed obvious that few people had chosen to leave Regina. I toyed with the thought of stealing another vehicle and splitting up to make our escape. It would increase the odds of at least some of us making it out of the city alive, but even then the idea of stealing someone's car at gunpoint disturbed me. Besides, only Will knew the location of Roland's farm.

I'd grown so used to riding on carriages, the swift movement and the noise of the Jeep were disconcerting. I was tossed about in the seat. The wind whipped at my hair, roared in my ears.

Will knew the city and was able keep us from most major avenues and intersections, but there were times when we had to cross over stretches of exposed roadways where we could be spotted for blocks in any direction. Near the northern tip of the city, we came upon Ninth Avenue North, and it was such a crossing.

Still in the relative cover of the surrounding houses, Will brought the Jeep to a halt. He shut off the motor and turned to speak with us. The abrupt silence was astounding, and I realized how thunderous our passage must have sounded to the people hiding in their homes—if anyone actually lived there anymore. "This is the last exposed stretch of road," Will said. "Once we're across here, it's another couple of kilometres through the suburbs, and we're out of the city. I don't want to just drive out into the open; we need to see if it's clear."

"Done." I swung my legs out of the Jeep, looking back to Will, "You should keep it running. If anyone comes, they'll see us before they hear us." I started walking. Before I'd gone a dozen metres, Katherine was at my side.

"Nice day for a walk, no?" It would have been a brave front, but her voice was unsteady.

"Stay in the Jeep, Kate."

"And get separated from you again? I don't think so."

"Better separated then dead." I said it, but I didn't believe it any longer.

Nor did she. "No, never again, Samuel."

We passed quiet houses where, I was sure, a phantom group of watchers regarded our passage. "What's this city going to be like in a year?"

"Hopefully, we'll never know."

It was unnerving to walk out beyond the cover of the street and cross into that bare intersection. The road we had been driving on was itself uncomfortably wide and open, but the one we needed to cross was a major artery that encircled the city, and, as such, had wide ditches on both sides—nothing to offer any real cover. When we set across it, we would be visible for over a half-kilometre in either direction. Once out on the exposed asphalt, we saw that the roads were tantalizingly deserted. We stood for a time, waiting, watching and listening, but there was no one to be seen.

Westward, the horizon was clear, and, aside from a few scattered clouds, the northern sky was pure with an impossible expanse of blue. It gave me a sense of freedom, then I glanced downtown to see the smoke that still rose like a malevolent thunderstorm. It was so unnaturally silent, I began to wonder if we had missed some form of mass exodus, and the five of us had been left alone in Regina.

When we were certain there was no threat, I looked back to where the others waited and raised a hand to wave them forward. Will drove to us slowly, as if trying to make as little noise as possible. I listened to the tires grinding small stones on the asphalt, when a loud, high-pitched shriek made the two of us jump with terror, then crouch down as if we could hide there out in the open.

The cry had come from my left. With one hand touching the road, I scanned the distance. Nothing. I glanced at Katherine, and she shook her head, eyes wide. Will had stopped, startled by our actions. I stood, looking wildly in all directions. The cry came again, terribly close, and this time I saw movement. Katherine saw it too and barked a short laugh. Ten metres from us, a crow hopped along the shoulder of the pavement. I would have sworn it stared directly at us, and I squinted to focus into those black eyes. It cawed one last time and then took to wing, the sound of its ascent flapping hollowly.

"Good omen, or bad?"

"Let's hope it's not an omen at all," I replied, waving at Will to continue.

As the Jeep crawled into the intersection, and we stood where we did, exposed and vulnerable, I experienced a vivid flash of memory that pulled me back to Vancouver Island and the ambush by Victoria. Shaken, I took hold of Katherine's hand and rushed to meet the approaching vehicle. We leapt aboard and set off to travel the last kilometres to freedom.

A church, a school and a mall slipped by, then we reached Rochdale Avenue and turned westward. With such a small distance to travel, I imagined that I could see the golden glow of wheat fields on the horizon. We began to gain speed. I glanced at Will's face, noticing how his jaw muscles rippled. His knuckles shone white upon the steering wheel.

"We're almost there," I said to calm him. I looked back at Simon, seeing him being shaken about in his seat. Christina was at his side. Her eyes were closed and set in a face that was ghastly pale. Katherine stared at me, eyes wild. I had a good idea as to what was in her mind. I called back, "Hey, Simon."

He cocked his head. "Samuel?"

"We're almost there, buddy. One more klick and we're free."

I turned forward again, grimacing into the wind. As we passed a gas station, I looked through the front window, seeing the haunted face of an attendant staring back at me.

Scarce heartbeats later, William began to curse vehemently. Stomach churning, I followed his line of vision and saw a truck approaching us on the other side of the boulevard. It was N.C.A., and they had seen us.

Without hesitation, Will slammed on the brakes and spun the Jeep into a wheel torturing spin. Rubber screamed on asphalt, Christina too screamed as she grabbed the cloth of Simon's shirt, barely keeping him from toppling out the vehicle. Some of our bags flipped onto the road, lost to us. The Jeep almost rolled. Once around, he stomped on the gas, and we sped back the way we'd just come.

With my left hand on the roll bar and the other gripping the top of the windshield, I half rose and twisted in my seat to watch what the N.C.s would do. At first, it appeared that they sped up to give us chase, then their vehicle lurched to a halt. I shouted out to Will that they had stopped, but he just grit his teeth and continued to drive. As I looked back again, a sharp pain cut into my right hand. Grunting with surprise, I let go of the metal above the window and slumped back into my seat. The glass on my side of the windshield was cobwebbed with cracks. My wrist bled.

I cried out, "They're shooting at us! Get down! Get down!" and tried to sink as low into my seat as I could. In the back, Katherine and the others hunched over, but they were still open targets. Will twisted at the steering wheel, making us zigzag across the street. I couldn't hear the next shot either, but something spiraled past my neck and hammered a chuck out of the windshield.

Less than a half block back the way we'd come, there lay a drainage ditch which intersected the street. It had steep sides that were thick with weeds. They grew longer and more dense as the ground sloped down to a trickle of water less than a metre across. Will spotted this and sped toward it. The tire on his side crashed into the curb; the front of the Jeep leaped. We all snapped forward, and my head cracked against the windshield. I was almost thrown from my seat. We rocked across the sidewalk, then he steered us straight down the sharp drop of the ditch.

The Jeep stayed upright, just barely, and more supplies toppled out the back. Straightening, yet hardly stable, with the sound of the engine echoing in a thunder at the close quarters, we sped along the length of the loose, slippery earth toward the next intersecting road which suddenly seemed so high above us. The spinning tires tossed clumps of dirt into the air behind us.

"Are they following?" William shouted.

They were. They must have jumped the boulevard and imitated the mad descent we'd just made. I yelled to Will, although I didn't know if he could hear me. He kept his head down and pressed ahead. The Jeep angled sharply upward as the intersecting road came rushing closer. We all leaned forward, fearing that the Jeep might flip backward as we tried to exit the ditch. Will struck the edge of the sidewalk running along side the road, and for a sharp second, it seemed like there was no more earth and that the tires were reaching for sky, then we dropped forward onto concrete.

Will hammered down on the gas pedal, and we lurched ahead, roaring onto the street. Then, without warning, he stomped his foot on the brake, bringing us to a screeching halt. Before the vehicle had stopped swaying, he was out and rushing to the ditch, firing his rifle at the approaching N.C.s. As soon as I struggled from my shock, I grabbed my own rifle and followed. Katherine came close on my heels. Christina stayed frozen in her seat, still clutching Simon.

I was breathing heavily, and my hands shook. I tried to shoot in controlled bursts, but the automatic kept pulling up and away from my targets. Even in the excitement, I could hear the sound of bullets hitting the metal of the N.C.A. vehicle as it raced toward us. Little crystal explosions erupted on the windshield, and then the driver attempted to swerve away from our fire. Already on unsteady ground, the truck swayed and flipped, rolling twice. It came to rest upside down in the tiny creek. Even as we watched, soldiers scrambled from the wreck like angry hornets.

Will raised his rifle to cut them down, then hesitated, and I understood what was going through his mind. "They're on foot," I said.

"I know, I know, but if they have a radio…." He shouldered his rifle and fired. Momentarily, the overturned vehicle erupted into flames, incinerating those still inside. Without a word, Will turned, and we followed him back to the Jeep. Five minutes later, we were free of Regina.

Trying to force as much speed from the Jeep as he could, William concentrated on controlling the steering as we swerved and twisted along the loose gravel roads. The rest of us were thrown and jostled in our seats, and, excepting Simon, scanned the sky for any sign of pursuit. We were kicking up such a cloud of dust that if we were followed by land, it would be impossible to see our pursuers anyway, but the real worry was that they would send a helicopter or small plane to track us down. Will had said that twenty minutes would see us to the farm, then we could hide the Jeep. It was a concern that the dust we were raising would not have dissipated or that the Coalition would launch an extensive land search for us, but I thought that unlikely. Even if we'd been reported, surely they had no idea that the Blind Prophet was riding in that particular vehicle as it fled the city. And if they did know, would I still be of any importance to them?

It was a question that I didn't want to dwell upon. With Joseph Adams dead, perhaps an old figurehead was better than none at all.

I shrugged off the thought and focused my attention on the darkening skies. Almost unnoticed, the day had slipped away.

Will swung off the gravel road and turned into a farmyard. Roland's shadow clad figure ran out, waving us into the open door of a barn. The Jeep sped into its dimly lit interior, and the large door slid shut behind us. As we disappeared inside, I caught a glimpse of someone standing on the roof of the house, apparently keeping a watch on the road.

The engine coughed for a moment after Will switched it off, then silence settled like a pall. But it wasn't an absolute silence, nervous at the clamour of our arrival, the crowd of horses already in their transports, moved uneasily about, stamping their feet and breathing noisily. I could smell the thick odour of hay. After the open highway that we had rushed along, the confines of the building made me feel protected and secure.

I climbed out of the Jeep and reached to help Simon. *With all I've been responsible for*, I thought, *at least I'm responsible for this.* Simon, the most innocent of us all, was free from the Coalition.

"We're here, Simon. Come on down."

He raised his hand, and I guided it to my elbow, telling him where to step. "Where are we?" he asked.

Poor guy, he's gone all this way with no idea what was going on. It had been too noisy on the drive to speak, and no one really possessed the presence of mind to explain things to him. For all he knew, we had been pulled over by a patrol. "We're at Roland's. He's hidden us in a barn."

Roland came up as I spoke, and the others climbed out of the Jeep to join us. He regarded Katherine. I introduced her and began to explain, but he raised his hand, cutting me off. "It's okay. There're a couple of extra seats. Some of our party didn't make it."

"What do you mean?"

"They got mixed up in that trouble this morning." I wondered what being "mixed up in" it meant. I was beginning to get the impression that a great deal of our difficulty had been caused by Will's group of would-be rebel fighters.

Will came closer, a pained look upon his face. "Who was it?"

Roland frowned, paused for a moment. "I didn't know them that well. The married couple, Susan and James. They were really friends of Ben's, not mine."

"Who's Ben?" Christina asked.

"You'll meet him in a minute. Everyone's been waiting inside the house."

We were all anxious to join the people with whom we'd be spending the next period of our lives, but the vehicles needed to be packed. Shortly after we began organizing what remained of our supplies, Roland's wife came out to join us. He introduced her as Alicia, and following the introductions, she moved about, assisting where she could. Simon stood by my side and talked to me the entire time. It felt strange, like we hadn't spoken for weeks. I found myself looking forward to all the time that we would have to share and explore our philosophies together. I was glad to have him there. I was also so thankful that Katherine and I had found one another for a second time. Katherine. Katherine had only been back in my life for one short day, but I was once again wholly captivated by her. I could hear her voice and looked over to see her speaking with Christina. Whatever she said made the doctor smile, and I felt my heart lighten. Perhaps they would be friends.

It took us little more than half an hour. Once the supplies were packed, everyone gathered outside, hungry for fresh air and the serene evening of the prairie. Night had fallen, and we hadn't been followed. Except for the stark light that shone above the porch on the house, we stood in darkness. The moon was nowhere in sight. Roland said that it would rise in about another hour and then we would set out for the mountains. Adrenaline tingled through me.

There was a slight wind, hardly a breeze, which brought with it the sound of crickets. I heard the bark of a gopher in the not too far distance. A moment later, it was answered by another. I always thought they slept at night, but it was no longer the world that I once thought I knew. Simon was at my side. I half expected him to ask me once again to describe what I saw, as he had that time in the park. As we stood there under the cold rain of the stars, I could feel all the tension of the last twelve hours begin to seep from my body. The soft earth beneath me took it in and finally, finally, I dared to hope about the morrow.

I turned to Roland, thinking to ask him how long it would take for us to reach the mountains, then I heard the screen door of the house open. Turning slowly toward the sound, I saw two men exit the building and stride toward us. This was obviously Ben, whom Roland had referred to earlier, as well as one of his friends who was also to accompany us. Something about the two of them struck me as familiar. Warning bells began to chime.

William whispered, "Oh, shit."

Then I recognized Ben's friend. It was Braxton, and I realized that I knew Ben as well. Ben Hallings. From the Island. I remembered seeing him on Scarth Street Mall. Then I remembered the rest of it—Stephan lying at my feet, bloodied and dead, the woman whom I had killed—and my desertion. I recalled as well the bodies of the three deserters that we had discovered on the road to Victoria, how Ben had said to me, "They deserved what they got."

He recognized me, and he remembered too. "Jacob Harrison," he rasped. His voice was chilling. Who could hate me so profoundly to utter my name in such a way?

"Deserter," he hissed with the same brutal tone.

"Oh Sammy," I heard Katherine whisper.

Braxton finally pieced it together. "I knew I recognized you," he said.

"You couldn't possibly understand, Ben."

He'd drawn his handgun. "Remember Stephan Low?"

Remember him? Was I going to be forced to relive that horrible moment? "He died in my arms, Ben."

"You mean, you left him to die, you son of a bitch. He didn't. At least not right away."

"I didn't...." I stopped. If Stephan had still been alive, then what Ben was saying was true. I had run out on him. *Oh God,* I thought, *was that Stephan's last remembrance of me?* Add that to the list of my sins. What then was there for me to say? I shrugged, vainly starting, "I thought he was dead; I'm sorry."

"You're sorry?" His voice was incredulous. He lifted his gun, flicked the safety and fired.

Releasing the safety made a faint but audible click. At the sound of it, Simon stiffened, then slipped quickly in front of me, his sightless eyes boring into my own. When the bullet struck, he was slammed into my chest. He grunted, his shoulders going slack. I caught him in my arms, holding him tight. Christina cried out. There came angry shouts and more gunfire, but I couldn't take my eyes from Simon's pain lined face.

"I was wrong, Samuel," he rasped into my ear. "There are some things worth dying for."

I groaned, lowered him to the ground, cradling his head in my hand. The other moved over his chest, stupidly searching for a wound.

He raised an arm, fingertips touching my face, seeing its features. He smiled. "I always knew it was you." Then he gasped, and with sudden strength clutched my neck with his right hand, drawing my face to within an inch of his own. For a moment, I breathed the same air he breathed, then his final words to me: "Never let this moment pass, Samuel."

He slipped minutely away, turning slightly; cool air swirled in the void between us.

Suddenly Christina was pushing me. "Move, Samuel! Let me help him." She shifted Simon to one side, searching his back for the wound.

He turned his head to her, his expression now empty and cold. "It's out of your hands, doctor." His head rolled down, hanging limply. Christina bent over him, sobbing.

Simon was dead.

I crawled back to his side and cradled his head in my hands. Ben may have still had a rifle pointed at me; it didn't matter. The outside world was forgotten as I studied Simon's face for a final time. It was then, ironically, that I saw him for the first time. He looked at peace; he looked…. I gasped, and at long last the Blind Prophet could see.

There is a silence that stretches into eternity, in between words and doing, between the end and the beginning of things, timeless but for the remembered beating of your heart and the rasp of breath. I've felt that silence; I know, where Destiny pauses and the future lies open and clear, and anything, anything can be written upon it—moments of beauty, moments of truth, moments of love. You can step into such moments, let them swallow you like a tranquil sea and let yourself drift forth, searching, into its warm waters. Every small ripple will spread out to touch others, creating…anything. All we need to do is watch and listen, then we need to act.

A third piece of the puzzle slipped into place.

Katherine knelt beside me. "Are you hurt?" I shook my head, dazed, not really sure if it was true.

It was only then that I looked about me. Ben and Braxton lay twisted and dead on the ground. Will was standing unsteadily, blood darkening his shirt. I realized that he'd been shot, but wasn't sure who had shot whom. His rifle hung at the end of his limp arm. "Braxton was a bastard anyway," he croaked between pants.

Christina stood from Simon's still form and walked slowly to Will. Her eyes were lifeless. She helped him to sit, removed his shirt and wordlessly examined his wound.

Roland said nothing.

Epilogue

We left William behind. Christina said that he needed to get to a hospital, and she stayed to take care of his wounds. Her only reason for wanting to escape Regina was Simon, and we left Simon behind as well. Roland had expected a group of ten; four of us set out for the mountains.

The flight from Regina took four days travelling mostly by night on the grid roads. We were dogged by hunger and exhaustion, by a fear that tracked us relentlessly.

By the second day my tears were spent, but I remained haunted by Simon's final words to me.

By the third day we knew we were safe; we hadn't been followed.

The prairie landscape began to roll and heave, finally thrusting skyward and reaching for the stars that watched over us on our journey. The thin and scattered vegetation of the great plains gave way to thickly forested valleys.

Roland's ranch was everything he'd told Will it would be. There was room for all of us to stay and to live. His parents, old, alone and afraid, welcomed us with relief driven tears. For the first time since the revolution, I began to plan for the future.

On one cool morning weeks after fleeing the city, I hiked up to what had become my favourite lookout over the valley. At first I'd gone there to watch for what I believed to be the implacable advance of the Coalition. As time passed, however, I found myself going more and more simply to enjoy the view and relish the solitude.

Upon an outcropping of weathered, rust coloured stone, I sat with legs dangling and thought of Simon. Never let this moment pass, he had told me. At the time, with his beautiful blood bright upon my fingertips, I was certain that he'd meant for me never to forget him—never to let the memory of what he had said fade from human ken. I had decided that once again I would take up pen and record his short, extraordinary story.

But, as with most things, time weakened my resolve. I was no longer so sure that I understood anything he had said, let alone his softly spoken farewell.

"I'll never forget you, Simon," I muttered, unsatisfied, confused.

A breeze feathered up from the valley, carrying with it my whispered name. Briefly, it spoke to me of the infinite. *Never let this moment pass, Samuel. This magnificent, this indolent, this sweet, sad, eternal moment.*

"Sammy?"

I looked down to see Katherine standing on the trail beneath where I sat. She had followed me. Still breathing heavily from her hike, her breast rose and fell deeply. Matted with sweat, her hair was a tangle, and with her fingers she carelessly combed it from her eyes. A smudge of dirt marred her forehead. She smiled and was beautiful.

A last piece of the puzzle fell into place, making the image complete. Then I knew, finally, at last, that where I was, was a place to be.

In the distance, far beneath where Katherine stood, I could see the valley river raging within the confines of its stone prison. The current thrashed against the rock and the echo, softened by the valley trees, reached my ears like the melody of an ancient song, undisturbed by our struggles and our pain, even by our joy. The mountain air was crisp within my lungs, scented by wild flowers and ponderosa pines. The sky deepened with a remarkable azure and the sun was born over and over.

ABOUT THE AUTHOR

Currently, Kenneth D. Reimer lives and works in Regina, Saskatchewan. Literature is the passion that has shaped his life, and he can trace its genesis to a single day in his youth when his older brother, Rolly, gave him a copy of *The Fellowship of the Ring*. Robert E. Howard and H.P. Lovecraft soon joined the ranks of Tolkien, and Kenneth found himself on a path of literary exploration that has yet to reach its culmination. When he is not writing, he is teaching. He has three degrees, including a Masters in English, and he spends his working hours teaching at Luther College High School.

He is married to Lisa Powell, who edits everything he writes, and they share a love for trekking the globe. Their most recent wanders took them to Peru where they hiked the Inca Trail, then watched the sun rise over Machu Picchu. The Great Wall of China beckons, and they are determined to stand on the summit of Kilimanjaro before the title of Hemingway's short story becomes an anachronism. Kenneth combines a passion for photography with his love for travel, and their house is decorated with images that document their explorations.

The Lamb White Days is Kenneth's first published novel. His next major work, *Zerotime*, is a time-travel story in which wanderers from the near and distant future travel back to our present day. It will soon be followed by a horror novel titled *Ashes*. This tale explores the lives of an underground society where modern-day werewolves and vampires seek their prey in the moonlit streets of Canmore, Alberta. Kenneth is also working on a collection of short stories.

LaVergne, TN USA
27 October 2009
162088LV00001B/2/P